Mike Lunnon-Wood was born
and New Zealand. He worked in
moving to West Sussex. His writ
of research he conducted, spend
airman in support of each book. 1
2008, survived by his son, Piers.

CW00539148

SOMEWHERE
OUT THERE

Mike Lunnon-Wood

SILVERTAIL BOOKS • *London*

PROLOGUE

Lubimbi, Zimbabwe. April 16th. 1986

The young boy walked along behind the cows urging them on. He was still two hours from home and he wanted to be there before dark. He swung his stick at the old red cow with the twisted horn and she darted to the left and ran into the trees. Cursing himself for his impatience, he swung deeper into the shade of the msasa trees to intercept her. He was twelve years old and his father's herd of nine cattle were his chief responsibility. They represented all the family's wealth.

He ran faster and then he smelt it.

Death has an odour that is unmistakeable. He stopped and walked forward towards the stand of rocks, large weathered boulders that stood as high as the modest two room breezeblock house in which they lived. He moved forward further. A neighbour had reported losing a calf some weeks before and had offered money for news of its where-abouts. Looking across the scrubby grass at Twisted Horn, he saw that she had stopped and was grazing. He put down the stick, and, careful not to tear his pants, which were good and for school, he carefully climbed the steep side of the boulder.

At the top he looked down at the large crack below and inched forward on his stomach. The smell was now pungent. Looking forward and down, he held his nose. Something was there. He looked closely, down some four or five feet and saw maggots crawling in a greenish black putrefied mass and suddenly recognised the shape below him. It had been human.

Pulling back, he scampered down the rock face and stood at the bottom, his chest heaving, his eyes wide, frightened at his discovery. It wasn't the horror of death that upset him. He had seen corpses before in the hondo, some as decomposed as this. It had simply been the fright of the unexpected. He collected his thoughts and looked at Twisted Horn. She still stood upwind grazing peacefully.

His youthful curiosity got the better of him and he climbed the rock again. At this distance the stench was acrid. He looked closely, couldn't tell if it was man or woman. The clothing on the corpse was still intact but covered in places with the blood and dirt and slime that had seeped from itsy cavities, and dried crusted and hard. A trail of ants moved up and down the opposite wall of the rock's cleft, feeding on the body. Maggots crawled and squirmed on all the exposed areas, while large blue flies hummed around the rotting carcass.

One thing the boy did notice and later remarked on to his father was the hank of hair still attached to the skull. It was brown and long, not like one of their own kind. It was the hair of a murungu, a white. His father suggested he was mistaken – it was a bushpig or a monkey, and less time exploring and more time with the cattle and he would be home sooner. In truth his father did not doubt the boy's eyes but was wary of becoming involved with the police or the dissidents who operated to the East. Life was peaceful and he liked it that way.

CHAPTER ONE

August, 1986

It was a warm and friendly wind that had risen up from the water like a lover leaving her sleeping companion's bed. The wind had travelled thousands of miles across the South Pacific and finally, just short of the wide sprawling sunburnt continent, it swirled and rustled leaves on the hill above the house.

The house itself was a low solid structure with a wide verandah, overlooking the bay below. Horseshoe Bay ran from Magnetic Island's northeastern end all the way to the Pacific Ocean – but there were, however, none of the gigantic rollers one usually finds on a Pacific shore. Miles further out, and just below the surface, was the Great Barrier Reef, and within the reef, and all the way to the Australian mainland, the ocean was more subdued and perfect for the tourists who came to frolic in the all year warmth. The island itself was only five miles from Townsville and with the ferry plying back and forth it was not difficult to get to. Even so, it was always quiet and, even in the busiest time for the island's few tourist hotels, there were beaches that were deserted.

The house above Horseshoe Bay was on its own at the end of the long winding dirt road. Even for Magnetic Island it was quiet up there. Seager sat in a cane chair on the verandah and idly thought about laying the table for breakfast, then put it off and enjoyed the warmth of the morning instead. Flicking his cigarette ash into an Ali Baba jar containing a green succulent plant, he reached for his coffee cup. An anguished squeal broke the silence, followed by chastising words, and his daughter entered the verandah from the house clutching a huge marmalade coloured tomcat.

"Daddy! Fudge just ate the gecko!" she announced indignantly. The cat had a look of bored indifference, as the child swung him up more comfortably and looked at her father.

3

Seager laughed softly. "Sarah, cats do that sort of thing. They're hunters," he said. He stood and walked over to her. "Come on squirrel, help me lay the table. And let Fudge finish his gecko."

"Uuuugh," she said, dropped the cat, and followed Seager into the house.

"Its tail fell off," she said. "Why?"

At that precise moment half way round the world, a man picked up his telephone and dialled a number, and four seconds later the phone in the house above Horseshoe Bay began to ring.

"I'll get it, please!" the child shouted, running for the phone. A moment later she called back, "Daddy it's for you," rather disappointedly.

"OK, you get the knives and forks and things and start the table. We'll be in trouble if your Mum gets home and it's not done."

Taking the instrument, he watched the girl run into the kitchen, never believing that he could love a child so much that wasn't his own.

"Hello?" he said.

"Max? Richard Vickery. Did you get my letter?"

"Yes, yes I did. The answer is no."

"Max, it's a lot of money on offer for a routine missing persons report. Think about it."

"It's not routine. They've been missing five months in the middle of the bush. Bush thick with hostiles, dissidents and other assorted pricks. I'm not even welcome there anymore. Besides, the spoor is cold, and the army have been searching for months. No. It's a wild goose chase, and I don't need the money." Max looked worried.

"I know you don't need the money. I authorised the last payment you took." The man named Vickery paused. "Max, please?"

"They aren't your kids, Richard, and I mean no. Now then. I have to lay the table so be a good boy and say goodbye."

"Can I at least tell them you're thinking about it?"

"Richard, I have a nice quiet life here now. I don't want anymore of your sell-job. Tell them no."

Seager put the phone back on the cradle, walked out onto the verandah and watched Sarah put the finishing touches to the table. The knives were on the wrong side, and steak knives at that, but when she

4

beamed at him and asked how it was, he said great, and together they went out to the car just as Svea Seager stepped from the door, little Jannie on one hip, and a bag of groceries on the other.

"Mum!" shouted Sarah. "We laid the table and Fudge ate the gecko."

"Really darling, do you think it was tasty?" she asked laughing and gave Seager the groceries. She had only been round to Picnic Bay and the store, but that was the kind of family they were, and that was why Seager didn't want to go back into the African bush – not for anyone.

It wasn't that Seager didn't like the bush. He loved it as only those who really know it can love it. He loved the sunsets, the silence and the savagery of it, but what Vickery wanted him to do made the difference. Vickery wanted him to go into the area illegally, look for three people who had been missing for five months and prove that they were or were not alive. One mistake and he would be hunted like an animal and he had been down that road before.

They were sitting eating breakfast, with the steak knives, when Seager thought he had better mention the call. He looked across at Svea who was buttering a piece of toast for Jannie, their two-year-old son. She had her flax blonde hair up in a functional bun arrangement, and with just a hint of makeup over her tan she looked healthy and vibrant. The freckles across her nose only served to make her look more natural and her cornflour blue eyes were deep and twinkled when she smiled. The laugh lines were there now but she was not one pound heavier since Jannie's birth. She was one of those rare women who get better looking as they get older.

"Vickery phoned this morning," said Seager casually.

She replied without looking up from the toast. "Not offering you another job is he? If you have to be a spy, do it for someone respectable, like the C.I.A."

"He's not with the South Africans any more. Working somewhere in the Middle East I think. He wrote to me last week." There he paused.

"Oh?"

"Ja. Anyway, I said no," he finished, feeling less guilty. He hated keeping things from Svea. She usually dug them out sooner or later so it was better to come clean.

"Said no to what darling?" asked Svea, handing Jannie his toast and licking her fingers clean.

"You better read the letter," he said.

"Sarah, elbows off the table please." She looked up. "Sorry darling?"

"I said you better read the letter," he repeated.

It was later that morning when Svea eventually curled up in one of the overstuffed chairs to read Vickery's letter. The manoeuvre was not a success because, although Sarah was at the beach with friends, Jannie wasn't and, between him and the dog, the telephone and preparations for the following day on the boat, she never got past the first few lines.

Eventually she asked Seager to just read it out.

"No," he said.

"Well just tell me what he wants then." She looked up at him. She even looked up when standing. He was big, just over six feet tall and heavily muscled, and his skin was a deep brown, leathery from a lifetime in the tropical sun. Crows' feet only served to emphasise his slate grey eyes. His thick brown hair was long and curled at the back, and on top was bleached by the salt and sun. At thirty-four years of age, he moved like a fighter and was fast and well coordinated.

He sipped his coffee, his fourth of the day, and looked into the cup as if expecting to find something, swirling it round before finishing it.

"Remember, it must have been back in March. Three people got stopped on the road above Gwanda. Two Brits and an Arab girl. They weren't seen again. Oh it was the usual story. Simple abduction."

"I remember it was on the news," she replied.

"Right. Well they had police, army, everyone and his bloody dog in there looking for them.*Hapana*. Nothing." He paused. "Richard Vickery is now working for an associate of the Arab girl's father, and he reckons I can prove one way or another what happened to those kids. I don't want to go back, Svea. It's too risky, it's too soon, and it's too intangible. The sum of money on offer is ridiculously high and that makes it all suspect."

Svea paused. "How much are they offering for the information?"

"Enough to buy four *Sveas*," he answered.

6

Svea was their fifty-four-foot steel hull deep-sea ketch, and Seager loved the boat almost as much as he loved her namesake. His wife still blushed when people asked what the boat was called, but it was an indulgence she appreciated. Seager looked at her awaiting a reply.

"That," she said, "is a lot of money."

"It's a lot of boats." He grinned, then turned serious. "I know babe, it's an awful lot of money, but we don't need it. I said no."

"Good. I sort of like having you under my feet all day."

He grinned and walked away.

Svea knew why they wanted him. They wanted him because, in his ten years with the old British South Africa Police in Rhodesia, Max Seager had been in a class all on his own. His specialty was rural areas and intelligence gathering and he knew the area concerned quite well. If anyone could put together a team to find the victims it would be ex Inspector Seager, Special Branch, the B.S.A.P. However, if he thought the trail was cold, then the chances were that it was – and if he thought that he would be risking his life unnecessarily by going back, then he probably was. That was the other problem, and the one that truly concerned Svea. Max was a wanted man in Zimbabwe and, while there was no price on his head as such, it was only because the authorities believed he would never be back. He had been responsible for considerable embarrassment at every level in the current administration and they had long memories.

*

The big ketch had her toe rail in the water with her main, mizzen and genoa trimmed and tight. Seager sat at the wheel and watched the course occasionally on the big floating compass set into the binnacle. Both children were sprawled, with life jackets on, asleep in the saloon, and Svea lay on the leeward cockpit cushion, a large gin and tonic in her hand, taking occasional sips but mostly lying with her eyes shut in the sun, and enjoying the spray that occasionally showered her as the boat shouldered westwards and home. They had stayed out overnight, the big Danforth anchors holding her in the lee of the reef on an evening so idyllic and calm it was more like the Mediterranean than the Pacific. They had found the spot two years before, soon after arriving in the area, but it did need a night stop, so, late the previous afternoon, Seager had contacted Marine Radio in Townsville. For a small fee they would relay a message on a land-line, and with someone organised to feed the animals at the house, they had settled in for the night. Svea and Sarah both wanted the fairy lights and, after the regulation pleadings and threats, Seager agreed and strung the row of forty watt bulbs from the main boom.

The bank of batteries in the upper bunk in the passage aft, and the big punchy Onan generator, could cope with that without a problem, as well as running the Decca Autowatch radar simultaneously. The radar would alert the crew with a bleeping note if any vessel approached within six miles of their anchorage, but ignore the occasional blip appearing on the edge of the screen twelve miles to the south where the main route through to the Flinder's Passage and the open sea lay.

They had set up the gas barbeque on the folding table and grilled groper fish steaks and sausages, and as the children grew tired they were folded, unresisting into their bunks. The fairy lights festive, if landlubberish, reflected on the calm water and were only turned off when Seager, tired of no night sight, shut them down and drew the big Zeiss binoculars up to look at the stars. That eventually subsided into farce after Svea, the better part of a bottle of French red in her, thought it would be more fun tickling the stargazer and they finished the evening making love on the squabs in the cockpit. Now, only an hour from the anchorage at Picnic Bay; someone who had travelled a long way to see them was arriving at the airport on the Mainland and hoping to be in time for the last ferry to Magnetic Island.

The woman arrived at the house as the sun dropped over the horizon. The northerly that had given the *Svea* the steady run home had veered and was now coming from the east, and as the woman stepped from the old taxi, the only one on the island, it plucked at her skirt and swirled leaves on the driveway.

The verandah lights were on and, in the pool of light, she still looked out of place and uncomfortable in her cotton dress and sensible shoes.

She paid the driver, who called a cheerful farewell and rumbled on down towards the bay. With one hand on her hat, and another clutching her large bag, she approached the steps hesitantly. She was in her fifties and had once been pretty. She had the pale complexion of those who have lived their lives beneath cloud, and she looked very tired, as though she had reached the end of a long journey.

Svea, who had heard the car arrive, came out wiping her hands on a tea towel and opened the screen door at the same time the woman was about to knock. They looked at each other for a moment.

"I've come to see Mr. Seager," she said and smiled.

"Oh, he's still down at the boat. I'm Svea. His wife." Svea stopped for a moment. "You better come in."

"Thank you," said the visitor. "I'm Mrs. Nolan. Mary Nolan. I have come rather a long way to see Mr. Seager."

They walked into the lounge together and, as Mrs. Nolan settled into a chair, she seemed to let out an audible sigh.

"You look exhausted," said Svea. "A cup of tea or something stronger?"

"I don't want to put you to any trouble," she said.

"Nonsense," said Svea, looking at the woman in the same way she did at Sarah when she was being difficult.

"Well, a small sherry perhaps?"

"That's more like it," said Svea, heading toward the liquor cabinet. "I might even join you." She smiled at the woman. "Max shouldn't be too long, he always potters round the boat after we've been out."

At that point Sarah came in scowling.

"Mum. I can't find my school socks and Dingaan is on Jannie's bed again."

"Sarah, this is Mrs. Nolan," Svea said and when Mrs. Nolan shook the child's hand she smiled. It was timid and warm all at the same time.

"I've got a daughter too," she said, "but she is bigger than you."

With a sudden flash of insight, Svea knew who the woman was.

Seager arrived home in time for Sarah's story. It was something he had always done, a bedtime story. As he tucked the Land Rover into the garage Svea met him.

"We have a visitor. She's come a long way to see you, so hear her out at least."

"Who is it?" asked Seager, his arms full of sleeping bags, a tool box and bits and pieces from the boat.

"I think it's the mother of the English girl that Richard Vickery wrote to you about," she said softly.

He looked away for a moment, then nodded and walked toward the kitchen door.

Seager showered, brushed his hair – and, in a clean pair of white slacks and a pale blue shirt, he finally entered the room twenty minutes later.

"Mrs. Nolan will be having dinner with us Max," called Svea from the kitchen. "There's a beer for you on the table."

He walked to the woman and held out his hand.

"Max Seager, Mrs. Nolan," he introduced himself, and then bent down for the drink on the table.

It was small talk for a while: the weather, the island, children and, when Fudge entered the room, animals. Seager watched her as she spoke and the impression he gained was one of genteel defeat. She hadn't quite given up but it wasn't far away.

It was when they were at the table that Seager thought it time to get to the point. He wasn't one of nature's most gifted exponents of circumlocution. "Well Mrs. Nolan, you didn't travel all this way to eat my wife's moussaka, as good as it may be."

The pause was long and awkward.

"Mr. Seager, you seem a man of some unusual abilities," she trailed off. She paused to fidget with her napkin, gathering her thoughts. Then she looked across at him and saw the depth in his eyes. Grey eyes that said more than he ever spoke.

Come on, he thought, *let's have it. Out with it.*

"Mr. Seager, I want you to find my daughter for me. She was –"

"– on a touring holiday in Zimbabwe, and was abducted in March of this year with her two companions," Seager finished for her. "Yes, Mrs. Nolan, I'm familiar with the incident, Mrs. Nolan, tell me? Have you spoken to a gentleman called Vickery lately?"

Svea kicked him under the table. He winced and carried on.

"Richard Vickery can be very persuasive indeed. I told him no for the following reasons. Firstly, while your daughter and her companions may still be alive, the chances are." He tailed off, realising the insensitivity of his tone. "Mrs Nolan, I am afraid to say that the chances are extremely remote." It is likely they were dead and cold by the forty-eight hour mark, he thought. "I would not like to give odds on it, and I am sorry, but I'm being the devil's advocate here. The trail is cold and confused by now because of the amateur endeavours of the initial searchers. Lastly I am not very welcome in that country. That means that, if I went in, I would have to be covert. That's a word the Americans love, it means-"

Now she interrupted him, her voice soft but firm. "Don't patronise me Mr. Seager. I know what covert means." She paused. "Will you at least hear me out? Then I will leave your house forever."

Seager sat back with a sudden new respect for the quiet little woman. Svea stifled a grin.

"My daughter's name is Maggie. She is my only child. Her father died some years ago." At this stage she held out a photograph and Seager took it. "She will be twenty this year. She is the most wonderful person I have ever known and I love her very much. She is bright, intelligent, compassionate and hasn't a mean thought for anyone. This trip was something they had planned all year." She trailed off again, then found the strength to continue. "Mr. Vickery said that you were the only person he could think of. He said that you used to be a policeman in the same area. He said you were a hard, resourceful bastard with just enough soft spots to make you likeable." She smiled at the quote. "I don't have much money. I believe people like you charge for this sort of thing."

"Mrs. Nolan, I am neither a private detective nor a bounty hunter."

"No, but you are a father. Please? She is all I have." As she began to cry to herself, she rummaged around in her bag for a tissue.

"Don't cry Mrs. Nolan. Please. Look, I," Seager stuttered and was growing impatient. "ALRIGHT!" he cried out. "No promises though. I'll make some enquiries. Stop crying now for Christ's sake!" Angry at his weakness, Seager was trying to be consoling and rational all at once. "I'll think about it, O.K.?"

The meal was tense, with Svea breaking the long awkward silences as best she could.

Seager's dilemma was pure. While he wanted to help Mrs. Nolan, he had his own responsibilities. The turning point was graphic. Svea went out to get the coffee, and while she was clattering cups in the kitchen Sarah awoke and came through to the dining room. Rubbing sleep from her eyes, she clambered up onto Seager's lap for a cuddle.

Mrs. Nolan watched this take place, half a shy smile directed at Sarah. Then her eyebrows creased and she rose and walked towards the big bay windows overlooking the moonlit sea. When Seager looked across a moment later she was mirrored in the window, a hanky in her hand as she dabbed at silent tears alone in her grief. Sarah seemed to understand from her position on her father's lap and looked up at him as if he were the cause. He smiled sheepishly at her as she stiffly lowered her head to his chest and watched the woman's back, before squirming down and walking timidly across to the window to stand beside Mrs Nolan. A moment later a quivering hand came down and pulled the child closer. It was then that Svea entered with coffee cups and, taking it all in within a second, she began to pour, angry and impotent.

Later, when Sarah was back in bed and Mrs. Nolan returned to the silvery night, Svea looked at him and knew that Vickery had won.

"You're going aren't you? Why?" She demanded.

He said nothing. She could feel him breathing against her.

"You have never even met these people. I don't want to risk losing you. Max," she said softly, "please?"

He turned in the moonlight, the curtains billowing against his back and faced her.

"It's not them," he said, "it's the others left behind."

"It's not bloody Laos with 'American Missing in Action'," she retorted hotly.

"No," he said. "It would be O.K. if it was. I could ignore it if it was. Don't you understand? They were kids, not troops."

"That is different Max. You don't have to go back."

"Someone does. These kids have been left behind, by the whole world. No one gives a damn if they're dead or alive! Maybe." He trailed off and looked out at the silvery water again.

"You can't bring the world's forgotten back by going in again," she said urgently.

"No, but I can try and bring back *someone*. Can't you see, they have been left by the whole frigging world!"

"Don't shout. You will wake up the kids!" she retaliated.

"At least ours are here," he said softly.

The tears were brimming in her eyes. "That was unfair, you bastard."

It was just before dawn when, still awake, she rolled over and faced him in the big bed.

He looked across at her and made to speak, but she put her finger on his lips. "Shhh. If you'd said no, you wouldn't have been the man I married. One day I might be that mother looking for my daughter and I'd like to think that some hard resourceful bastard with a soft spot would help me too. Just be careful."

CHAPTER TWO

It was 0300 am and the big Quantas 747 SP was an hour overdue at Bahrain's small airport. A Pakistani man, one of thousands of expatriate workers on the small Gulf Island, waited patiently by the World Travel Desk in the main hall for his passenger. He had a card with Seager's name on it and eventually smiled to himself as the little red light on the arrivals board indicated the aircraft was down. A small video monitor on the wall beside the arrivals board showed the images from a camera in the customs hall. A sign below that indicated it was sponsored by Caltex but the waiting man didn't watch the monitor. He didn't know what the man he was meeting looked like so that was pointless.

Two tired air stewardesses limped out of the sliding doors from the customs area pulling little trolleys behind them. Their headdresses looked limp and sweat stained their blouses. A local Arab wearing a traditional thobe and ghutra sat nonchalantly, picking his toenails and occasionally conferring with his companion. Two other Pakistanis in pale blue uniforms moved up and down, endlessly sweeping a vinyl floor already spotless. Two local veiled women held the hands of two small children and a knot of English expatriates stood and chatted to a young couple with bags and a ghetto blaster. The couple turned and walked towards the departure area, sweating even in the air-conditioned coolness of the terminal.

A group of people moved down the stairs from the offices above, all with little badges allowing them access to the operational areas. Their ties were loosened and collars grubby, grateful for the end of the night. The Pakistani waiting for Seager moved toward the barrier and held up the sign as people began to come out of the hall and stood looking for familiar faces. A big man stepped forward.

"I'm Seager."

"Welcome!" said the man. "Welcome, please be coming this way sah!"

14

Seager followed him out into the hot and humid night, the porter with his one suitcase trailing behind. The driver stopped at a new Mercedes 500 SEL and opened the door.

Seager smiled as he entered the car but his eyes had a flicker that was menacing.

"Hello Vickery," he said softly. "You're out a bit late, aren't you?"

The man chuckled.

"Hello Max. Welcome to Bahrain. How was your flight?"

Seager looked at him witheringly. "All the better for seeing you," he said.

"Well, you can rest up now. I've got you in the Sheraton. Tomorrow you meet my illustrious employer, and we go over the details. Tonight you sleep."

"That was a shit trick Richard," muttered Seager, fishing for a cigarette. "Sending the mother. You're still a real prick."

"I still get results," justified Vickery, smiling pleasantly.

The Mercedes powered past a large taxi and its driver waved his hand in a gesture that was almost Italian. Seager went for the window button as he lit his cigarette.

"That's unnecessary, sport," said Vickery. "About ten grand of the purchase price of this little number is the air-conditioning system."

Seager grunted noncommittally.

The car entered a narrow bridge and ahead of them were the lights of the main city. Seager picked out several landmarks and immediately began logging them in his memory banks: the Diplomat Hotel, the large sign behind Gulf Air, the statue in the foreground. The car moved into the extreme right lane and surged around the coastal highway before turning left and then swinging up a steep ramp to the main lobby of the Sheraton Hotel.

"I'm here as well," said Vickery. "Mohammed will bring your bag. Come inside, Max. The food isn't bad, the bar service is excellent, but otherwise it's like any other hotel: overstrained smiles and overpriced everything."

A pretty Phillipino receptionist checked Seager in, and as he signed the registration form he noted the account details; they were to go onto

Vickery's room bill and an American Express billing voucher was attached. Someone had written GOLD CARD! in brackets in a scrawled attempt to avoid anything embarrassing taking place. He noted the number.

As they walked toward the lift Seager turned to Vickery. "How long have I got, if I can find them?"

Until that moment, Vickery still wasn't sure that he had Seager committed and he tried to cover the elation with a casual answer. "Oh. Two, two and a half months. I think that's the most we can give you for the fee."

Christ, thought Seager, *by the time I have a team in the bush, settled and running I'll only have sixty days. Sixty days to assimilate activate and infiltrate.*

"We better get on with it then," he said.

"Right. Breakfast at nine?" asked Vickery.

"Make it seven," he replied.

Sixty days.

When Seager got to his room, he went straight to the minibar and rummaged amongst the bottles. He pulled a bottle of Fosters Lager from the back with a grin, and sat on the bed, sipping from the bottle and looking at the photo of Maggie Nolan left with him by her mother.

She had a shock of dark brown, almost black, hair that had been permed into a soft Afro style of curls. Her eyes were brown and large and her complexion was what the English called peaches and cream. She was wearing bright red lipstick and a choker of pearls. The photograph had obviously been taken with the girl dressed for a night out because a corsage of white orchids was pinned to the black evening top. Her smile seemed genuine and honest and she was startlingly attractive. In the background Seager could make out a hallway of some kind but it was out of focus and indistinct.

He finished the beer and walked to the minuscule dressing table that doubled as a desk, then threw the plastic blotter pad arrangement to one side and began making notes on a piece of the hotel paper. In one column he wrote "Personnel" and beneath it one name and followed it with a question mark. PASCOE? Below that he simply wrote 6-8 and then added another name, 'Solomon' in smaller letters. In the second column he wrote "KIT".

When finished he walked to the phone and dialed the operator. It was to the hotel's credit that they answered immediately.

"I want a person to person call to Perth, Western Australia. A Mr. Pascoe on Perth 2424365. I'm room 711. Seager."

They spoke for a while, Seager being deliberately vague, and then finally convincing the other man to join him in London, just for a chat. "Ring Qantas tomorrow," Seager smiled to himself. "They'll have a ticket for you. Buy some bush kit, anything you need. Stick it on this Amex Gold Card Number. Don't worry, they will authorise it. See you early, day after tomorrow."

Then, at last, he showered and fell into bed without booking a wakeup call. He never seemed to need them.

*

Vickery walked into the coffee shop in the hotel's ground floor and looked around for Seager. It was a strangely decorated room of cool blues and greens and lots of glass. It had set out to be cool in atmosphere but ended up being starkly cold. It was also very quiet. He saw Seager and walked over.

"Morning Richard," said Seager, "you're late. I've ordered you scrambled eggs and coffee. They keep saying they're closed and don't open till eight and I keep quoting your room number. It seems to work."

"It's early for that kind of humor isn't it?" countered Vickery, reaching for coffee.

"We have much to do. Now then. You remember Ken Pascoe? The laddy who got my arse out of the Buybe River?"

Vickery nodded, sipping his coffee

"Organise a ticket for him to join me in London. Tonight. Here is a list of things I will need in seven days. Oh and, by the way, Ken's ticket, have it collectable in Perth at the Qantas office. How soon can we get on with the meeting? You and I need to talk before I go. Awake yet Richard?" Seager smiled at Vickery's groggy demeanour.

"Lighten up Max. It's still the middle of the bloody night."

In spite of the way he felt, he looked immaculate, as always. A three piece bespoke suit, hand made shirts, silk tie and Italian shoes were standard day wear for Richard Vickery. He was a very urbane sophisticated man with a mind like a steel trap and a reputation the length of Africa for being the most effective spymaster that South Africa had ever produced. His more inferior opponents greeted his retirement from active intelligence with sighs of relief and they blessed the capitalist system that paid such men to move to the private sector. Ironically, those blessings came from societies that were either rampantly socialist in a very African fashion or where complete despotism reigned.

Yes, Vickery was a man who would use any means to get the right people in the right place to get the job done, and he didn't like losing. For all of Seager's initial dislike at Vickery's methods, he knew that they would make a formidable team. Vickery with the contacts and the money, and Seager on the ground, with Pascoe and his team of heavyweights in case things got nasty. Where they were going, that was a distinct possibility.

"The Sheikh will see you at eight-thirty. In real terms let's say ten. Hear him out. He is paying the piper, to use a favourite expression of yours," advised Vickery, adding, "he's very quick, you may even call him learned. He's a neoconservative too, so no swearing or silly jokes. He's fluent in English, so watch what you say. Memory like an elephant."

Seager nodded. "OK," he said, "no jokes about the Israeli Air Force, or offering him a bacon sandwich."

"I shall ignore that," said Vickery. Then he beckoned the waiter. "Scrambled eggs are for children. Bring me Eggs Benedict, Devilled Kidneys and more coffee. Also toast, hot and lots of it. Thank you." He smiled charmingly at the confused man. "Off you go, there's a good chap!"

*

"Your Highness, may I introduce Mr. Seager?" Vickery turned and presented his large companion. "Mr. Seager, his Highness, Sheikh Rashid bin Ahmed Al Khadem, Emir of Ras Al Qaleem."

Seager stepped forward and took the proffered hand. The grip was firm and the gaze was direct and open. "Nice to meet you Sir," said Seager.

"Good! No fawning sycophant. Come we must go." The Sheikh turned to one of several men around him, all dressed alike in robes and headdresses. "Seager will ride with me, yalla!" he instructed, walking from the room, the phalanx of robed figures following.

Vickery pushed Seager after him.

"Come on sport, you're in the front of the car. We're going out to see the Emir of Bahrain. You can talk to Sheikh Rashid on the way."

As they arrived, the car doors were opened for them. The Sheikh looked into the front where a robed figure had sat with the driver.

"Abdulla," said the Sheikh in English, "please allow Mr. Vickery to sit there."

The man scrambled from the car and held the door for Vickery while Seager climbed into the back with the Sheikh, looking at his watch. Ten o'clock. He smiled and, as he looked up, Vickery raised an eyebrow in warning. Too late.

"Not keeping you from something am I Mr. Seager?" asked the Sheikh.

Seager shook his head quickly like a guilty child.

"Good." The Sheikh was about to say more when he was cut off by a warbling sound and Seager had to stifle a laugh as the man answered a telephone set into the Mercedes door and began speaking in rapid Arabic. It gave Seager his first chance to study the man who would be footing his not inconsiderable bill. Swarthy and elegant, the Emir of Ras Al Qaleem was certainly an imposing figure. He was tall, at least Seager's own height and sported a trimmed goatee beard. His eyes were quick and alert and widely spaced above a sweeping hooked nose. A small scar ran the length of his cheek and disappeared into the beard. He was, Seager estimated, in his early fifties and was ageing well. His hands were long and powerful and on his left wrist a gold Rolex, studded with diamonds, peeped beyond the edge of his sleeve.

He hung up the telephone and looked at Seager.

"Yes, the watch. Overdone as only the Swiss can do it. I don't share my countrymen's love of flashy jewellery, but it was a gift, you understand." A smile lit up his eyes. "And I'll satisfy your curiosity on the other matter. Oxford."

Jesus, thought Seager, *Vickery was right. He misses nothing.*

The Sheikh continued, "We only have ten or so minutes, so let us begin. I need you to perform a task for me. I believe the remuneration has been discussed by Mr. Vickery so we can dispense with that. Wealth, Mr. Seager, brings a certain disdain for material things. I'm sure Freud would have something to say on that but I don't remember. However, there are few things a man can give another that are truly worthy. One of those things is life itself and the opportunities to buy life, are rare indeed." He thought for a while. "I have a friend. A man who has stood beside me for forty years." He laughed mirthlessly. "There are those who would speak ill of him and say bad things, but he is my friend. His daughter was taken by some godless heathen in a country you know well. I want you to find her for me, that I may give my friend back his daughter." He paused. "I also had a daughter a long time ago."

The Sheik paused and watched the buildings flashing by as the convoy of cars raced down the coastal highway. Ahead a police car with lights flashing turned on its siren as the convoy approached a set of traffic lights.

"There is a chance that his daughter is dead but, Inshallah, if she is still alive I want you to find her. She was with an English girl and a man but you know this. Find Layla Rakkafian for me – or at least prove beyond doubt that she is dead, and let her father grieve openly. Mr. Vickery will give you whatever you need." At his side, Vickery nodded quickly. "What we don't have we can provide. We are not without influence. So, Mr. Seager, ex-policeman, will you do this for me?"

The question was direct and required an answer.

"Yes," he answered. "But I will need to recruit others."

"*Malish, malish,*" the Sheikh waved his hand theatrically.

"The fee will also go up if I need to use force to get them out," said Seager.

Fuck it, he thought. *I'm the one sweating and eating shit from cans and sleeping under bushes. Malish that,* he thought, grasping the meaning.

In the front, Vickery shrank into the seat in embarrassment.

The Sheikh turned and looked.

"I'm not a desert camel herder, Mr. Seager. Don't try and rip me off. Is that how you say it?" he murmured to Vickery, who nodded.

"It's not a rip-off. I'm talking about spending months looking for them and then, on the off chance they are alive, finding a team of experts, a team of five or six men, who will take on fifty and win. They are not cheap. We will get one chance only, and I wouldn't risk it with anything but professional soldiers, bush troops."

"I can give you soldiers. My own Palace Guard," the Sheikh said, again waving his hand like it was all of no consequence.

"No offence, Sir," said Seager, unsure of the correct title, "but the people I want would eat yours for breakfast." There was a sudden silence, broken only by Vickery who sank lower into his seat and actually groaned in embarrassment. The Sheikh turned and looked at Seager and surprised everyone by bursting into laughter and slapping Seager's knee.

"Done!" he exclaimed. "Done! Very well. You may put your invoice into whatever bracket is necessary." He laughed again. "I like you. You look me in the eye and insult my Palace Guard. You name your own price. Tell me Mr. Seager do you have children?"

"Yes, a daughter and a small son."

"Then you know what this means to me." He was serious now. "Find Layla Rakkafian and her friends."

"I'll do my best. If I can't find them, they can't be found," said Seager, equally seriously.

The Sheikh tapped the driver on the shoulder and the car screeched to a halt, the convoy pulling off the side of the road. The leading police car turned in panic, only to see Seager and Vickery alight the Mercedes and walk to another smaller version, which did a U-turn and headed towards town.

"Jesus Max," swore Vickery, "you really do push your luck."

"It's tough in the Gulf, but it's a lot tougher in the bush. He can afford it."

They returned to the hotel and spent the rest of the day working on the lists of requirements that Seager had put together the night before: passports, cash, contact numbers in a chronological sequence.

At four the following morning Seager was on a Cathay Pacific flight northbound to London. The Qantas flight that Pascoe would have been on was fully booked and Seager turned down Vickery's offer of pulling strings to get someone bumped from the flight to make room for him. While at the airport he placed a call to Svea and talked to her and the children. Later, feeling guilty, he bought her a string of pearls in the duty free shop.

CHAPTER THREE

As Seager walked into the lobby of Heathrow's Excelsior Hotel, he recognised a familiar figure at the check-in desk. He walked forward and addressed the receptionist.

"Miss, don't let him in. This man is a well known troublemaker."

The man turned. "Kanjani Max! How's things?"

It was Ken Pascoe. He seemed fitter than ever, his small stature belying his lithe power and unending stamina. His hair was parted conservatively on the right and was the same colour as his brown eyes. The years had aged his face and its lines deepened when he smiled. He wore a faded pair of jeans, docksiders, and to fend off the chill of the morning a bright red ski jacket.

"Good," replied Seager, and then without waiting for a reply, he turned to the receptionist who was smiling sheepishly. "Have our bags taken up please, Mr. Pascoe's bill on my room. We will be eating breakfast. Where do I sign?"

A few minutes later, they sat in the restaurant, having got past the woman at the door, and waited while a chubby blonde girl with a punk haircut poured coffee. She lent forward. "It's a buffet. You have to serve yourselves," she whispered. "But I can bring you toast if you like."

Seager appreciated her willingness to help, and decided to tip her accordingly when they left.

As they ate he began briefing Pascoe by pulling from a briefcase several clippings given to him by Vickery. They were from local Zimbabwean press and International press at the time of the abductions. He handed them to Pascoe.

"Remember this little scene?" he asked.

Pascoe looked and nodded.

"What chances do you put on their being found?" Seager asked.

"Not much," Pascoe replied. "Depends who's lookin' though."

"We are," said Seager.

Pascoe raised an eyebrow but said nothing.

"We have sixty days plus what's left between now and the end of August. Here's the offer. Remember Vickery? Good. He's the contact man with the client. If we find them – or should I say, find conclusive proof of their death – you get fifty thousand U.S. dollars. If nothing, the retainer is half that. Twenty five grand. If we find them alive, and take them back you get seventy. There's more money for a team. What do you think?"

Pascoe looked evenly before speaking. "That's a lot of money for a maybe."

"Its clandestine," said Seager. "They can't know we are there, and it could get hairy." He paused. "How's things at the Marina?"

Since Pascoe and his wife had left South Africa they had bought a small Marina in Western Australia. It was a love affair that was not as financially rewarding as they had hoped. In fact, they were in debt and Seager knew it. He had offered them a loan the year before but Pascoe had refused the offer.

"We could use fifty grand, that's for sure," Pascoe replied.

"We'll be a couple of months. Think about it and let me know tonight. If you decide you're in, you will be responsible for recruiting a team and the infiltration, day to day discipline – and if we find them, the extraction. I'll liaise with Vickery, run the search pattern and make the final decisions."

Pascoe nodded, and Seager continued, "I'm going over to talk to the English girl's mother, get a full profile and try some general information on the boy. I'll be back around four. If I get through early I'll go straight down to Brighton. I want to talk to the kids that the Rakkafian girl went to Varsity with."

"Right," said Pascoe. "Check you later. I'm going to sleep."

"Don't sleep," admonished Seager. "Think about my offer!"

"I have," grinned Pascoe. "I'll be in the shit with Donna, but I'm in. You can't be trusted on your own anyway."

As Seager argued the rates with the kid at the car hire desk, Pascoe settled in his room and went straight to work. As Seager drove away in a new 380 SEL, Pascoe placed a call to a Victoria Falls number in

Zimbabwe, and settled back to wait for the connection. Seager would be pleased. The contract was neither police work, nor one of a military nature. It wasn't something that a private detective could take on either. It would require a mixture of all three talents and the men to match. There were still fine police officers in the Zimbabwean Police, but their priorities were different. There were still professional soldiers, but men like John Peters and Jack Schramme were either dead or retired. The man who made his name a legend in the Congo, Mike Hoare, was too old and since his tactical fiasco in the Seychelles, his credibility was shot. They would need to spend weeks looking for anything, long, hot patient weeks of police work, and if they found something, then they would need to be soldiers too. The men chosen would have to do both roles equally well. There were agencies in London who could supply ex-Special Air Service Regiment men on specific contracts, usually for training or bodyguard duties, but the sort of men Seager needed, would have to be ex-service re   recruited from civilian life, and Pascoe was the man with the contacts.

As Pascoe went about his search, Seager took the M4 into Central London, the big Mercedes relishing the wide road. Once in Kensington he turned right to head towards the river, and hopefully pick up the Albert Bridge. He got snarled up in the one way system and eventually paid a taxi driver to go to the address so he could follow. Albany Mansions was a four floor, old building that ran the length of a block and had three or four entrances. The number Seager wanted was in the second entrance, and he parked the car and walked toward the door. After pressing the bell, he waited for a moment before the door was opened.

"Hello Mrs. Nolan."

They sat in the front room, and Mrs. Nolan poured tea. Eventually Seager spoke.

"Mrs Nolan, I want you to talk about Maggie: her habits, her quirks her thoughts, her ways. I want as complete a picture as you can paint. Any photographs, letters, anything that will show me the way she may think or react."

They talked for two hours, and Seager spent a further three reading old letters, and looking through pictures. By lunchtime he had a good grasp of the girl and her ways. He said a goodbye with a cheery, "Be in touch", and walked up the road to a rather dismal Victorian Pub. It was full of odd people, a mismatched collection of working class young professionals, full time drinkers and life's losers. There he ate a tasteless cheese sandwich, finished his beer, and asked the bored barman the way to the South Coast.

Several wrong turnings and a full hour later, he was on the M23 outside Croydon heading South. It had begun to rain and the road shimmered in the wet, and as he passed the Gatwick exit, he turned on his headlights, the big car easing through sixty kilometers an hour in the light mid-afternoon traffic. The motorway ended abruptly and a few miles further on Seager had to ease his way around a pile-up where the road from Cuckfield and Haywards Heath entered the A23. Twenty minutes later he was on the main road into Brighton and racing through the Old Stein, towards the beach. The town looked worn and tired and reminded Seager of a pensioner trying to make ends meet. He looked for a sign to Hove. The sea was slate grey and the brisk winds swept the wave tops into white horses, blowing spray ashore over the sea front road. The rain still fell and the windscreen wipers beat a reassuring tattoo as he moved westward along the road. A family of holidaymakers had given up even trying to remain festive and stood forlornly in a shop doorway, only the two children clutching candy floss and nibbling at it seemingly unaware of the rain and cold. Seager wondered how anyone could live there and thought of the woman he had known who had left Rhodesia some years before and come here to settle. He didn't know whether to admire her courage or marvel at her stupidity.

He passed a derelict pier, shuttered and wreathed in barbed wire to prevent people gaining access to its rotten surfaces, and soon realised that Brighton and Hove were one place, divided only by bureaucracy. Swinging left to find the main road, he passed a statue of Queen Victoria which looked like everything else: in need of a good clean and facelift.

A pair of punks at the traffic lights walked by oblivious to the weather holding hands. The male had orange hair, the girl blue, and both had a pasty look about them, the look of a lifetime of poor nourishment and smog and insufficient sunshine. For all that, they laughed as they walked and as the lights turned green and Seager swung the big silver car down into Hove proper, a blonde girl in boots and sheepskin jacket gave him the eye, but he was realistic enough to admit to himself it was the car that was attractive, or more correctly the money it took to buy it. How many illusions had been shattered by the return of expensive hire cars he thought. An old woman stepped into the road as if she owned it, pulling a trolley behind her, her mean mouth set against the wind and rain, her slippers wet and muddy. It was all very depressing and he thought of the sunshine and warmth of his home half way around the world.

He decided to walk to find the address he wanted, and parked the car. It wasn't far, two blocks up the road and on the right, and as he stood in the doorway he shook the water from his jacket, its expensive polished leather impervious to the assault. He pressed the bell, and waited as a muffled voice and clumping boots signaled someone's approach. The door swung open, and a bright round face beneath mousey permed hair and granny glasses peered at him. She appraised him and smiled appealingly.

"Yeah?"

"I'm looking for Sandy or Rebecca," he said. "My name is Max."

"You missed them," she said, "it's gone six, and Woodies is open."

"Woodies?"

"That wine bar around the corner. What do you want them for?"

"I'm a friend of Layla and Maggie. I'm going to look for them, I need to know more about them."

"Okay," she said, "you buying? I'll walk round there with you, introduce you."

"I'm buying," Seager said, smiling his boyish smile. "Just as long as it's not port and lemonade."

"Oh no! Terribly plebian anyway, that drink! Come on," she said, and held out her hand. "My name is Allie."

They began to walk.

"Are you doing something at Cambridge, Allie?" asked Seager.

"One *reads* at Cambridge," she said. "Political science with Maggie,

Layla, Sandy and the beautiful Rebecca and a million other hopefuls." She stopped, her face looking up hopefully at him. "They're dead, aren't they? They couldn't still be alive now, could they?"

"That's what I want to find out," said Seager.

"Are you a South African?" Allie asked.

"No. Rhodesian," answered Seager.

She beamed at him. "Oh good, couldn't stand another boring evening discussing bloody South African politics."

"I quite agree," said Seager. The girl linked her arm through his and a moment later they entered the crowded smoky cosmopolitan atmosphere of the wine bar.

"All Hove's beautiful people come here," whispered Allie into his ear.

"Jesus. The rest must be a bit rough," said Seager and the girl burst out laughing.

"I like you," she said.

They pushed their way forward toward the bar. The patrons were the wine bar's usual mixture of art and antique dealers, car salesmen there to pick up something feminine, girls out together, a few regulars and unemployed actors. It was appealing and casual and the smell from the kitchens was delicious. Allie pulled back a seat at a table, and pointed to the occupants.

"Right to left, Sandy, Kevin and Rebecca. Everyone, this is Max."

The young man stood and offered his hand. The grip was firm and even and he looked Seager in the eye. Seager liked that. The two girls were very similar both fair and blue eyed. Although Sandy was almost Slavic with high cheekbones, Rebecca's face was fuller and more sultry.

"Max is going to look for Layla and Maggs," Allie said, matter-of-factly. "He needs some behavioural aspects, stress patterns and predictability factors."

Seager looked surprised.

"Not just a pretty face," she advised. "Look, there's a waitress, I'll have a bloody enormous Bloody Mary."

Seager laughed out loud, and turned to look for the girl with the tray. Their order taken, he got down to business. They talked for a while and Seager finished by saying, "So, I need a picture of the both of them, and whatever you can tell me about the young lad."

Rebecca said nothing, just watched over the top of her glass. It was Sandy who spoke, her voice firm and direct.

"Who's paying, you?" she demanded. "Magg's Mum hasn't any money, she's on a grant like me, and don't say Layla's father. He hasn't written to her in years. He doesn't give a damn one way or the other, just puts money into her account."

"No," Rebecca corrected, "that's from her grandfather's estate."

"An old friend," said Seager. "A man who is wealthy and feels he can help." He stopped, then continued, "So has anyone a recent photo? The one I have is a few years old."

By nine he was through, and walked back to his car. He declined the invitation to stay offered by Allie, it would have meant in her bed. Being faithful was one thing, but undue temptation was another entirely. Best to avoid that, he thought.

The hotel he found was on the sea front, and looked outward at the stormy night. He checked in, went straight to his room, and after setting the kettle to boil, he called Pascoe.

"You won't believe it," said Pascoe.

"What?"

"A bit of luck. Rob Stockly is here in the U.K."

"Rob Stockly?" Seager asked, yawning into the phone.

"An ex-lieutenant from the Scouts, a recce specialist. Real good with troops too! He's everything we want, he's only been here three weeks and will know where to find the rest."

"Where?"

"Somewhere down near you. Place called Littlehampton. I asked him to meet us for a beer tomorrow night."

"Okay," said Seager. "tell him there's a wine bar in Hove called Woodies. Make it about seven. You come down tomorrow and we can start on the logistics."

Seager was awake early the next morning, and caught the 0650 train to London. Eventually he was disgorged at Victoria's platform 12 along with the rest of the commuters, and wanted to laugh when people virtually ran to the exits. Taking off his jacket, he walked to the gate. His mahogany tan left him different from the rest of the people and,

29

feeling very conspicuous, he put his jacket on again. There was a queue, but eventually he got into a taxi and asked to be taken to Zimbabwe House, but first a department store.

The driver was truculent and unusually un-cooperative for a London cabbie. "I don't wait, right!"

"You don't wait, you don't get paid," snapped Seager. "Now move it!"

Seager's patience was already at a limit. He wasn't good in a city of over ten million people. The cabbie looked back, saw the size of the man in the back seat, and drove away deciding that perhaps today he would wait after all.

He bought a cheap tie at a shop and, hoping he looked like a teacher, he walked into Zimbabwe House and told the receptionist he was one, that he had a class doing a project on Zimbabwe and wondered if they perhaps had any maps he could borrow? A call was made, and the girl eventually said "Sorry. out of stock." So Seager left and asked to be taken to the London University School of Cartography.

"Never 'erd of it!" the driver said.

"Well, stop and ask a policeman. There's a good chap!" He paused for a moment. "Before I come over there and take the wheel and smack you with it." They weren't getting along, and Seager paid him off twenty minutes later.

Without a student's I.D. card he was refused there too, but in the end two crisp brown ten pound notes into the private benevolent fund of a hard up Geography undergraduate met the need. By the time he was ready to leave, he had a complete set of relief maps taking in all of western Zimbabwe, the Caprivi Strip and the tips of Angola, Zambia and Botswana in three scales, complete with a cardboard tube to carry them in.

"Here's my number," said the student as he rolled the maps, "just in case you want to colour in Siberia or something." He handed Seager a bit of a Macdonald's serviette.

"Thanks," said Seager, "I'll bear that in mind."

The student paused before speaking again. He was small and intense and kept pushing his glasses back up his nose.

"I've got a friend who has access to some very hi-tech stuff. If you need it. He's a postgrad in electronic engineering and is into chips and things. Not salt and vinegar either. He moonlights writing programmes and can get into any piece of hardware in the country."

"What makes you think I would need that?" asked Seager.

"People like you, who want accurate maps of Banana Republics and won't go to legit sources? Who have five hundred quid leather jackets and don't give a shit if they get wet? People like you can always use technology. Someone else's that is."

"Maybe," replied Seager as he walked off into the rain to find a taxi.

After stopping at an Interflora to send six dozen roses to Svea, he was back at Victoria by 1400 hrs and walking through Brighton Lanes by 1600. It seemed to him to be all silver and jewelry but he eventually found a stationers and bought some clear polythene, some china graph pencils, and was back in his room by 5, working on the grid pattern of the initial search area.

Later that night, Pascoe and Seager stood up near the bar, each nursing a pint of lager from the jostle of people around them. They had arrived early and parked Seager's car right across the street. They watched a traffic warden ticket it, and Seager shrugged.

"Vickery's gold card taking a hammering again," muttered Pascoe into his Heineken.

"It's tough in the bush," agreed Seager.

At exactly seven the door onto the street opened again and a man walked through. As his eyes swept the room taking in everything at once, he ran his hand through his hair and straightened his tie. He looked uncomfortable in the jacket and the collar was too tight. "That's him," said Pascoe, "that's Rob Stockly."

He waved and held up his drink. Stockly nodded and moved toward him, gently edging his way past other drinkers, with muttered apologies. "Hello Rob, how's it?" greeted Pascoe.

"Ja okay, how are you sir?" he replied.

"Not Sir anymore, not for the moment anyway." Pascoe turned and indicated the big man behind him. "This is Max Seager."

"Nice to meet you Rob, what's yours?" asked Seager, shaking his hand.

31

"Lager sir, thank you."

"Max," he said. They took their drinks, and went and found a table by the window. The place was filling up fast, and Seager wanted to be able to talk without shouting, or being overheard.

"Rob," he began, "earlier this year, three kids, students were snatched on the old Wankie road. One of those kids has a rich benefactor. He wants them found, or conclusive proof of their deaths. I used to be in the police there. Ken Pascoe you know. We are going to put together a team of ex-Scouts, and useful types to try to find those kids. We have sixty days from the end of August. Funds pretty much unlimited. I will run the search, and Ken will run the day to day operations. If we find the bodies, we take evidence and piss off. If we find the people alive we will have to take them back by force if necessary. We contact a group of anything from five to seventy-five, we are on our own. No back-up, no casevac, and we must not, repeat must not be compromised." He stopped and watched the young man's face. When there was no reaction, Max continued, "We will be there on fake passports. The fee will be handsome for each man, and Ken thinks we will be operating with a team of ten or eleven men, including locals. If you agree to be in with us, then Ken will be relying on you to help recruit the stick."

"Sir," Rob began, before correcting himself. "*Max*. I'm not popular there. If I'm found, there will be some hassles. How much is handsome?"

Seager smiled. "If we get them out alive, enough to buy into a place like this. If we come out with nothing you, as an officer, get twenty thousand US dollars as your retainer."

The man thought for a moment, and then began to speak.

"I left with nothing. Hapana. Went to Jo'burg and didn't like it too much. Came here a few weeks ago, and it's done nothing but rain. If there's enough for a place like this, then there's enough for a payment on a farm somewhere. I'm available, but." He paused. Pascoe looked up from his beer and Seager leant back in his chair. "We go in to get them back alive. No half measures." He suddenly smiled for the first time. It was wide and open and frank. "I want a whole farm," he explained.

Seager breathed a sigh of relief. If Pascoe said this guy was good then they needed him.

"Right," said Seager, "I suggest you complete your commitments here and move up to London with Ken. You have a lot of work to do. I think Ken will run with military ranks while the operation is on. You will be 2 1C reporting direct to Major Pascoe, who in turn will report to me. Okay? Right let's get a few beers in and take the night as it comes. Tomorrow it's on."

CHAPTER FOUR

The Palace of the Ruler of Ras Al Qaleem stood halfway up the side of a hill that had seen much traffic in the last thousand years. Traders plying their wares had crossed the ranges since the time of the Old Testament, and for some of the residents of the small Emirate life had changed little – but for the ruler things were very different. The palace was a huge sprawling complex on five levels set into the hillside and surrounded by gardens that rumour said took millions of dollars to build. The palm trees, all thirty-one varieties, were planted as adult trees, imported from, of all places, California. Fountains and marble walkways crisscrossed the complex and everything was the best money could buy, from the giant Persian carpets to the pink marble, to the solid gold faucets in bathrooms the size of double garages. Yet, for all its splendour, the man who lived there disliked it intensely. Sheikh Rashid had watched the palace being built as the last wish of his father, an ageing conservative autocrat who believed that appearances were all important.

Now he lived there with an ever present entourage of advisers, staff and confidantes. He had no family as such. His wife and daughter had died in an automobile accident over twenty years before, and his last remaining brother had finally given in to complete liver failure and died on his yacht four years earlier in the South of France. He would rather have lived in something more modest, but whenever he thought of the expense of the palace he felt obliged to reside there. It lacked much, but in reality no more than the feeling of loved ones around him, the sight of children and the warmth of the family unit. At fifty-two years of age, he wasn't old, but old enough to know what he had missed. He crossed the wide expanse of the main hall outside his rooms and, after telling the servants to leave, he strode into the main public area of the Palace. He liked a few moments of privacy before the day began. This morning he had cancelled his other appointments. Vickery was back and he took real pleasure in the smooth South

African's company. Vickery was one of those rare men who manage to serve without being servile and, in a palace riddled with fawning idiots, he found that most refreshing. He entered his office, and strode to the sideboard where a pot of fresh Brazilian coffee stood on a warming unit. The blend was mixed especially for him, but for all the notice he took of its flavour it may as well have been instant Nescafe.

Scanning the cancelled appointments, he smiled to himself. A minor African diplomat wanting short term loans for his country headed the list. Following that he had a member of his National Security staff, a man who saw treason under every tree and bush; then lastly, before lunch, there was a plea for clemency from a French contracting company whose Middle East negotiator was in jail after trying to bribe the small Emirates Minister of Development, for preferential treatment on a motorway bid. The French, thought the Sheikh, ate snails and frogs' legs, invented the bidet and never used it and had an army with no Frenchmen in it. Strange people, but strong. He would see what the idiot with the motorway tender had to say for himself.

There was a knock at the door.

"Yalla!" he bellowed.

The door opened quickly and an aide stepped forward, ushering in Richard Vickery.

"Good morning Sheikh, how's things?" Vickery was more informal than ever.

"Ah! Mr. Vickery, come sit. Chai? Coffee? No? You have eaten, yes?"

"Yes thank you Sheikh, I have heard from Seager. They are on schedule."

"Good. Let's cover the other items first. Then your pirate friend."

They settled down and began going over the items on the agenda Vickery had prepared. All concerned dealings with the multi-nationals and huge corporations that fed like parasites on the petro dollar. That was Vickery's role, keeping them honest, the first concern being an American supplier of advanced surveillance systems.

"Its a bit dodgy," said Vickery, "but it seems they quite often change the boards for cheaper ones after the job has been inspected. The boards are the integrated circuits in the hardware."

"Why?" asked the Sheikh. "There must be a reason other than expense?"

"They usually have the maintenance contract as well and new boards are chargeable at six times the price of the originals." explained Vickery.

"Tell the manager that, if he does that, he will rot in a prison and his balls will rot separately on a rock in some wadi somewhere."

"Right," said Vickery. He would relay the message, word for word.

"Next!" said the Sheikh and so they continued until eleven o'clock when they finally got round to the subject of Seager and the search for Layla Rakkafian.

"Tell me about this Seager," said the Sheikh. "Tell me why he costs so much."

Vickery sat back and crossed his legs, the knife-like creases in the lightweight suit trousers folding perfectly. He put down the yellow legal note pad, and began.

"Born in Rhodesia, well Southern Rhodesia as it was then. Must now be thirty three, thirty four. Only child, who only ever wanted to be a policeman. Completely fluent in both major language groups of that country, although he would deny that. Something of a lay expert in witchcraft as practised by the locals in the western part of the country, which he learnt as a boy on his father's farm. Outstanding recruit of his intake, and boasts an exemplary career. Just a bit too successful for the new regime, which lost a lot of men to Seager's intelligence. He doesn't like losing and always plays to win – has a rare talent for making men do what he wants and getting the best results. He's a loner, a very hard man when it's needed. Otherwise, the perfect policeman. Honest and straight, until the system doesn't work. Then he does it his way. Now independently wealthy, and doesn't need work ever again. I had to get Maggie Nolan's mother to visit him to get him to agree to try this job."

"Will he succeed? Will he give me my friend's daughter back again?"

Vickery considered it. "If she is alive then Max Seager will find her. If she needs to be taken back with force, then he will do so. He is the only man I can think of, who wouldn't just go in and sit and while away the hours and days getting a suntan on your retainer. Oh yes, he will succeed – if Layla is still alive."

"You have done well Mr. Vickery. Let us hope he does as well as you. Now, let's see the French, who think we award road projects over the perfumed delights of some whore."

It was two days later when Seager and Pascoe arrived in Lusaka and, after a call to the Emirates local Ambassador, they immediately headed South East for Livingstone and the meeting with the transporter truck that was to move some 'basic' equipment over the border. A gregarious young black man met them later that evening and they followed him to the yard where his huge Ford flatbed truck was parked. They spent the remainder of the night sliding the oil wrapped weapons deep between the hollow floor of the container beneath the load of twenty tons of machine parts that were being returned to a warehouse in Bulawayo. The small consignment that was to be smuggled was all they would need if an armed assault became necessary and to protect the party in an area controlled by dissidents, where even the Zimbabwe Army wouldn't go in under platoon strength.

The dustproof parcels also contained a set of brand new General Electric MPR P2 B-C hand-held radios with base station, surveillance microphones, logging recorders and – Pascoe's pride and joy – a set of six new Sony hand-held video cameras. They used battery units that could be re-charged on a generator, and tripped into operating by the V.U. meters on the logging recorder.

"I can't get the fucking things to work at home," muttered Seager, who preferred old fashioned eyes to high technology, "let alone in the bush."

"Stop moaning and have some faith," consoled Pascoe. "With this kit we can cover heaps of ground, six times what we can with the team and your bloody telescopes."

Seager grinned as he pushed the case of four Ziess telescopes onto the truck. "At least they don't need batteries," he said.

The last major item under the load on the trailer was a spun aluminium case containing a selection of odds and ends used by on site teams on a homicide investigation. Containers of Plaster of Paris for moulds, weights, scales, basic ballistics measurement tools, camera and specimen bags. "Lets hope we won't need those," said Pascoe, "or we are out heaps of bucks."

"And three people are out their kids," finished Seager.

They spent the night in a local hotel, after watching the trailer disappear down the highway towards the bridge that crossed into Zimbabwe, where the truck would wait until the next morning. The evening was uneventful, and Pascoe entertained Seager with stories, while they both absorbed the pleasure of being back in Africa. The pleasure paled a little when the waiter in the hotel laughed at their request for eggs with breakfast. It seems they had run out of eggs three weeks before and hadn't seen any since. They crossed the bridge themselves just before nine the following morning in an Avis hire car and presented their Emirates passports – courtesy of Vickers and the Sheikh himself – to Immigration Control. They were waved through with minimum fuss and Seager almost purred with pleasure as they entered the village of Victoria Falls, its familiar sights and sounds flooding his brain with memories. He resisted the impulse to get out and walk around in case by chance they were recognised, and they drove to Deka where the truck would be waiting to hand back their precious cargo.

Arriving early, they spent forty minutes waiting off the road for their first rendezvous with Andre, a man Seager had known for some years. Andre, once a Warden with the Department of Parks and Wildlife, now ran Photo Safaris and would allow the team the use of his camp. They watched his battered old land cruiser draw to a halt on the shoulder of the road. Andre stopped and looked around; then, finally seeing their sand coloured Peugot in the trees, he drove over to them and climbed down from the cab.

Sitting on the bonnet of the car, Seager grinned widely. "Kanjane Andre. Howzit my mate?" His accent immediately thickened into the full clipped almost South African sound of native Rhodesians.

A small wiry man with tight brown curls and a full beard, Andre walked over and extended his hand.

"Jesus, Max. How long? Three years? Good to see you!" His grin was marred by a missing tooth, and his face was dark brown from the sun, his eyes brown like a squirrel. "Andre, meet Ken Pascoe."

The introductions were made. While talking, they transferred the load left by the truck into the back of Andre's vehicle, Pascoe fussing over the electronics like a mother hen. The men stood for an hour and talked before Pascoe drove south for Bulawayo and his meeting with Stockly. Seager headed west with Andre, down the same road until the Kamativi Mine turnoff, where they left the main road and headed yet further west into the bush. Here Andre's camp lay on the banks of the Sengwa River, placing them at the heart of the search area. There for three or four days, they would make further preparations until the arrival of the team, and then the job could begin.

As the land cruiser pulled onto the dirt road, Andre broke the silence. "So Max, what's the sitrep? The camp is set up roughly where you asked and I have cancelled my parties for the next three months."

"You know why we're coming in, yeah? Well, as far as you are concerned, we are surveying for this company." Seager held up a legitimate survey permit made out in the name of Petro-Search (U.A.E.) that had been waiting for him along with the other equipment in Zambia. "We have theodolites and some geological survey gear coming up with Ken, just for appearances. You and your blokes know nothing, but obviously we would appreciate any help we can get."

"Well, they're good blokes. Simeon you know from your last stay with us. The rest have had their problems with both the authorities and the dissidents, so they're pretty much available for anyone who has a dig at both. See them right with some bucks and they're yours." Andre paused momentarily as the vehicle lurched over a rut in the road and he paused while he corrected the speeding machine. "Just have them drive for you and then tell them what you need. They can probably put you on the spoor of dissidents in a dozen places on request. Just as long as what you are doing isn't political they won't give a shit."

Seager offered him a cigarette, an imported Benson and Hedges, and Andre took one, smiling. They were still short of luxuries. "Thanks Max. How many of you will be there? Should I get some more tentage up?"

"About ten I think, all ex scouts, R.L.I. S.A.S. That type of thing.

Ken is recruiting now. We'll be bringing some local boys on board. I'll just have to trust his judgement. Ever hear of a guy called Stockly? Ex Lieuey in the scouts?"

"Name rings a bell. I think I may have met him years ago with Dave Hodgeson at their camp at Kariba."

"You may have done. He's one of them."

"Could have a good unit eh?" Andre asked, smiling.

"We better. If it gets hairy, there's no chopper or help. We just grab the kids and fuck-off quick smart into the bush, and hope whoever gets hostile doesn't like being shot at by some crazies."

"That's you Max – a crazy bastard. But clever crazy. How's Svea? You have a son now too I believe?"

The small talk carried them for the next six hours of nerve-wracking driving over bad roads and worse tracks. As the sun began to settle, Andre pointed to the south. "In there, below the gomo, is the camp. Just the place for some surveyors!"

They arrived at the camp as dusk draped the bush and the cook's fire burned cheerfully off to one side of the main tents. The tents were large and laid out to preserve the maximum privacy for the paying guests while still keeping an open casually arranged air about the place. Haphazard planning is what Andre had once called it. The main mess tent was surrounded on three sides by accommodation tents. Behind the accommodation tents there were three smaller shelters, two with canvas baths and the third surrounding a long drop toilet. To the south of the main tents lay the cooking fires and sleeping quarters for the camp's five fulltime staff. There was a cook, a mess waiter, and two drivers who doubled as guides and a bossboy. Ever since Independence, Andre had tried to call him a Supervisor but old Simeon had worked camps for twenty years to become Bossboy and no change of regime or terminology was going to deprive him of his title. He remembered Seager well from the time, three years ago, when he had spent long periods in the Chalala camp near Kariba, and greeted him effusively.

The camp's only use for electricity from the old generator chugging away in the trees was to power the big freezer and fridge. From that fridge came the ice cold beer that sat on the mess table under the hurricane lamp's bright glow. The tent sides were up and the mosquito netting did little to stop the moth's kamikaze attempts on the hot glass of the lamp. Reaching for a beer, Seager wiped his hands across his trouser bottoms in a vain attempt to clear the grime of the road. Away in the night to the north lay the Chizarira National Park and to the south and east the wild bush and Tribal Trust Lands that would be the search areas.

Andre saw him look into the night and spoke. "It's a big area, Max. A lot of places to cull a couple of people and just leave the bodies for the jackals and hyenas."

"There's never been a proper search," Seager replied. "Not by a policeman. I'll have people on the ground, good people. We will infiltrate their camps, we will drink in their beerhalls, we will eat at their fires. We will find who took them and then find the kids, dead or alive." He stopped and took a long pull at the bottle. Andre knew that, if anyone would find them, Seager would, with the same bulldog determination that had made him the talk of intelligence circles during the bush war.

They were disturbed by Simeon who arrived with more beer, usually the mess waiter's job. Seager knew immediately that something was afoot, because the old man did not immediately leave but stood respectfully to one side and waited to be addressed in the old fashioned way.

"Speak old one," said Seager gently. "Three times the rains have been and gone, there must be much to say. Tell me, has the one in Harare given you all a vote again as promised? Is sudza cheap? Are there farms for all?"

The man cleared his throat. "Sekuru," he began, using the term of respect, "there is as much chance of these things happening as there is of you having a baby." Seager chuckled delighted at the analogy, and the other continued. "There is as much chance of these things happening as for Boss Andre to take a wife and have strong sons."

"Simeon, you think with your dick," Andre said in English.

"It's better, Boss, than not thinking at all, which is as one does with his balls full of seed and no ground to plant," Simeon replied with a twinkle in his eye.

This time both men laughed.

41

"Boss Max, Boss Andre said that you would have extra work for us. Good wages. Is this true?"

"Eeeeh," Max replied in Shona, "work for each, but you work for me and not the mujibas in the bush, or the ma-policemen."

"It shall be that way. What is it you have for us, Boss?"

"At the end of last winter, on the road from Hwange to Bulawayo, two murungu –" He used the Shona term for 'white' "– young women, with a man as escort, were taken by the ma-dissidents from the road and have not been seen since. Their mothers grieve, their families wish them to be found, whether they are dead or alive." Max paused, handed the man a beer and indicated for him to sit. The man settled a little self-consciously and Seager continued. "I want your men to remember where they have seen spoor, movement of groups of men, old camps, hidden shelters, places where men have stopped and camped. Where they go for umfazis and beerhall girls. When we find the groups we will find news of those who took the people from the road. Then we will find them or the bodies. Your men will be paid double wages till the job is done, and if we are successful with good news for their families then bonus time for you all. Enough for a car each." He paused again, then continued, over a burst of laughter from the cooking fires behind, "Your drivers will move my men as ones who search the ground for gold and iron with levels and marked poles, all the time guiding them to where they have seen the sign of the hyena shit that steals girls from a road."

The old man drank deeply and then, wiping his hand across his mouth, he spoke. "They will agree. It will be like the hondo, the bush war, but this time we work for money and for ourselves. Boss, these girls and the boy they were with, this was not ma-political?."

"No politics. No trouble with the people in Harare. They won't even know we are here. All we're doing is trying to return three young ones to their families. What we do here is a good thing, Simeon. Fear not," Seager reassured him as best he could. The threat of political reprisals by troops was ever present in Africa. Toe the line or become a casualty. It was simple enough.

"One more thing Boss, there was one asking for word of you last Christmas time in the lowveld. My brother worked in Chiredzi. I was visiting him."

"A murungu?" asked Seager, interested.

"One of the lowveld, one who spoke of a chase and a hunt with you. He is called Solomon, but said you would know him as Chimkuyu."

"Chimkuyu? Aaah! I know him well. How is he, still stealing game?"

"Yes, still stealing game. He may be of use in the weeks ahead, what say you? Shall I send for him?"

Seager looked out into the dark and remembered the tall sinewy black man: Chimkuyu, who could smell water and track over rock, who could stalk antelope close enough to touch and who was the scourge of the Parks and Wildlife Management wherever he went because he hunted where he pleased and took what he wanted. Yes, he would be of enormous use here. A pair of eyes and a heart that loved the hunt would be invaluable.

"Eeeh Simeon, send word. Tell him the one who speaks with the spirits, the one who uses the *swikwiros*, needs his help and, if he would join us, I promise him a hunt like he has never seen," Seager said softly.

"It shall be done."

Simeon stood and, thanking him for the beer by clapping cupped hands, he moved off into the dark towards the men gathered around the fire, each of them awaiting news of bonus pay and a sure few months work.

"I'll organise a bath," said Andre. "Then we'll eat."

They ate grilled fillet steaks and washed them down with beer, Seager relishing the sounds and smells of the bush. It had been a long time and he truly felt at home here in the grass and trees and heat. They slept and rose early, and then the mound of preparations began. Extra tentage went up, an ops tent, an extra mess tent and smaller quarter for Seager and Pascoe away from the main camp. While all seemingly casual it would be run as a military operation. Pascoe insisted on that. Weapons were unpacked and cleaned of grease, and a large table set up in the ops tent. The collection of small scale maps were laid flat with hunks of granite holding down their corners. Two men were dispatched to Wankie to start buying supplies, the hundred-and-one things a group of fifteen men would need in the next weeks.

*

The curly-haired young man looked up from the engine as the woman walked into the workshop. He was lithe, swarthy, with quick brown eyes and a fast smile that offered much to any member of the opposite sex, an offer that was frequently taken up.

It was one of the few decent things about the job; the rest was boring and repetitive and he hated living on the Rand. It was crowded and fast and he felt constantly ill at ease there. It was nothing like his homeland to the north, and as good an automotive engineer as he was, he was a better soldier. He wiped his hands along his overalled thighs as she walked closer, his eyes appraising her frankly. She smiled demurely back.

"All done?"

"All done," he replied, holding up the keys to her car, "you might like to bring it in next month and we'll look at the timing."

She thought for a moment. "Timing? Is that important?"

"Timing," Pirelli answered grinning, "is everything, if you know what I mean?"

"I know exactly what you mean," he replied, her look saying, *I'd love to but I'm married.*

He was about to pursue the issue when the voice of a man thick with anger carried across the shop floor. Pirelli smiled charmingly and excused himself, saying, "Next month then?"

She smiled as he walked toward the commotion, relishing the prospect of a tumble between her heavy thighs, but the smile faded as he neared the shouting customer. The man was big, red-haired and solid, his heavy pudding-shaped head resting squarely on his shoulders, seemingly without the benefit of a neck. The object of his anger was a middle-aged Xhosa mechanic by the name of Jacob, a man as talented as any Pirelli had ever worked with.

"What's the problem?" he asked.

The man turned on him, spittle on his lips, his nose red and veiny.

"The problem is I didn't bring my car here to be worked on by a black man. I expected someone who knows what they are doing to do it!"

"Jacob is fully conversant with all models of BMW seventy-three," Pirelli answered. "This man knows what he's doing better than any. He's one of the better mechanics in the Rand area. Now what specifically is the problem?"

"I told you! You stupid little pork shit, I don't want a kaffir working on my car. Now you get the manager down here!"

Pirelli smiled charmingly for a second, the complete fawning servant, before allowing his demeanour to change.

"You have insulted me. I am not Portuguese. I am of Italian descent. You have insulted Jacob who is a good man and a friend of mine. Now pay your bill, take your car and fuck off out of this workshop before the pork and the kaffir get pissed off!"

"Just you try you little."

The man never finished the sentence, for Pirelli's foot swung up into his testicles, the months of frustration boiling out of him. As the man doubled over, the boot came up again into his face, flicking his head back in time to meet a short sharp punching combination that cut flesh with every punch. The man went down groaning, holding his face and his groin, blood running down his fingers onto the filthy workshop floor.

Jacob spoke for the first time, "Now we're in trouble." Then he beamed a wide smile at Pirelli, "But it was worth it! Just to see that!"

"You didn't do it, I did, so don't worry," Pirelli said. "I was sick of this job anyway." He bent down to the moaning man, "So just remember next time, I'm Italian and Jacob is Xhosa, not Kaffir." Pirelli stood and looked at his friend. "Check you around sometime," he said, and walked to the locker room to clear out his things before the police arrived.

That evening, at home at his sister's house, the phone rang and Robert Stockly, a man Pirelli had served with in the Rhodesian Army, asked him to come and meet him. He also asked where to find another they had served with, Keith Buchanan. Pirelli told him and they agreed to meet in two evenings' time.

*

45

The cow in the crush was in pain and bellowed loudly, fighting the steel bars around her neck. The long raking cut in her flank was fly-blown and maggots crawled in the putrid wound. "Hold her steady!" the man called.

He was big, very big, sporting a bushy blonde beard that brushed his faded khaki shirt. Raising his arm, he gently probed the wound with the end of a ball point pen. The animal bellowed again and thrashed against the bars of the crush. "Boss Keith!" one of the herders said. "Make her sleep." They had seen him do it before when another injured animal fought in fear.

"Get the muti," he said.

The herder nodded, ran to the truck and pulled an old plywood box from the cab. It contained basic remedies for stock and Keith Buchanan wanted a broad spectrum anitibiotic. As the man returned with the box, he walked up to the cow's anguished head, feeling behind her ear with one large hairy hand. Then he pushed two fingers into the pressure point swiftly and the cow collapsed in the crush. Buchanan used his knowledge of anatomy and karate whenever it was necessary.

"Quickly now," he said, pulling a knife from his pocket and quickly scraping the wound clear of maggots and cutting away the rotten flesh. A minute later he was finished and, dusting the wound in sulphur powder, he threw in a hefty dose of the antibiotic as the cow came round.

Confused and still sore, the cow clambered to her feet. Buchanan opened the crush and the beast darted clear to join the herd. Watching with some satisfaction as she was joined by her calf, Buchanan finally walked back to the truck and eased into the seat and drove away slowly. He was appalled by the attitudes on the farm; no-one seemed to care, the stock were thin and, even allowing for the drought, there should have been supplementary feeding. The fences were falling down, the dip tanks leaking, the buildings shabby. The owner didn't care and neither did his employees. He had spent six long months trying to improve the place but, without the money to spend on both the land and the labour, it was futile. He also found the attitudes of the local farmers difficult. He was by no means a liberal in the Western sense of the word, but he found the deeply ingrained dislike of white for black and black for white intolerable. They couldn't even get along enough to build something decent; the entire Orange Free State was like living in a time warp, quite different to the progressive attitudes in Zambia and Zimbabwe that he was used to.

He looked out at the dry red earth and stunted grass as he drove and thought about the richness of the bush in the lowveld, the game and the warmth. Here in winter it was bitterly cold. *Jesus*, he thought, *I have to get out of here soon.*

That night, the farmer's daughter Suzannne rode over on her little Honda to his place and gave him a message to phone Louis Pirelli in Johannesburg urgently. There was also a message from a bloke he hadn't seen since leaving the army up north, Robert Stockly. *Maybe something is going on,* he thought. *Christ I hope so, anything would be better than this!*

Suzanne smiled coyly at him, twirling one finger in her dark straight hair. "I don't have to go bed for a little while," she said hopefully, and Buchanan felt a sudden welling of pity for the girl. She was stuck on this farm just the same as him.

"Good," he said with a flash of inspiration, "you can help me feed my snakes."

It was not as the girl had expected. She recoiled back, her eyes wide. "Well actually I do have to go."

Buchanan watched her waddle back to the motor bike and rode away as he began to chuckle to himself.

Got to get out of here, he thought. He looked at the message and walked to his phone.

CHAPTER FIVE

In Bulawayo Ken Pascoe had already begun the recruiting process. The first man he sought out was a wiry alert ex Selous Scout Sergeant by the name of James Nyamadze. Nymadze was a product of the old colonial mission school system who had been raised on the stories and dreamed of the days when the Rhodesian African Rifles had served abroad. Like Seager's lifelong desire to be a policeman, Nyamadze had wanted to be a soldier. He left the school system, a reasonably bright scholar, and went straight into the R.A.R. after lying about his age. There he served his apprenticeship in a regiment that had served with honour in Burma in the Second World War and, as the terrorist emergency increased in Rhodesia, he simply continued to be a soldier. He had considered crossing over several times, to join the ZIPRA Army of Joshua Nkomo, but he never did because they did not impress him sufficiently as soldiers. They were good if properly led, but no match for his Regiment or for the Selous Scouts which he joined on the first intake.

Like Seager, Nymadze had been a casualty of the new administration, but because Nyamadze was black he had serious problems. He wasn't just an ex-Smith regime soldier, he was a hated ex-Selous Scout and, as soon as Mugabe came to power, he had very real fears for his safety. The Scouts had been too good. Their kill rate too high. Pascoe had met and been impressed with Nyamadze on several occasions and Stockly had been able to provide a contact address. Tonight they would meet and choose the rest of the locally-based members of the team.

Now Pascoe waited in the bar of the hotel, noisy with a mixed crowd of drinkers of all colours but one background: working men. Pascoe wore scruffy jeans and a T-shirt and drank his beer from a bottle like most of the people in the room. The first Pascoe knew that Nyamadze was there was a hand on his shoulder. Turning around, he saw the bright smiling face and the laughing eyes.

"Kanjane Nyamadze!" greeted Pascoe, putting out his hand. The man took it and held it.

"Mushi," he answered. *Good.* "How are you Sir?"

They bought more beer and found a seat at one of the tables. A local prostitute smiled appealingly at Pascoe, her bright red lipstick contrasting against her coffee skin tone. He shook his head and turned to Nyamadze and began to tell him the story. He told it straight, without glossing over the danger to the local men in the unit if they were found bearing arms or compromised by either the local authorities or the dissident gangs in the area.

"What will I be doing?" asked Nyamadze.

"Scout," said Pascoe. "You find them and we get them back. That will be the quickest way. You will lead the local troops. We may split them or use all at once. If we contact and get the targets out alive then you, as an N.C.O., get ten thousand dollars. We think maybe two months to do the job. If dead, half that. If nothing at all, a thousand American a month. Are you in?"

James Nyamadze thought of the years since the war had ended, of the low profile he had always kept, just in case someone somewhere put the pieces together and shopped him to the Party. He thought about his two small sons who would need good schools and his wife who took in washing and mending to make ends meet. He also thought about the smell of cordite and the thrill of the contact. He was a father but, first and foremost, he was a soldier. With the money he could move to a new location, put his boys into a school and have money about the house, maybe enough for a business.

"When and where do I report, Sir?" he replied.

The others arrived later and Nyamadze introduced them. There was a small sinewy chap in his mid forties called Cave Ncubi, an ex corporal from the scouts and his offsider, a younger man with cheeky eyes and a quick smile called Timothy Sibanda. The last ex-scout of the group was a tall loose-limbed individual named Mpakachana but just called 'Chana' by most. He was, Nyamadze informed Pascoe, sometimes belligerent and would not abide fools. On the other hand, his abilities as a deep reconnaissance operator were nothing short of brilliant and made up for his general dislike of humanity. It meant he would work on his own without problem. He would also carry an M.A.G. without complaint but preferred an old Lee Enfield Mark 111 and was a superb rifle shot.

The last to join was a gregarious bright humoured man of middle height and barrel stature. Nyamadze explained that Silas was not an ex-soldier but currently a serving policeman. His record was impressive and he had served with the Support Unit which was paramilitary in nature, before posting to C.I.D. Now, a few years on, he had seen many promoted above him simply because they had better connections in the Party. He was frustrated and ready to strike out on his own, but needed money. "He's serving in Binga but can move anywhere in the area," Nyamadze said. "And Sir, he was involved with the original search."

Pascoe's immediate suspicion was abated with the prospect of having someone with access to files of the original case and, more importantly, someone who could warn them of any police interest in the group of surveyors.

"Will you help us?" asked Pascoe.

"As long as what we do is not against my country or my people, yeah."

"We just want to find three kids and get them home for Christmas," said Pascoe.

It was the second piece of incredible luck and James Nyamadze smiled over the top of his bottle, at a very smug Pascoe.

*

Far away to the south, Robert Stockly met his group in Johannesburg. All were living in South Africa except a man named Richard Masters, who had flown from England the night before. Masters was tall, about six foot four and lean. He was one of those Englishmen who had spent so much time abroad that he was more at home there. A career soldier, he had served with the Special Air Service Squadron in Rhodesia and had become an Officer in that unit. He also had a special love for the bush. Since then, his career had taken a different turn. Masters was still a soldier, but he no longer swore service to King and Country; now he swore service to whoever was paying the bill. Some said this made him a mercenary, and Masters was not against using the word. Until recently he had been in the Middle East, in the pay of the Sultan of Oman.

Stockly had reservations about keeping a professional soldier interested long enough without action, but in Masters' case he would regard the whole episode as a safari that someone else was paying for, until things began to happen, if they began to happen. He had told his wife that he was going back into the Oman for another three months spell with the Sultan's Forces and had promptly gotten onto the Johannesburg flight after Stockly's call, relishing the prospect of some time in the world's last wilderness. Now his eyes seemed to pace the room like a caged animal. He had that look about him, something contained, something wild.

Pirelli and Buchanan arrived together. Then came Keith Buchanan. Buchanan was a far quieter individual than the rest, with many facets that he rarely spoke of. He was a keen ornithologist and expert on venomous reptiles. He was also a second dan exponent in karate and a keen rugby player. For all this he was a shy, sometimes inarticulate person who only came into his own in the bush with the birds and snakes. He had once admitted to Pirelli that he would rather watch ants on the ground than television and was the perfect foil for Pirelli's happy chit chat and girl chasing.

Stockly had brought them all together at a Sandton Steakhouse and, when he made the offer, Masters and Buchanan seemed unimpressed with the money offered. Both would have gone along for nothing, just to get back into the bush.

Pirelli worked out on his calculator how many gallons of petrol he would need to sell to make that sort of money and muttered, "Jesus man, I'm in. So is Keith. He can watch the birds and things."

Buchanan just ploughed through a steak that was so rare it bled. Stockly looked at him. "Keith?"

Buchanan looked up.

"You in boet?"

"Ja, sir." He took another bite. Working on the farm in the Free State was boring and repetitive. The labour was sullen and hostile and so was the boss. His fluency in Sindebele and Shona meant little there. Better go north again, even if it could get heavy.

Stockly looked over at Masters. "Richard?"

Masters would be the man who, with Pascoe, could draw up a battle plan if it came to that. Stockly knew that his limitations left him clear of that and Pirelli and Buchanan were basically bushmen. Masters was the assault specialist and would take care of that side of thing if necessary.

"Sounds like fun," he replied flippantly, "but I have to be back in Muscat by January. Yes, under that condition, I will make myself available to Max."

Pascoe looked at Pirelli. "Louis, your parents still live in Harare don't they?"

"Ja, I'd like to leave them out of this."

"So would I. That's why you will all be travelling on new passports with new names."

Stockly began to go into details and they lingered so long into the steakhouse that, some time after midnight, the steakhouse manager had to move them on. The following day, photos went by courier to Vickery for the new travel documents and they all left with instructions to meet in Francistown in Botswana three days later.

*

Deep in the bush south of Chizarira National Park, preparations for the arrival of the team were almost complete. Pascoe, Nyamadze and his team would be arriving tomorrow, with Stockly and his team through from Botswana later tonight. They were all on schedule.

Seager watched the two drivers and the cook rolling drums of petrol from the back of a big Ford seven tonner. The expanded fleet would use plenty of petrol. Seager didn't like logistics, but it had to be done and, since the other two were better used in recruiting, it fell to him. A service pit was ready, dug into the hard clay. Stockly said he had a guy who could fix and maintain vehicles as well as his other duties. *Don't let me down Rob*, thought Seager as he walked towards the stores tent. *Without vehicles we are buggered.*

That evening, they sat around the table in Seager's tent. Stockly, his hair clean and wet sat sipping a beer in shorts, while Pascoe, still dusty from the road, leant back in his chair cradling his beer in his lap.

"Right," said Seager, "who have we got and what makes them special?"

Pascoe started going over the men he had brought with him, each one's attributes, talents and shortcomings and Stockly followed him with the same exercise.

"Right, that's seven, plus us three is ten. Add the two drivers and Chimkuyu if he comes and that's thirteen – unlucky for some."

"Fourteen," said Pascoe, firmly.

"Explain," said Seager.

"Forget the trump card. What would you say if we had a serving member of Binga C.I.D. on the team?"

Stockly and Seager both looked at Pascoe disbelievingly.

"Say it again?" said Seager.

"Detective Sergeant Silas Ndlovu, Binga C.I.D, now works for us. He was on the original inquiry too."

"Where did you-"

Seager was cut off when Pascoe suddenly said, "Nyamadze found him."

"Christ. If he's legit then he's going to be worth his weight in gold. Fucksakes, what a stroke of luck!"

"He's taking a couple of days leave and will meet you on Saturday for a briefing," advised Pascoe smugly.

They talked late into the night until they were joined one by one by the other white members of the team in the tent. Seager watched Pascoe talking to each evaluating them and their worth, scheming about who to put with who when they started work, and gradually the beer worked its usual way and the talk got loud, along with the laughter. Finally, they were joined by Andre who couldn't sleep through the noise. Away down the camp, the Matabele troops were sensibly asleep and only old Simeon wandered the camp, bringing more beer and stoking the main fire that crackled cheerfully into the night air.

The dawn crept over the hills like a late arrival at a party, with the camp already awake and productive. The cooking fire had been stoked and a huge pot of porridge bubbled to one side. It was the mealie meal variety and would be served with butter and salt and tinned milk and followed with as many eggs and as much bacon and toast as anyone could eat. The men were gathered around shaving in a large metal baby bath that steamed in the early light. Nyamadze looked over at Pirelli who was certainly the worse for wear, hungover and bleary.

"Mujiba," he said to Pirelli, calling him the name of the young boy who tends cattle, "has all that drink gone to your head? If you think you have a babalas now, wait till we run to the river." The river, the Sengwa, was three miles away to the east.

"The river? I think I'm going to puke."

Nyamadze laughed loudly and spoke again. "Relax Pizza, we begin running tomorrow." He was the only one of the Matabele who would use Pirelli's nickname. "Today we listen to Major Pascoe and the policeman."

An hour later they were gathered under the shade of a Mopani tree, all waiting for the policeman Seager to begin. He didn't keep them waiting long. He arrived from his quarters with Pascoe trailing and holding maps, a folder, coloured pens and a large flip chart pad.

"Right," he began. "Listen carefully. I am running this search. Major Pascoe takes over if the locals get nasty, or if we have to do a snatch that involves firearms. Until then I'm Sunray. You all copy that?" He paused for a moment to let it sink in, then continued. "You are all going to be paid a fair day's wages, until we hit the target. Anyone of you wants to fuck about, or is just here for the ride, say so now. Once we begin, you are committed."

They all just looked at him, a couple of Matabeles shifted nervously, and Masters sat with half a smile on his face. "O.K. here we go. That tent –" He pointed to his, "– is the local office of Petrosearch Company. You are all employees of the company and have various job titles, you read me?" He nodded to Pascoe who began handing out sheets of paper to each man. "Learn your job descriptions, some of you are geologists, some surveyors, some assistants. We are here prospecting for gas and oil. Over there –" He pointed to the shaded area under the awning of the mess tent "– are theodilites, measuring tools, rock hammers and some fairly hi-tech gear that will all look good. All of you have some handy at all times. If you are sussed by a local, collect rocks and look intelligent, make notes and things till they piss off. O.K.?"

54

He paused there and ran his hands through his hair. Away in the trees a bird cried but, except for that sound, and the soft murmur of the staff at the fire, the bush was quiet. He walked across to the gnarled trunk of the msasa tree, brushing a fly from his face and pulling three photographs from his shirt pocket. Digging again in his pocket, he pulled out drawing pins and pinned the three pictures up on the rough bark at head height.

Pascoe stood stock still in the shade of a tree motionless in the heat, watching the small spurts of dust as Seager's feet moved on the dry ground. When he turned his slate grey eyes had the glitter that Pascoe knew so well, a smouldering glitter like a leopard. Those who had been looking at each other and talking softly felt the air change about them and everything fell silent.

"Somewhere out there–" he swung his arm in a sweeping gesture at the bush to the west, "–are three people who were kidnapped in March of this year." He paused to let the statement sink in. "They may be dead, they may be alive. Either way, we are going to find them. Initial intelligence shows they were snatched by dissidents." He used the generic name for the Matabele gunmen who had never given up their arms after the bush war and used politics as a reason to plunder and steal, and not by army people looking to discredit anyone. "So this is the situation. Somewhere between the Falls-Bulawayo road and the Tribal Trust Lands South of Gokwe are a group of dissidents that took part in that kidnapping. We are going to find the group and from there the victims. Any questions so far?"

To their credit, no-one raised a hand or spoke.

"First job is to isolate all such groups in that operational area. We are restricting the search to this side of the Falls road because Intelligence at the time tells us that there was too much military activity the other side in March. They would have come this way."

Pascoe had pinned up a map on the tree below the photos. Seager pointed to an area that corresponded to roughly the size of Wales.

"We are going to watch, listen, and track. All will be covert and each team will have a frozen area. You will spend three to five days in the bush and then come in. You will be dropped, supplied and picked up by one of the surveying vehicles. I'm not going to tell you how to do your jobs, you are all experts – hand picked, that's why you are here. No heroics, just weeks of bloody hot thankless watching and hiding and boring. Yes, I said boring stuff. Any questions?"

Again, no-one raised their hand and Seager smiled dryly; he knew his men.

The briefing lasted most of the day, with Seager and Stockly spending more and more time speaking Sindebele, making sure that Ncubi and Sibanda knew exactly what was expected of them and their crucial part in the operation. The teams were split. Pirelli was teamed with Mpakachana. They had worked together before. Nyamadze and Stockly would work together and the big silent Buchanan would hunt with Cave Ncubi. Tim Sibanda would track and listen for Pascoe and Masters. Seager remained uncommitted, hoping that Chimkuyu would soon arrive.

That night was more subdued than the last, with most of the men making personal preparations for the day to come. Pascoe broke open the arsenal and issued weapons to those that wanted them. All were takers, as all were aware just how easily they themselves could become victims to those they were looking for. Most opted for AKM's, the Soviet 7.62 Intermediate with the familiar banana shaped magazine, that was so common in the developing world. The M Model had a folding stock which made it easier to conceal, which in this instance increased its attractiveness. Masters, ever different, chose the only AR 15. It was Colt's answer to a folding stock Armalite and, although it needed cleaning often, it was his personal favourite in fold-up guns. Chana gazed longingly at a scope-fitted .303 in Andre's personal gun cabinet, but Pascoe shook his head, saying it was too long.

"But I can always be a poacher," appealed Chana.

"You are a surveyor," replied Pascoe firmly. "Hide an AKM."

As the night hardened around them, the men sat round the fire that blazed outside the mess tent, stripping and cleaning their equipment and drinking cold beers. The beer would be the last till they were back in camp at the end of the week. Already they had split into the working teams and what impressed Seager most was they had done so without being asked to do so. He looked around himself. Pirelli and Chana were testing the hand held radios and Cave Ncubi and Buchanan were doling out the goodies that would accompany the ration packs. There was biltong, both beef and kudu, tinned peaches and guavas, both an important source of sugar, and there was the cheap tobacco. Pascoe couldn't stop them smoking but he could give them the sort of leaf smoked out there and the smell would be less alien. There was also Keith Buchanan's chief penchant in life. Flakey bars. Dozens of them were in the fridge, and he would take as many as he could eat before they melted in the hot sun. The heat was becoming remarkable. It was only September the first and the hottest month of the year was still to come. October, called by many the 'suicide month'. Within a few weeks it would be so hot that nothing would move in the midday sun. The predators would hunt at dawn and sleep during the heat of the day. That, in turn, affected all the other animals. Men were the same; none would do any more than was necessary between the hours of eleven and two. Seager had planned on this and it would become a major part of their strategy. The team would move anytime they wanted. In the dead of night, or in the heat of the day.

The only time they would lie and watch would be between dawn and mid-morning and then again at dusk, when the dissidents they were hunting would move along the tracks hurriedly to make their destination before nightfall. When men move quickly they leave signs and they make noises. They get careless. That was what Seager and Stockly had planned for. Someone getting careless, a track used once too often, a pile of faeces, too many in one area. It's surprising how many flies a pile of excrement attracts and, if you look for flies, it's surprising how often you see them. More than one hide in the Liberation war was found because a man was too lazy to bury his own waste. That kind of carelessness costs lives.

Breakfast was the same as the first morning: large steaming bowls of maize porridge and fried eggs, bacon and toast. It would be the last for a week for the men so they ate with gusto. It was while the mess waiter was placing huge plates of food before the men that he leant over Seager and spoke.

"Boss, there is a man here. A stranger. Shall I tell him to fuck off?"

Seager turned to see who it was. Beside him, Buchanan had risen to his feet and grinning said to the Mess Waiter, "Only if you have plenty of sick leave."

Then Seager saw the man in the shade of the msasa tree, still carrying the photos of the abductees. He was tall and lean and sinewy, his hair was short, almost shaved. He wore only shorts and carried a Lufthansa plastic overnight bag in one hand and a walking stick in the other.

Seager's face broke into a grin. He stood clear of the table and walked towards the man, Buchanan following. Stopping a few feet away, he extended his hand. The other man took it and smiled, a bright beaming thing, exposing a missing tooth.

"Kanjani Chimkuyu, how go things?" he asked.

"Mushi, he who talks to the spirits," was the veiled reply.

They both sank to their haunches to go through the traditional greetings and talk of families, crops and the affairs of men. It would be unseemly to get straight down to business. There were formalities first and protocol demanded they be met.

Eventually the man looked at Buchanan and spoke directly to him. "There was one, a young one without beard or years in the bush with another young one. The other stayed and learned from Chimkuyu but the first walked a different path."

Buchanan grinned widely. "You remember me Solomon? We were young, as you say."

Seager turned and looked at Buchanan and then back at the Shangaan. "Chimkuyu, I have a hunt here. We hunt men. Men who took these children from their mothers." He pointed to the tree above Chimkuyu's head. "We seek the children to return them. If they who have done it have killed them, then we seek proof of their death, to let their mothers grieve openly and before all."

Chimkuyu said nothing for a moment and then nodded. "Men are no more difficult to hunt than animals. They are stupid and lazy, they have habits. Study the habits and then finish the hunt," he said.

"Will you hunt with me old one?" asked Seager softly. "I have much to learn of the bush."

Chimkuyu took some snuff from his old tin and nodded. "I am here, am I not?"

Buchanan voiced Seager's relief by laughing softly to himself and said, "Come Solomon, eat with us."

Chimkuyu had walked most of the night and was hungry, eating on long after the others had finished. Pascoe had begun his last briefing of Seager's orders as he finished eating and set about slurping loudly from an enamel mug of very sweet, milky tea.

"We deploy as follows. Pirelli and Mpakchana, Sector One here." He indicated the map now on a flip chart easel. The area they were to search was divided into four roughly equal slices, but each with its share of tributaries and cover, tracks and possible hiding places for small groups of men.

"Buchanan and Ncubi, Sector Two." Sector Two took in sections of the Shangani and Kana rivers. "Stockly and Nyamadze, Sector Three." Sector Three was the northern edge of the Mafungabusi Plateau stretching up to the headwaters of the Lutope and Sengwa. "Captain Masters, Tim Sibanda and I will take Sector Four." Sector Four was the Sebungwe Mlibizi and Busi Catchment area bordered in the south-west by a small settlement called Lubimbi.

Pascoe looked at Seager and he shook his head. "Let your man rest up, tomorrow you can go north, Siabuwa through to Binga. Meet the policeman then move back through Chizarira over the course of the week. Organise a pick-up by two way on Friday. O.K.?"

Seager looked at Chimkuyu and nodded.

Each team would move into an area and set up a crude camp. They would then range far and wide each day, locating tracks used by people recently, roads which the dissidents would never be too far from, water holes, deep bush they might have used for cover. Seager knew this was not going to be easy. His men would search for news, but only the people who committed the actions knew exactly who was guilty. The dissidents out there were not one people. Normally, they would have very little contact with each other. Their few common denominators were similar racial background, language and a dislike of the Shona and their ZANU party who ran the country. Organised, these Matebele gangs could cause havoc, but until now their actions had been sporadic and self motivated. Try as he might, Seager could not put his finger on why that had changed. And above all else, one question had been bothering him. The question *why*.

The dissident gangs in this part of Zimbabwe could be unpredictable, but at least their actions were understandable. They were self-serving. What they did, they did for their own tangible gain. But why take three tourists? There was never a ransom demand that Seager knew of – and tourists would only be a hindrance in the bush.

Seager had not yet given it voice, but he had one fear that eclipsed all the rest. What if the two girls and their companion hadn't been abducted by dissidents at all? What if they'd been abducted by troops *masquerading* as dissidents? That would be almost impossible to prove and they would almost certainly be dead. It would have been hugely embarrassing if they had been, in fact, taken by troops and then released or found. They would have been murdered immediately.

*

The first vehicle got back just after nine that night and Seager helped the driver to work the hand pump, refueling the tanks and the ten jerry cans on the roof. He and Chimkuyu would leave at first light north to Siabuwa and their later contact with Silas from Binga police. The driver, an overweight quiet man called Roger, was understandably exhausted and went straight to sleep, but only after telling Seager that he had put both teams on spoor before lunch.

Day one was over. Fifty-nine to go.

The second vehicle limped in just before dawn. The driver had hit an anthill at speed and sheared the wheel's nuts of the left back wheel. He had jerry-rigged a skid from a branch and travelled the distance back at three miles an hour. By the time Seager and Chimkuyu left the camp. the vehicle was over the service pit with Andre at work with a welding set.

It took them the best part of the morning to work their way through to the road, stopping frequently to look at likely places they could come back to later. Chimkuyu quickly grasped the concept of a map and, once he understood the legend and colours, he began marking places he wanted to look at.

"Here," he said, "this sky colour means water? And this colour of a kudu female is grass and this leaf colour is trees?"

Seager nodded and explained the contour lines. Chimkuyu looked for a minute and then said, "Here and here and here. If I wanted to

60

build a camp near to water and a track with high ground to watch from, these are the places I would seek out."

"We will begin there tomorrow," said Seager.

"Women," said Chimkuyu.

"Ipi?" asked Seager. *Where?*

"They will have women in their camps. Women like fires and shelters. Do you have farlookers?" He meant did Seager have binoculars.

"Yes," said Seager.

"We want high ground at early evening. See the smoke of their fires and, if lucky, we will see the flame."

Seager was pleased. Already Chimkuyu had taken his thinking beyond what he would usually ponder. The man thought like a hunter. Seager thought like a policeman. Together they might succeed.

Some time later, they emerged from dense scrub to find Silas Ndlovu sitting on the spare tyre to his vehicle at exactly the place he had told Pascoe he would meet Seager. As Seager approached, he felt the heat radiating upwards from the Land Rover's bonnet. In his cheap suit, Silas was obviously uncomfortable – and, as he climbed down, he tried unsuccessfully to smooth the wrinkles before he met his new boss. His appearance was completely incongruous with his surroundings. The Siabuwa Binga turnoff was no place for a suit even for a chap to meet his new boss.

"In my day," Seager said as he approached, wanting to put the man at ease, "we didn't wear suits. No good for mixing with the masses."

He put his hand out to the smiling black detective who took it and shook.

"In your day," replied Silas with surprising wit, "you didn't get the opportunity to earn five years salary in a few weeks."

"True." Seager was pleased to get straight to the point. "Can you help?"

He was tired of telling the story now. The smaller man beamed widely. "I think so. I raided Wankie and Nymandhlovu files to compare. This is the way it looks. Furthermore –" He paused, giving the moment the correct importance, "– we got new material only yesterday." He began to spread pages on the bonnet. "These are all copies, you may keep them, but I will give you an overview now if you like."

Jesus, thought Seager, *we never had guys like this in my day.* "Go ahead," he replied.

"Sources at the time had them heading east towards Silobela. Tracks that we found said the same. They were spooked by an army patrol somewhere in there and turned north. That's when we lost the spoor. A constable on that follow-up now works for me. He loves to talk about it. It was his chance of glory, you understand?" Seager nodded. Silas continued, "So nothing new since then, until three weeks ago, again four days ago and finally yesterday."

"Continue," said Seager, reading the pages.

"Five buses robbed, two stores and an armed incident here." He pointed to a place on the map. "All within seventy miles on the main road. These don't reach the press. We have some information from members of the public indicating increasing movements in here and here." Again his stubby finger stabbed at the photocopied map. "They seem to be consolidating and meeting in here. We have a couple of informants in there and it's political again. But–" He paused again and dropped into English, "–we aren't planning anything until the rains are finished. The army have washed their hands of it. You'll have the area to yourselves. That is good and bad. You won't be disturbed but you won't have their interference either or their diversion. If you need more, just get a message to me at the camp. I will meet you again here."

Seager held out a piece of paper. "On here, Silas, is the ops frequency we are using. We'll have a listening watch each night from eight until nine. OK? Twenty hundred to twenty-one hundred. You are Zulu Six. I am Zulu One."

The man took the paper and read the frequency, memorised it and began to eat the paper in mock security. Seager began to laugh before adding, "Anything more Silas, let us know eh?"

Nodding, the policeman spat the paper out into his hand .

"I won't advise you if we are successful," said Seager. "Your sources will tell you that. How do you want your money? Post Office will be risky. I don't know what internal security the police now has."

Most police departments has access to employee details in the constant battle against corruption. Any officer suspected of taking money in return for his involvement in the suppression of evidence would have his personal financial details under scrutiny very quickly and most of the serving police had accounts with the Post Office.

Silas nodded and pulled a variety of items from his side jacket pocket. There was a pen knife, a couple of bus tickets, some change and a button. Finally out came a piece of paper. He handed it to Seager.

"Barclays Bank in Harare, First Street Branch. Account in the name of Joshua Nkala."

Seager nodded. It all made sense. A bank account hundreds of miles away in Mashonaland in the name of a Shona. Very careful indeed. "Don't worry. You will get paid," reassured Seager.

"I know, Mr. Seager. I did some checking on you. There are men at Kariba Police Station who still talk about you." Silas firmly pushed the other items back into his pocket. They shook hands and, as Seager crossed back to his vehicle and the waiting Chimkuyu, Silas sounded his horn in farewell

After the policeman had accelerated back onto the road, Seager and Chimyuku sat in silence as Seager read the top sheets. All were incident reports and completed enquiry forms dating back months. He too picked out the common denominator and began to laugh, softly at first and then more firmly.

Chimkuyu looked across nonplussed and waited for an explanation. Finally Seager said, "I know where to take you with the farlooker old one. I can place the boys within seventy miles of every fucking dissident in the top end of Zimbabwe."

He began to laugh again. He had reason to be pleased. The information Silas had provided meant that Seager could now recall all the teams and re-deploy them in one area. Still large, but now manageable – particularly with the logging recorders and video cameras with their solar packs and trigger system. The area they wanted was the headwaters of the Mlibizi River across as far as the Busi and westwards to the edge of Lubimbi, smack in the middle of what was Sector Four.

He started the engine. The camp was still six hours away fast going, but if he could make the eight Papa Mike broadcast he would recall the teams and they could have a briefing by tomorrow night. He lit a cigarette, pleased with the day. In twenty four hours they had almost totally eliminated three of four sectors. He had expected to take weeks doing that. Now, with the audio and video recorders and the telescopes with some high ground, they could plot the locations of every group in the sector over the next weeks until they found what they needed. For the first time, he was confident of the sixty day limit and sang softly to himself as he drove. It was an old Nat King Cole tune and he wished he could remember the theme to 'Out of Africa.'

They eventually rolled into a very quiet camp just before nine and Seager ran for the big base radio transmitter. "This is Zulu One, Zulu One who copies ova?"

One by one they came back and Seager, pleased that they had maintained their watch to the letter, began. "Have news. New Sitrep. Uplift tomorrow. Sunray first then in sequence."

CHAPTER SIX

Pascoe sat with Seager in the ops tent, his shirt open to the waist, ripped and torn and filthy. He had scratches above his eyes, in spite of the floppy hat that was thick with dust. One knee was sporting a large scab where he had slipped and scraped himself.

They had arrived back, the two pickup vehicles within an hour of each other. The men were washing beneath the forty-four gallon drums shower units before de-brief and new orders. Seager wanted the time with Pascoe to ascertain what immediate success they had had in Sector Four, and the deployment procedure for the next day. Pascoe sipped at a beer and began to talk as Masters entered the tent, cleaned and in fresh kit.

"The bloody place is thick with them. Tim picked up six sets of spoor in one day and we visually contacted two groups. Richard was within twenty feet of the one mob, about seventeen of the buggers. Moving north. A bit of a rabble, but the weapons were clean." He took another sip from the bottle.

"Rasta types," said Masters, "one was smoking dagga and one was trailing his weapon like a tired man with a stick."

"How much ground did you cover?" asked Seager, walking to the map on the wall and picking up a hurricane lamp as he went.

"Fuggin' heaps," answered Pascoe in a most unmilitary fashion.

Masters walked over and looked at the map. He moved his finger as he calculated but, before he could answer intelligently, Pascoe thought better of it. "About thirty five miles."

"What direction?" asked Seager.

"Figure of eight starting here." Pascoe rose and walked to the map and pointed, "And finishing here."

Seager looked at the map, both men watching him, waiting for the news that had brought them all out ahead of schedule.

"I saw Silas," Seager said, "very good stuff. All their intelligence point to one place." He turned and looked at them. "Sector Four.

They're in Sector Four somewhere, I'm sure of it. I feel it in my bones, Ken. I want to re-deploy everyone in there, break up the sectors again and take in the cams, recorders and the telescopes."

Pascoe's face broke into a grin. The tiredness washed away and he started to laugh softly. "Shit! Are you sure?"

"Yeah, I'm sure," answered Seager. "I've never seen such conclusive evidence."

"Alright then. Let's do it."

The three of them were joined by Rob Stockly and they began with the small scale maps, selecting the one that covered Sector Four. It was spread on the table and a clear polythene plastic lay over the top. The fibre tip marker pens were produced and they set down the divide area amongst the men again. The area Seager wanted to cover was some four hundred and ninety square miles.

With five teams in on the ground, it would be roughly ninety square miles each. If the search was for anything smaller than a group of men living together the task would have been daunting. But men use the same routes by habit, those routes become tracks and the tracks eventually become a bare path through the grass or bush. They need to cook so they build fires, they need shelter so rough lean-to's go up. Very soon you have something very obvious to the trained eye. All they would need to do would be to monitor movements along the tracks and eventually follow the tracks to their destinations. Eventually a camp would leap into focus in the telescope's eye. Then they would isolate which camps could hold someone against their wishes, or which camps displayed evidence of visitors. Something unnatural.

Seager had once sent a man to the gallows because the individual had taken a liking to the briefcase he had purloined from the body of his victim. Here in the bush, the belongings of a tourist would stand out from the usual odds and ends. It could be a scarf or a handbag or a camera or a suitcase – but something would lead a watcher to think that this camp could be one worth sneaking a look into. Those dissidents living in the camps would have become careless in the recent months. The army had not been in here since the war ended. There was no reason to suspect they might, so the incredible security they had observed during the war would have slackened, or so Seager hoped.

He held the blue pen over the polythene. "We want thirty by thirty ideally. yeah?" He looked over at Stockly, who was the most experienced for this covert type of search.

"Ja," he said, "then we can just crisscross it for spoor and tracks. Can you define the edges geographically? Makes it easier to know when you're entering some other frozen area."

Seager nodded. Stockly's reference to 'frozen' was a term used when covert teams were put in, usually wearing the enemy's kit. The area was frozen for their use and theirs alone to prevent the possibility of the operators being shot at by their own people. In this case it was slightly different, but it would ease the situation to know that any tracks you found were the enemy and not your own people. "OK," Seager said. "Thirty by thirty it is. The bottom corner, Zulu Four, Pirelli and Chana. Above them, let's see. Zulu Two, Buchanan and Ncubi?" He looked at Stockly and Pascoe. Both nodded, approving his choice.

"Right bottom, Zulu Three, that's you Rob and James, and above you that leaves me and Chimkuyu. Sibanda and Masters can range around the top and right-hand edge of the quadrant." On the map he wrote Zulu Five and two arrows, one along to the right and one down the edge. "Ken, you just tag along with whoever has something interesting to see." Seager finished and looked at them.

"We better put together a briefing," said Pascoe, "just give me twenty minutes to shower and change and I'll join you." He got up, stretched and walked yawning from the tent.

"Oi Madala!" called Stockly to Pascoe. "Don't overdo the speed now!"

"Fuck off," Pascoe replied tiredly.

Pascoe was the oldest of the group. He and Buchanan were by far the fittest of the team and the others were feeling the effect of the long hours of walking up and down hills. By the end of the month, Seager knew they would all be in top condition – but now they were feeling the abused muscles. He smiled at the exchange and looked at Stockly. "Give him another couple of weeks, Rob. He'll walk you into the ground. That's a promise," said Seager softly. "I've seen him on a follow-up."

"I know Max. That's why I'm rubbing it in now," Stockly replied wearily.

The briefing the next morning was over quite quickly. Everyone was pleased that the area had been narrowed down and they could get on with what they were good at. Finding people who wanted to remain hidden. Seager's part over, Pascoe began talking about the cameras and microphones. When he had finished, the men began familiarising themselves with their sets. Ncubi handled his like it would explode any moment until Buchanan took it from him.

"You handle it like a new baby," Buchanan said in English.

"Be more fucking trouble," replied Ncubi shaking his head, speaking Sindebele.

"Cave!" replied Buchanan. "If you can't eat it, fire it or fuck it you aren't interested, are you?"

The Matabele creased up laughing at the truth of the statement and covered his laugh genteelly with one hand, as if embarrassed by it all. The two had developed quite a friendship in the few days and Pascoe was delighted. It was one of those relationships that made the difference when the going got tough. Mutual respect and time spent together made for good teams.

Just before dusk, Seager took over again and went through the call signs, warning them about radio procedure. They established codes: *theodilite* would be the word for any kind of equipment malfunction, *samples* for visual contacts and, if they required Pascoe or Seager's attention, they would need *lab analysis*.

Seager broke out the beer later and Andre's cook had laid out a buffet by the fire for a *braaivleis* – or, as Masters insisted on calling it, a good old-fashioned barbeque. The night was spent relaxing and they were all in their sleeping bags by ten, knowing they would be woken at four thirty by Simeon who was sulking at having been left out of the search. Seager's consoling talk about marching on stomachs and the like had no effect; the old man wanted action and walked about muttering to himself, much to Chimkuyu's amusement. Chimyuku was beginning to think of the camp's aging major domo as a stork with spindly legs and a long neck.

The next day, as vehicle three slowed to turn north, Seager's vehicle turned back to give them their rations. Buchanan was eating a Flakey bar and had bits of chocolate in his beard as he looked from the window at Seager.

"Want some?" He offered, talking with his mouth full and smiling.

"No thank you," replied Seager, who thought that anyone older than his daughter who ate chocolate at this hour of the day was not all there. "Keith, keep your eyes open eh? This place is thick with them."

Buchanan took another bite of his Flakey and prodded Ncubi who was asleep.

"Cave, wake up bastard! Max reckons we should be careful. Oi, wake up!"

Ncubi muttered something and Buchanan turned to Seager.

"He said they're all Tsotsis. No problem." Taking another bite, he threw the wrapper on the floor. Tsotsi was the word for punk-trouble-maker.

Seager just shook his head and, as the door slammed shut, he nodded once to the men in the other vehicle and they pulled away, Masters' feet jutting from the window the last thing they saw through the dust.

*

It was after lunch that the men in vehicle one eventually climbed clear of the oven hot cab and began unloading the cargo from the rear. There were the extra boxes, each containing two days rations for two men. There was, however, no soap, toothpaste or tobacco, nothing at all that would produce an alien smell. A man can smell toothpaste or soap a mile downstream of where another has washed if he himself doesn't use it. There were their packs, the geology gear, the radios and the autosurveillance units, and finally their weapons. All in all, a heavy load that would take the rest of the day to carry deep into their sector to whatever base camp location Seager selected. From there they would range miles every day, sometimes staying overnight, watching tracks and waterholes and the kraal-lines, the routes between the hundred tiny settlements that pockmarked this corner of the world. They struck out immediately, Chimkuyu to the point and Pascoe trailing behind, doing limited ant tracking and watching their backs.

It was late afternoon when the tall Shangaan first displayed his worth. He stopped, looked about him and, dropping his packs, wandered up the side of a small ridge. He was back a few minutes later.

"Small crack in the earth from which water flows," he said. "A spring."

"Where?" came Seager in reply. By this point he was tired, hot, and sweating freely.

Chimkuyu pointed into the bush below the ridge.

"How did you know?" asked Seager, forgetting his tiredness, now fascinated.

"The birds." He pointed. "The small ones with yellow beaks only have their young very near water. They eat from the edge."

"You may have good eyes, but they're not that good," said Pascoe disbelieving.

Chimkuyu gave Pascoe a lordly stare before offering a smug smile. "Little one, he who talks to the spirits tells me you know much of war, soldiers and men. Since you are so close to the earth, look down more often and learn of other things." Chimkuyu bent down and picked up a tiny yellow brown feather. "When the young have plumage such as this, they can only fly short distances. Therefore the water was there in those trees where the colour is greener and the leaves thicker."

Seager chuckled at the rebuke. The place now pointed out was the only possibility; otherwise the vegetation was sparse and thorny.

From that time on the Shangaan only ever referred to Pascoe as "Small Feather" and in time the rest of the group caught on. Pascoe then began to treat the man with considerably more respect and would often sit and talk with him in halting Sindebele, learning what he could. The little brown feather incident was the beginning of many lessons for the two white men from the Shangaan.

They set up their rudimentary camp seventy or eighty yards from the spring. Far enough from prying eyes if anyone else came to the water and far enough away to allow the few small animals and birds to use the spring without fear of the intruders. The shelters big enough for one man were a few yards up a slope. A dyed woven fruit bag was suspended up a tree with provisions away from the ants and other scavengers, its new green colour blending with the foliage.

Once the camp was established, the auto-surveillance unit was broken out and checked and the weapons were cleaned before Chimkuyu produced matches and lit a small cooking fire built of three stones in the traditional way. The dark settled as the smoke dissipated into the leaves of the canopy over their heads and Seager lit his first illicit cigarette as Pascoe produced some equally illicit chewing gum. Both had smells that were alien.

"Be thankful I am not looking for you," admonished Chimkuyu. He stood and, collecting his rifle, wandered out of the camp and up the hill.

Seager guiltily called after him to wait and he would come too. The cigarette in his mouth, he broke out the telescope from its stainless steel box and, taking one last wistful drag, he dropped the butt to the ground and stamped it in deep before scraping more dirt over the top. The Shangaan nodded approvingly and they both walked from the camp as Pascoe began testing the abilities of the tiny SONY microphones, still stubbornly chewing his gum.

Fifteen minutes later, Seager was spreading the legs of the tripod and pulling the lens covers clear. The telescope was roughly thirty-three inches long, with the end front the size of a tea cup. Seager looked through the viewfinder and tilted the eyepiece towards the stars appearing in the sky. Focusing on a particular star, he indicated to Chimkuyu to look. The older man peered into the eyepiece made a startled "Aaah!" He looked quickly up at the sky and then back into the scope, swinging it first left and then right, making the same pleasure noise each time he found a star.

"How is this done?" he asked finally, looking up.

"Like those who have poor eyesight and wear ma-spectacles. This is a spectacle of many pieces of glass, thick, like the bottom of a coke bottle, each in turn making that which you see larger."

He looked into the eyepiece again and spoke as he did so. "He who talks to the spirits. What do you think is out there?"

Seager wondered how to answer that one and settled on honesty.

"Each of those small lights is another sun, many thousand of years travelling in the fastest aeroplane, and between them nothing."

"A sun?" the Shangaan laughed gently. "For one who talks to the spirits you are naive like a child. How can there be nothing? There is never nothing, and there is only one sun."

"What do you think is there?" Seager asked firmly. "O great teacher?"

"That is not for me to know," he replied with dignity, "but be assured young one, it is not nothing, for there is never nothing."

"You talk with a winding path," said Seager, trying to pin him down.

"How can you have a straight path going nowhere?"

Shit, thought Seager. *The bugger has had me again. The man's logic is mindboggling.* "Look to the bush, Chimkuyu, find me some gun-dungas."

The Shangaan chuckled softly and swung the telescope down and began to slowly scan the black bush for a pinprick of light somewhere below them.

They spent the next two hours on the ridgetop taking turns to bend over the eyepiece. They saw two flames in that time and Seager took bearing on each with a hand compass. In the morning they would seek out the sites of the fires. It was on one of these occasions that Seager was bent over the eyepiece that the Shangaan spoke for the first time since they began. He looked up at the moon, a bright solid disc in the night sky and said, "What a thing that is," with some wonder in his voice.

Seager looked up at him and then the sky. "It was barren without life or water or air," he replied.

"How do you know? Even the farlooker can't show you that," he said defensively. Seager looked back at him and smiled.

"The Americans. They have put two men up there in a special aeroplane. They walked on the surface in special suits like a fireman."

Chimkuyu looked at him quickly. "Is this true?"

Seager nodded.

"How dare they? Is nothing sacred? Do you ask a woman why she will die for her child? Do you ask the earth why rain falls in one place and not another? Do you ask the sun why it rises?"

Seager could have said yes to each, but the old Shangaan's disappointment in the modern times was raw enough a wound without rubbing in the salt of further revelations.

"Some things are sacred and should not be asked, seen or questioned," he finished with.

"You are right, Madala. Some things we seek as hunters, end up hunting us."

Chimkuyu motioned for Seager to step back and bent to the eyepiece for his turn, slowly swivelling the telescope on its mounting.

Seager was stretching, trying to ease the ache in his back when Chimkuyu clicked his fingers twice. The silence was unnecessary, simply a routine instilled over years of poaching other men's game. Seager looked down quickly.

"North needle," said Chimkuyu. It was his name for a compass. He never used one – his natural sense of direction absolute – but he knew Seager would want a bearing.

Seager squatted and held the compass over the telescope to get the angle, then stood to read off without any influence from any metal in the instrument.

"Marked," he said and scribbled the bearing on a piece of paper. "What have you got?"

"Light moving, three of them. White light, not from a fire, moving fast."

"How far?" asked Seager.

Chimkuyu shrugged into the telescope. "We will have to wait till daylight to tell. This farlooker shows some things but loses others."

"Do not move it," said Seager. "In the morning we shall look through again and judge better."

The Shangaan rubbed his eyes and together they walked down the hill to the camp, slowly picking their way through the tracks, scrub and fallen branches.

When they arrived, Pascoe was steadily stirring a pot of soup on the small fire and turning the foil-wrapped cakes of maize meal in the ashes at the edge. On the far side, tins of beef stew and cups with tea bags were laid out in line. They settled on their haunches and, without speaking, began to eat.

"Whenever you say nothing, something is on!" Pascoe said profoundly.

Seager grinned in the firelight. "We have two fires and a torchlight march to pick up on in the morning."

"Good," said Pascoe.

They ate quickly, talking little, and as Seager and Pascoe drank tea, Chimkuyu walked from the camp, carrying his cup and headed back up the slope to the telescope.

CHAPTER SEVEN

Seager was up before dawn, after another hot and sweaty night beneath mosquito nets, with the sounds of the crickets chirping all around. "I'm getting too old for this shit, sleeping on rocks," he said to Pascoe as they readied for the out.

Beyond the camp perimeter, they split up, Chimkuyu going after the torch group to find tracks and the other two moving off just towards the place they had seen the fires. Chimkuyu went alone because he could move faster and cover the tracks a longer way towards where they were going. Seager and Pascoe would slowly approach the places where the fires had been seen and see if anyone was still there and how long they had been there.

It was late morning by the time they reached the point that Seager thought should hold the remains of the fire. They were moving on a compass bearing and it was slow going because they weren't sure just how far away the distant flickering light had been. It was, in fact, a great deal further than they thought and it was nearly two in the afternoon when Pascoe – who was walking ahead slowly, cradling his weapon – waved Seager to the ground and settled himself into the scrub, slowly like a predatory cat watching a mouse.

Seager settled just as slowly, thinking, *Jesus they are still here, Ken has seen something*. Easing his finger forward, he slid the safety catch on his weapon onto fire.

It was then that he smelt it. The wind had changed and there was the warm, slightly acrid smell of woodsmoke on the wind. Very slowly, Pascoe turned his head and looked at Seager, then tapped his nose with his finger. In silence, Pascoe rose and began to move into the trees.

Seager felt a drop of sweat developing on the end of his nose and, as he rose to follow, he wiped it clear. He could hear his own heartbeat and he felt the old half fear of going into an uncertain situation that could become extremely dangerous. It was a half fear because the other half was the old excitement of nearing his target.

It was very hot as they moved beneath the gnarled branches of the msasa trees. The rest seemed to shimmer and roll in waves with the smoky tinge in the dry wafting air. *Nice and slow Ken, nice and slow. Let's see them before they see us. We have got six weeks or so, nice and slow now.*

Pascoe needed no lessons; he moved like a chameleon, from one shadow to another, his sweat-streaked khaki shirt blending with the bush. Only his eyes seemed to flick back and forth, watching everything at once, looking for the movement that would give his eyes a point to focus on.

He froze.

Seager saw it too. A movement in the trees thirty yards ahead. A hand had brushed a fly. The figure was sprawled beneath a bush. Seager scanned the scene. To the right of the relaxing man was a very small fire, a tiny spiral of smoke dissipating into the wind. Behind the fire another man lay still, probably asleep, one arm across his eyes.

Pascoe began to move backwards, inching at first, then making more deliberate movements. Seager followed. A moment later, they settled against the base of a tree, obscured from view by a large granite boulder discoloured by lichen and dry moss.

Pascoe removed his floppy hat and wiped the sweat from his face. With a finger he wrote in the sand: "GOOD SCOPE!"

Seager smiled back and raised one thumb.

The telescope had shown them a fire no larger than a domestic barbeque at just over eight miles' range. Even considering that at night it would be built up and blazing, it was impressive – and Seager was pleased with the original decision to purchase the Zeiss instruments. He shrugged towards Pascoe. "What now? Wait?" he mouthed in silence.

Pascoe nodded and held up both hands open twice. Twenty minutes. He drew in the sand and then an arrow round to the right. So, thought Seager. He wanted to go and look from the other direction.

Seager nodded and wrote in the sand. 'MORE THAN TWO'?

Pascoe looked up quickly and held up two fingers, questioning. Then he shook his head, held up three fingers and drew the sleeping man in the sand.

Seager rolled back a few feet and looked into the camp from the rear of the boulder. It took him a full minute to see the arm on the third man obscured by grass, brown and tawny. Anyone could have missed it. He smiled and remembered why he had asked Pascoe to come and why they had recruited the men they had.

Pascoe signalled that he was going round the side and for Seager to shoot if something happened. Pascoe called it suppressing fire but had described it as "shoot the shit out of something and keeping it down while one of your people did something nasty from the other direction, or alternatively, get the hell out." He nodded and looked at the big Rolex on his wrist. Twenty minutes.

Pulling his lightweight pack on carefully, Seager drew a small pair of binoculars from the centre section. Stripping away the camouflage veil in which they were wrapped, he pulled it over his face and slowly rolled to his right, his eyes only inches from the ground. Then he lifted the instrument to his eyes and pulled the veil down to the far ends of the lenses, like a camouflage net over a gun barrel, and focused the scene. Stopping long enough to pull his rifle nearer, and ready to react to any problem, he began making mental notes on the scene. He began counting the tins by the fire. The round tins would be used for drinking from and there would be roughly the same number as men in the group. He could see a definite five and perhaps a sixth lying on its side. He looked at the tree supporting the end of a piece of twine that disappeared into the shadows. There was a garment over the line, perhaps shading the ground for a sleeping man on the other side. Four, maybe five. The sleeping figure beneath the bush stirred and rolled onto his side away from Seager.

The heat shimmered and danced and he pulled the binoculars down to wipe the sweat from his eyes, before swinging them to the right to see if he could see Ken's approach from that flank. The trees seemed lifeless in the glare of the day and beneath them nothing moved. It was forty-five minutes before Pascoe returned, clicking his fingers in the prescribed manner before appearing from the bush behind Seager. He crawled forward silently, then reached for the water bottle and took a few sips.

Seager waited patiently and finally Pascoe held up six fingers. Leaning closer, he whispered, "Six A.K.'s and an R.P.G. Nothing else of much interest."

Seager rolled his thumb to the left. Pascoe nodded and they began to backtrack downwind, away from the silent camp and its sleeping occupants. Half a mile away, beneath the tight canopy of an acacia thorn tree, they settled down and began to exchange notes.

"The one with the tea-cosy hat," said Seager. "He's the boss."

Pascoe looked up with interest.

"He had an expensive looking watch, better fed than the rest and bigger, much bigger. He wouldn't take shit from the others. Also the tree was the best possy. Best shade, near the fire – and he had a sidearm."

"Yeah," said Pascoe, "I saw that. The little one with the R.P.G., I reckon he's only about eighteen. Stupid little prick, should be at school."

"Did you see an automatic gun?"

Pascoe shook his head.

"How long do you reckon?"

"Couple of days. But they'll be moving out soon. No sudza, no nyama."

Hardly any food at all, thought Seager. This wasn't a permanent camp. "O.K., let's let 'em go and we'll come back with Chimkuyu in a couple of days and see which way they went. It's about four now. We could make the other site by dark."

Pascoe brushed a large blue fly from his face. "Yeah let's go. I'm sick of this fucking place already."

Seager pulled a map from the pack and began to work the bearing to take them to the second location, this time with more accuracy over the distance from the base camp.

"Just about due west, maybe two six six. About three miles, then turn north again for a bit. You take the point and see if you can smell them again."

They slung the light packs and walked from the shade into the softer afternoon light. Here Seager took a bearing on a hill in the distance and began to walk a steady tattoo, his long legs brown and strong.

They found the other site just before dusk, but to Seager's frustration it was already empty. After some time, they found the tracks and followed them far enough to establish the direction in which the men had gone; then they turned back to sift the camp's remains. Seager was busy until dark and, for a short time after, with a torch. He found boot impressions and a place where a rifle butt had been leant on. The fire was long dead and the ashes had been scattered. It was Pascoe who spotted them, grey and fine, hard against the side of a sizeable boulder. Had the fire been built on the north side of the rock they would never have seen it.

"Nine," he said looking at Seager.

"Naaa, seven. Only seven different prints here. These laddies were good. They've left virtually nothing. No tins, no butts. If you hadn't seen the ashes we would have walked right past. That was sloppy. My guess is, whoever runs this bunch, delegated that job and didn't check it. It doesn't gel. The rest is good. Whoever runs this bunch is very good. Very good indeed." He smiled at Pascoe. "Worthy of the chase."

*

The others all had similar results the first day: fires dead, camps empty, cold spoor. Only Ncubi, who had split up with Buchanan, had found a camp that was inhabited. He watched it for a half a day and then left to rendezvous with the big bearded man who was his partner.

They were going to head back to the site when, that evening – back at base camp – Masters and Sibanda radioed in that they needed help. Up on the northern edge of the sector they had found a leopard in a snare, alive and fighting but in real trouble. Abandoning their mission, they had immediately set up a small camp nearby to watch over it until Andre, back at base, could suggest help. Sibanda had shot a Thompsons gazelle and they threw the snarling spitting angry amber eyed beast a whole haunch. It watched them its eyes filled with hate, trapped and in great pain. The snare had caught its rear right leg at the edge of a stand of acacia trees and had more than likely been intended for antelope. Even, so the poacher would be pleased beyond his wildest dreams with his catch: the leopard's skin was worth many, many antelope.

Andre was about to leave the main camp with a dart-gun, one item he had relieved the Parks and Wildlife Department of on his departure, when he remembered Buchanan's expertise. Andre could sedate the leopard while it was still in its snare, but Buchanan's father was a vet, and years of osmosis had given him some experience in treating animals. So, rather than go back to investigate the inhabited camp, Buchanan and Andre left Ncubi to watch the camp and set out to rendezvous with Masters and Sibanda.

They arrived after three the following day and went immediately to work. Though its eyes were still angry and its snarl still menacing, the leopard was weakening fast and had eaten nothing from the haunch.

"He's been fighting the snare all night and all today," said Masters.

"Lucky he hasn't tried to bite through his own leg," said Andre. "Where's the nearest water?"

"Why?" asked Masters.

"He'll be thirsty after he wakes, but maybe not strong enough to travel himself if it's any distance. We'll move him doped." He looked across the grass flattened by the animal where it had rolled and struggled, fighting the thing that held him, the thing he couldn't understand. In his world he feared nothing except men. No animal would trouble him because he stuck to the trees and rocky slope of the hills. He had wandered far, obviously from the Chizarira Game Reserve, because out here his kind were few and far between. Their coats were too valuable to poachers and trophy hunters alike.

"O.K.," said Buchanan, obviously visibly upset by the scene, "let's dart him and get him clear."

Andre came very close from behind while Buchanan walked close to the front to distract him. The black lips exposed the savage feline incisors, and his coat rippled in anger. Buchanan crooned at him softly, but his ears were back and he was spat out ferociously.

Then the dart hit him high in the left rump.

The leopard spun at the new source of danger and immediately the drug began to work. Within a minute he was groggy and disorientated. Buchanan moved forward, carefully ignoring Andre's warning about the unpredictable nature of the drug and its sedating effect. "Come Ingwe, come my boy. Let's get that fucking wire off you, um?" He touched the cat and it remained inert.

The others moved forward, Andre pulling wire cutters from his pocket. "Let's move it. I want him down by the water before he wakes or he will rip us up."

They cut the snare clear and, as Buchanan stitched the wound as best he could, the others emptied the back of the land cruiser. After they had lifted the inert animal up onto the tray, Andre handed him a hypodermic syringe. Up front, Sibanda started the motor and, with everyone aboard, he began to head towards the nearest water, a good two miles away. The syringe contained a huge dose of penicillin and, after that was administered, Buchanan tightly bandaged the ugly wound.

"He'll tear it off in a couple of days," said Andre.

"Be O.K. by then. He'll have his strength back and can lick it clean and hunt."

They set him down by the stream edge, heavily shaded by the leaves. A few minutes later, the leopard woke groggy and confused, and limped painfully into the shade.

Dusk was already hardening to night, a whole day lost to the leopard while Masters and Sibanda's share of the sector went unscouted. Seager would not be happy that their best laid plans had been disrupted so early in the operation, but the leopard was as big as males go and well worth the effort to save. No matter, Masters and Sibanda would have to make up for what they had missed. The next day, they were up before dawn, determined to make up for lost time.

They spent the morning working hurriedly through the areas they had meant to explore the day before. Masters took point, Sibanda exhausted after the previous day's exertions. For long hours there was nothing – or, if there was anything at all, they overlooked it in their haste to make up time. It was the middle of the day, and both men flagging in the oppressive heat, when they picked up a set of spoor and began to track it.

By late afternoon they had followed it for seven miles east, before it swung north and out of the sector. They were moving back when Sibanda, walking on Masters' flank and eight to ten yards behind, swung his eyes off the bush to his side, long enough to take a compass bearing while walking. Normally he would have stopped, but today there was no time for lingering, so he continued apace. They were still half a day behind schedule.

In the four or five seconds he had taken to look down at the compass, men emerged from the tree line on Sibanda's side. With his eyes on the compass, Sibanda barely noticed that they were no longer alone. And perhaps it was the exhaustion of the day before, or perhaps he was too obsessed with making up for lost time, gazing into the trees on his own side of the track, but Masters didn't notice anything either..

By the time he looked round, it was already too late.

Sibanda never knew what it was that warned him they were no longer alone. There was no shot at that stage. He didn't remember any alarm amongst them. He just remembered going to ground as fast as he could and rolling round to present his weapon at the yet unseen threat.

Masters heard him roll and spun with reactions honed by three years of bush firefights. As he turned, he brought the AR 15 to his shoulder and dropped onto one knee against a tree bole.

Sibanda was nowhere to be seen. Fifty yards away, on the trail, three armed men stared at him, looks of surprise on their faces.

Masters mind emptied of all thought. Later, he would remember so little. Right now, it was only instinct. One weapon foreshortened in his vision as it was brought to bear on him and that was enough. Now he knew what he must do. The Colt bucked four times in his hand as he dropped two of the men in precision succession. The third man broke and, as Masters moved to stop him with another round, from somewhere Sibanda discharged a single round. The man fell in a sprawling mass of arms and legs and wire and sticks.

All three men were dead.

Masters and Sibanda hurried to the fallen bodies. All were armed with automatic weapons but a closer look proved them to be not dissidents at all but, in fact, poachers. The last man had been carrying the wire snares they would distribute, and they would shoot what they could, for skin, tusk, horn or meat.

Masters thought fast. He signaled to check exit wounds. All the armalite rounds fired from his AR 15 had exited and gone on. The only bullet still in a victim was the 7:62 intermediate fired by Sibanda at the last man. Both the others had the same weapon type. Anyone un-likely enough to come across the scene would assume that the men had argued and ended up shooting it out. They removed some rounds from the second AK and Sibanda, muffling the report, fired four rounds from his rifle into the ground, then dropped the casings by the single body away from the other two. Four rounds. Four holes. One round one hole.

"More," said Masters. "These boys aren't that good."

Sibanda fired another dozen rounds away and then liberally scat-tered the cartridge cases about the scene.

Upon finishing, they looked at each other, nodded and moved into the bush to put some distance between themselves and the scene. The whole thing had taken less than two minutes.

That night, Masters reported the incident to Seager as he knew he had to. Neither felt any remorse. To them, poachers were the lowest form of life, and even if the poacher hadn't shown his weapon first, Masters would have probably considered shooting anyway. He was a rare fanatic and would kill to defend the animals he loved so much. That was why Seager didn't believe it was a reflex to a potential contact. He thought that the pair had come across poachers, remembered the leopard and thought it might be appropriate to even the score a little. Seager could quite easily believe that, because he was capable of such himself. What angered him was the fact that these men, who were two of his elite, had almost compromised the operation. In fact, they were very lucky that they had not sustained injuries themselves, or had the police involved if the others had got away.

After Masters and Sibanda had been dismissed, Seager ranted to himself in the camp below the kopje, Pascoe listening and letting his friend vent his steam. "Fucking stupidity Ken. Rank fucking stupidity. They, of all people should know better. Sibanda should have seen those people long before it came to that and Masters should have known better."

"I'll have a chat when we see them on Saturday, don't worry. It won't happen again."

"It had better not. I came in with a team and we are all going out together. Next time they could be fucking killed. This is a rescue. Not a fucking Wild West movie. There will be minimum rounds repeat minimum rounds expended on this job!"

"Here," said Pascoe, "have some tea and stop carrying on."

Seager took the cup and sipped it. "I don't leave anyone behind Ken."

Chimkuyu arrived back that night. He had had a very successful two days and, by the light of a torch, he drew from memory a complex map of the tracks he had followed. He had visual contact with two small groups and produced small pieces of evidence for Seager: live ammunition, a shampoo bottle that had whiskey in it, an afro comb left behind at a camp and, lastly, a small blue casino chip.

"Nothing that would have been owned by ma-English girl or boy?"

Chimkuyu shook his head and then asked Seager what the chip was.

"Money for gambling" he said, "that came from someone who had been to the Falls." They ate whilst comparing notes and talking before climbing the hill to uncover the telescope and watch the dark wilderness below.

*

The remainder of that week was largely fruitless. Chimkuyu ranged far each and every day, finding many tracks and seeing various people at odd times. The hostiles he reported to Seager.

Pascoe bade them farewell on the Wednesday morning and walked out to call for a pick-up. He wanted to join Rob Stockly and Nyamadze for a couple of days before the weekly debrief. Collected on Saturday morning, all the teams were pleased to get back to main camp and hot showers from the drum. Andre's cook had fashioned a proper menu from a piece of folded card and, in a show of spirit, the men combed their hair and ordered from it, flicking ash into ashtrays instead of onto the ground. One even drank beer from a glass. The relaxation was most welcome and was followed by the debrief on the map. While the men took their turns in debriefing Seager, the others sat outside the mess tent and slowly demolished the rubbish bin full of bottles of beer.

By eight that night, they were finished – and, as they allowed the atmosphere to wash over them, and the soft chairs around the fire to become more comfortable, Seager alone worked on into the night. This was his forte, a fluid moving portrayal of what was happening out there in Sector Four. He was disappointed, but did not allow the others to sense it. He was hoping someone would have seen something more. Some tiny indication that Layla Rakkafian and Maggie Nolan had passed that way. Clues to the young man they were with would be harder to place. Not quite as incongruous, not quite as out of place.

Three young whites out here, where are you? He tapped the map with the big snowman marker. *Where are you? Leave me a clue somewhere. Anything. A ribbon, a hairclip, an English coin. Anything in a camp and my boys will find it.*

*

The next morning, the search resumed in earnest.

Sibanda and Masters began from the south of their sector and moved north slowly. The area was close to several settlements and what tracks they found were easily confused. Meanwhile, Stockly and Nyamadze, like Pirelli and Chana, dropped very quickly into their operating routines. They would go hours saying nothing, all communication by signals with the right hand. They covered many miles, crossing and recrossing the narrow paths and tracks, watching for spoor smoke or signs or habitation. At night they went to high ground and watched with their telescopes and through the days they sat by water holes, waiting for thirsty men to stop and fill their bottles. They all found snares, most abandoned and rusty, and on the Tuesday Pirelli came across an old woman living alone in a dilapidated hut. She was, as Pirelli later told Seager, as crazy as any person he had ever seen. They had watched her one night throwing handfuls of her own faeces at the moon, shrieking at it. Stockly and Nyamadze sat in the heat of the day by one stream edge and tried to differentiate the pairs of footprints that had crossed there. They gave up at sixteen pairs and made a note that this point was to be watched.

By now, the heat was monstrous. It wilted the bush, it dried the dust and all living things cowered before it. In Chizarira Reserve even the rhino sought shade as the sun blazed and baked the landscape. The rains were still a month away, and it would get hotter still.

The highlight of Buchanan's week was when Ncubi found a tiny grass snake and presented it to him. Most Africans hate snakes with due reason. Many on that continent were venomous and fatalities every year were considerable, not even worthy of news like anywhere else in the world. Ncubi delighted Buchanan with the gift. Most others would have just ignored it or trodden on it, but Buchanan spent the rest of that morning looking for a grasshopper small enough to feed it.

It was Friday morning when a break in routine gave Sibanda and Masters their first time off since the meeting with Silas the Binga policeman. It redeemed them in Seager's eyes, for the initiative displayed in spite of the pall of gloom it spread on morale at the base camp the next debrief.

They had begun that week in the southwestern corner of their 'r' shaped sector and had moved very slowly indeed, the tracks confused and tatty. By Friday they had covered the sector through to the road that linked Lubimbi to the main graded Kamativi Road.

Lubimbi was a tiny town, more a bus stop really, with a store and a school and the remains of a garage. Sibanda had suggested going in and wandering around, seeing what he could find. If no information was gleaned, then certainly a couple of Cokes and a loaf of bread could be in it for them.

"Find a shabeen," said Masters, "see what the talk is. These people are either sympathisers or pissed off with it all. They should be talking to each other."

Sibanda agreed and, dreaming up a cover story, he walked back down the road in shorts, tattered shirt and bare feet, having left his kit with Masters who was about to lie up for the day. After making enquiries, he was directed to the shabeen in the back of the store.

Shabeen were the unlicensed bars run usually by women to supplement their normal income. They sold maize beer, maybe some cheap whiskey by the shot and usually offered food of some kind. With his local accent, Sibanda was immediately accepted and sat near the front of the room where the breeze was warm through the long broken window. A dog, stiff-legged with the years, walked across the sunny bare earth in front of the store and two small children chased an old bicycle wheel with sticks. He exchanged pleasantries with the other drinkers as one might do anywhere in the world, and was soon engaged in conversation with a local man who drove a petrol tanker for two days a week in Hwange.

The day passed most pleasantly for Sibanda, Masters' money going over the bar like he was Aristotle Onasis, and the cartons of Shake-a-shake and Chibuku coming the other way like a production line. It was nearing dusk when be began talking to a much older man. Sibanda told him that he had just left his job and was going home to see his family. The man too had a family, a son and two daughters and they were the pride of his life. They talked of their children and then, without any prompting, the man leant forward conspiratorially.

"One must be careful of course hereabouts," he said. "The boys. They come through here sometimes. It pays to be home before dark, least you see what you should not see." Tapping his nose, he drew back in drunken over-reaction to his own statement, then bent forward again to his young companion. "Why, just a few months ago my son was bringing my cattle home from their grazing." He stopped and smiled. "I have nine cattle. Fine beasts whose forebears were the Royal herds of Zululand, after that the Royal herds of Mzilikazi and after that."

"What of your son?" Sibanda asked gently, steering him back to the topic as gently as he could.

"Oh, he was coming home and smelled something. He has a good nose, has my boy. Like his grandfather. A good nose."

"Carry on," said Sibanda. He poured the old man another dollop into the old cracked glad. "What did your son of the good nose smell?"

"In between the rocks. The smell." He tapped his nose again, "A body. Not no no no. Not one of the boys, or a traveller, but a murungu." His eyes widened at the thought. "I told him no, it was a monkey, best not to be involved with these things. But something terrible had happened out there. Times are hard, friend." The man smiled, his demeanour changing all over again. "But I was telling you of my herd."

It was midnight before Sibanda was back with his partner and they spent the next day waiting impatiently for the eight o'clock 'listening watch' at main camp. At precisely that time, Masters turned on his magic little General Electric with its space shuttle technology and began to speak.

"Zulu One, Zulu One, Zulu Five." He repeated it just once and Seager came back strength five.

"Zulu Five this is One, go."

"Zulu One – have immediate need repeat, immediate need lab analysis. Did you copy ova."

"Don't get excited, it's not too hot. Confirm following loc."

He read the coordinates fast, reversing them as agreed. Then Seager repeated them back and they both shut down for the night.

All across the sector, the teams who were able had heard the exchange and wondered what was so bad it could need Seager's attention.

To this, there was only one answer.

CHAPTER EIGHT

Morosely, Buchanan tried feeding his little snake, but it had only eaten three days before and didn't seem interested. He put it back in his pocket and settled against a rock to sleep.

Ncubi had already closed his eyes for the night, confident in his ability to hear things in that condition and wake if need be. As he tried to sleep, he was thinking about a camp he had seen earlier. Something about that camp had made him uneasy, but he hadn't yet explained himself to Buchanan. Buchanan would want to know *why* and *what*, but Ncubi could answer none of these things. Right now it was only a feeling, hazy and indistinct. He wanted to go and watch it again. Perhaps this camp was one to put the cameras on. Perhaps it was one to watch all day, every day. From the spoor Ncubi had seen, there was much coming and going but seemingly without purpose. It was too permanent, yet too basic. It was too busy, and yet too quiet.

Over the next day they circled the camp time and again. By the third time, Buchanan no longer believed it when Ncubi insisted he wasn't looking out for anything in particular. By the fall of Wednesday night he was deeply unnerved.

"There is something there," said Buchanan. "What is it, Sekuru? What have you have seen?"

Buchanan asked it over and over again until, at last, Ncubi consented to reply. "I don't know but it is there, or not there. I am not sure."

This time, Buchanan had heard enough. His frustration erupted. "We'll put the camera there then. *Then* we'll know, one way or another."

They did it on the Thursday before dawn, the tiny camera's zoom facility on its tightest focus, and yet still revealing only tiny figures moving in and out of camp. Buchanan had complete faith in Ncubi's instinct and they began to watch with the telescope from a nearby rise, the camera running lower and nearer. Every now and then the catlike

Ncubi would move even closer. Close enough to hear and to smell. All that day, they kept close watch on the camp, Buchanan making notes and sketches as he went.

By the time Thursday evening came, they gathered together in the light of a rising moon and began to compare notes and perceptions. Buchanan stroked his matted beard. His hair was thick with dust and grime and he had not seen water to wash for a week. Even if he had he would not have used it. Neither man smoked. Neither man had cleaned his teeth with anything other than a chewed twig and neither had eaten anything other than the staple sudza and meat in that time. They were as natural as they could be in their surroundings, with no alien smells or colours. They both spoke in whispers or used hand signals; they left virtually no track as they moved and they never slept in the same place twice.

"So," Ncubi said, "the camp lies here –" He drew a map on the ground in the dark, "– high ground. People come and go? You saw this from the ridge?"

Buchanan nodded. "They move in twos or threes, sometimes more. But the timings aren't regular, Sekuru. There isn't any pattern."

"What about the one with the woollen hat, the flag colours? He was there before, this time last week." Ncubi paused. "But the others, they come and go. Some we have not seen before and yet the camp only has five people most times. They coming and going Keith." Ncubi used Buchanan's Christian name for the first time. "It's too much for a small camp. It is like the main gate of Nkomo Barracks. Are you with me, Sekuru?"

Buchanan suddenly smiled. The moon was rising and Ncubi could see him clearly, huge and powerful like a bull elephant. He began to laugh very quietly. "I am with you," he grinned. "It's a fucking picket! The people coming and going are leaving another bigger camp some-where up her" He jabbed a huge finger at the ground where Ncubi had drawn his map.

"That is the way I see it too. But we have to find it and, with one picket, there will be more. There will be silent posts. Maybe many."

"Whoever put this together had had some training. Sovbloc," said Buchanan. "The ma-Russians use a twenty per cent rule. One in five men will guard in turn. With this picket, then, there are twenty or thirty in the main group. The more we find we keep adding."

"It's a big camp," Ncubi said. "Remember the tracks we found to the south of here? They may lead us to another picket, a route from the south."

Buchanan nodded. "I'll call camp. Tell them to hold off the uplift until we've checked the whole perimeter of those hills."

He looked south at the low rise in the moonlight. *Somewhere in there. Now I will seek you out*, he thought. *Me and Ncubi, the best scouts in the regiment, after Schullie and after Pete Clements. Mustn't forget to feed my little snake. Contact! We have a contact here!*

Delighted, he pulled his pack towards himself and rigged the Nicad battery transmitter booster to the little General Electric handheld. As he called in, Ncubi opened their last tin of meat and added water to the dried sadza from the day before. It wasn't much but they were hungry and had finished the last of their biltong days ago.

Ncubi rubbed his hands clean of dust and began to eat with his fingers, thinking how Seager and Pascoe would be pleased if they had hit the right camp. He wondered how his young comrade Tim Sibanda was getting along with the ma-English officer. They had shot the poachers, much to his delight – and he wasn't fooled for a minute. He had never seen Sibanda make a mistake of that type, although everyone did sooner or later.

Ncubi bit into the cake of dried mealie meal, then shoveled some of the braised steak into the mouth and looked at Buchanan talking into the radio. He had seen the big white man smash bricks with his hands and yet his eyes were that of a teller of stories, of someone who understands things. In Ncubi's experience, men of violence were often men who understood nothing else. He stroked the little inyoka, the snake, like it was a child and took delight in the birds in the trees. Sometimes, when he should have

had the telescope on something important, Ncubi believed he was watching a bird. But for this fault he was an outstanding bushman, and he slept securely when the other man was nearby.

Ncubi finished exactly half of the food and pushed it over to Buchanan, who was repacking the booster unit.

"Some faint traffic there," said Buchanan, but all around him the night was silent.

*

Dawn the next day saw Andre leaving to collect Pascoe, who was midway between Stockly's team and Pirelli's, and Seager. Stockly would run the debrief at the base camp while the other two reacted to Masters' and Sibanda's request for the lab analysis. It was after four by the time Andre ground round the side of a hill inflow ratio four-wheel drive over the rocky uneven ground. Seager rose from his shady spot and waved to attract their attention, then bent to scoop up his pack and rifle. Chimkuyu appeared from the trees to his left and together they waited for the vehicle to reach them, throwing gear in the back and climbing in.

"Kanjane" said Pascoe.

"Let's go" said Seager, tiredly taking a beer offered by Andre, and reaching for the cigarettes on the dash board. Chimkuyu refused a beer but drank water slowly, sipping as though it was a cocktail.

"How long to that location?" Seager asked, winding the window all the way down. It was hot.

"Another three hours once down on the flat there." Andre pointed below to the miles of waist high brown grass and trees. "We'll come out about twenty clicks up the road from Lubimbi and meet them a bit further down. They've left signs on the road."

The sign would be something innocuous, a Coke bottle or a tin can in a particular spot – and in the bush on the edge of the road would be a broken branch hanging, or grass tied in a knot.

They stopped an hour later and hand pumped petrol from the drum on the back into the tank. Dusk was already settling and, as they left, Pascoe put a magazine into his weapon and cocked the action. No-one asked why. As dark approached, the chances of their becoming the target of a dissident action themselves increased. Four men in daylight in a four wheel drive was too risky a target – but at night, headlamps picking their way through the bush at a crawl would be very tempting indeed to anyone within range.

They found the road at nine that night, after stopping for an hour and a half to make rough repairs to the fuel pump. After seeing what could have been Sibanda's sign on the road, they stopped and swung the big roof-mounted hunting lamp into the trees. There, high in the beam, was something white halfway up a tree thirty yards off to the left. They flashed the light and a smaller more yellow beam flashed back. Andre clunked the transmission into four wheel drive and gently nosed the Toyota back off the road and into the bush towards the signal.

"Hope it's them," said Pascoe.

"Andre stop!" came an order.

"Douse the lights and move off to the right there," came a hurried response from Seager. He turned and looked into the back seat. "Chimkuyu, see who it is please."

With the vehicle still rolling in the dark, the Shangaan slid from the door, his weapon low, and disappeared like a puff of smoke into the dark. "O.K., let's just wait and see," said Seager softly.

Chimkuyu came back a minute later with both the men they were to meet and they all settled down in the dark to allow Sibanda to bring them up to date. Then they decided to wait for the dawn and slept uneasily wherever they could.

Just before four, Seager shook Andre awake. "Let's go clear the village while it's still dark. Then we can talk to the boy when he takes the mombes out to graze before school."

Chimkuyu appeared from the dark and climbed into the back – he had been resting elsewhere – and together they edged back onto the road, quiet and lonely in the light of the moon. Following Sibanda's directions, they hissed through the quiet intersection without the benefit of headlights, and ten minutes later he tapped Andre's shoulder.

"There ahead. The house."

It was a two room breezeblock dwelling with a corrugated iron roof. In the dawn's eerie light they could see a chicken run, the door open and the fowls walking and stretching. As they watched, the rooster on the edge of a forty four gallon drum flapped his wings and crowed, almost overbalancing with the effort. Behind, cattle moved gently in a kraal. Nine of them.

"I could kill a cup of coffee," murmured Pascoe.

"Me too boet," Seager answered. "Not long now." He cupped a cigarette to cover the glow and watched the house, binoculars and patience the only requirement.

A few minutes later a woman appeared at the door. Adjusting her wrinkled dress and rubbing sleep from her eyes, she walked to the drum the rooster was on, irritably swinging the bowl at him. Dipping the bowl inside, she pulled it clear, then dipped her hand into the black interior and flicked water onto her face. She shifted her dress again, hoisted the bowl onto her head in the time-honoured manner and walked gracefully back into the simple house.

The smoke rising from the little house reminded Seager of his childhood, growing up on the farm. Back then, thirty years ago, there had been no breezeblock houses on farms. There were traditional huts of mud and poles, thatched roofs with steep eaves and cool interiors that always smelt of woodsmoke and sweat and ash and paraffin. Outside any line of huts there was always a cooking fire burning and the three traditional stones that supported pots containing the food for the family that day.

The smell of woodsmoke on the air was one that had always held fond memories. His earliest were of the father of the farm's spanner boy – the old colonial term for the man who handed the farmer tools, and maintained the workshops. The old man was a practicing witch-doctor, and also something of a Nganga, one who spoke to the spirits and foretold the future and cast spells. The two were often confused and rarely did one find a man who did both. As a child, Seager would sit at the feet of the old man by his fire and listen to stories of ancient kings and warriors. The old man would sit upon a carved mopani stool, his once strong legs now spindly and his stomach and chest wrinkled like his ebony face beneath the ash grey hair. His rheumy old eyes had always twinkled when he spoke. As Seager grew older, the old man had indulged his interests in the ways of the Nanaga and even begun to teach him the means to get into a man's mind and find his fears, which was the basis of the craft. Once supple through fear, the rest was easy.

Coming up out of his memories, Seager raised the binoculars and once again watched the house below. Twenty minutes later, a boy stood in the doorway pulling his shirt on and tucking it in. He picked up a stick from the ground and walked to the kraal, swinging open the loose wire gate. The cattle milled briefly and then walked clear of the gate, out towards the grazing ground. One old beast with a twisted horn bad temperedly kicked out at another as they cleared the gate and the boy swung his stick at the ground. Then they moved off into the growing light.

"Back up," Seager ordered, lowering the field glassed. "Let's intercept them a click or so away, nice and quiet now." Then he stepped from the early shadows of a young acacia, Chimkuyu at his side.

The boy noticed them immediately and stood, the stick in his hand, wondering what to do. He had only ever seen a white man this close half a dozen times before, usually in a speeding vehicle on the road. He shifted nervously and his eyes flicked to the cattle moving ahead of him.

"Do not fear young man," called Seager in Sindebele, "you are the son of Jacob?"

The boy nodded uncertainly.

"They are fine cattle. Talk to us and, if you help, I will give you enough money for a fine little bull and two heifers, befitting the herds of Mzilikazi your ancient king." Sibanda had told him of the father's pride of his mangy thin scrubby interbred cows.

The boy's eyes widened. "What is it you want of me?" he stammered at the two approaching men. Both were big, and the African was taller and stronger than any man in his village.

"Fear not toto," smiled Seager.

"I am not a toto," the boy said proudly. "I am nearly a man."

"So you are. I have come from England. You know England?"

The boy nodded. "At school we have learnt Geography."

"Good. I have come seeking news of three young murungus, taken from the main road to Bulawayo. I come from their mothers who grieve for them. I seek news only. Three months or so ago you found a body."

The boy looked surprised. He had only told his father and no other.

"Take us there. No-one else will know. I wish to see what is left and see if it is the friend I seek. Show me the place and I will give you the money. No-one else will know."

The boy looked suspicious, then nodded quickly. He pointed west. "That way. Three hours or so by footing it." This time, he spoke in English. "But if they find out, they will come and kill my father and mother and."

"They will not find out. Come, leave your cattle here. I will call my driver and three hours will be half."

They parked the land cruiser a few yards from the large formation of boulders the boy had indicated. Andre waited and, trying to find something to do, he began syphoning the drum into the tanks of the vehicle. Meanwhile, the boy and Seager walked forward and the boy pointed upward. There was no smell now, there would be nothing but some bone and hair left.

Seager scrambled up the rock face and peered over. Moments later, he reappeared again and signalled to Pascoe for the aluminum case in the back of the vehicle. Masters walked it over and threw it up to Seager.

"Yeah?" he asked.

"Yeah. It was a white alright. There's hair. Rest is gone but the skeletal frame is big, unlikely to be a woman. I'll need the lower jaw. I'll have to take the whole skull and crack it away later." He dropped into the crack and out of sight and Masters walked back to Pascoe.

"Max reckons it's too big to be a woman?" he said hopefully.

"If it's the bloke, then the girls can't be far away," Pascoe said. "Cross your fingers pal."

Seager reappeared again, holding the heavy case and a green plastic bag. Slithering down the rock, he walked over to the others. "Right, base camp let's go." He placed the bag with its grizzly contents into the back of the vehicle and turned to the boy. Then he reached into his pocket and pulled a wad of notes clear. "Three hundred dollars, young man. Tell no-one and we shall do the same. Buy the cattle in a few months, not until then – for all shall know that you came into money suddenly."

The boy nodded and then, cupping his hands, clapped them together twice in the Matabele way of saying thank you, before turning and running away into the trees and rocks that led to his home and school. Seager watched him go, then turned to Chimkuyu. "Know this place, old one, we may be back to search for more."

*

Keith Buchanan raised the small binoculars to his eyes and peered down the gentle slope. They had swung south before the dawn, almost jogging at times, and were now sitting absolutely still watching a track that had been used several times recently. They hoped that it would lead them to a second guard post nearer the base of the hills. Appearing from the south were five figures still a hundred yards away, but moving fast: all men, all armed from the first indications. As they came closer to his position, Buchanan nudged Ncubi, who lay asleep beside him. The man awoke, immediately aware of the change in his partner. Lifting his head, he looked and, without speaking, pulled his weapon forward and slid the safety off. Then he settled to wait.

Christ, thought Buchanan, *the place is crawling with them.*

They were close. Buchanan lowered his glasses and watched them with naked eyes, eyes rimmed with dust and fatigue. The leader was a good seven or eight feet ahead and setting a fast pace, obviously close to home and feeling safe. He was tall with dreadlocks rubbing his shoulders and the sling of an AKM folding stock assault rifle. He looked thin and jaundiced and had a plastic Woolworths bag slung over one shoulder. The rest were behind in single file. They waited for ten minutes and then stepped onto the track, looking for the camp that had to be somewhere between them and the low hills four miles northwards.

Have to establish the pickets first, Buchanan said to himself, *then somewhere equidistant in the middle in those hills will be the main camp. Could be sixty or seventy strong, must cover an acre at least, an acre of lean-tos and maybe even a few tents. Up there in a gorge or by a stream or spring.* He felt it in his bones, but first there would be the satellite camps. They pushed on, Ncubi reading the tracks fast enough to run along but creeping like a cheetah in the grass, smelling the air for smoke or tobacco or soap or meat drying on branches.

Just before dark, Buchanan – by then on the point – settled to his knee very still indeed. They were close, the hill rising above them dark and forbidding.

A match flared in the dusk fifty yards ahead. *Contact!* They watched the match drop. Another was struck and lowered carefully to the ground,. In the glow Buchanan could see a figure bending over the flame, obviously ready to blow on the beginnings of a fire.

Buchanan and Ncubi began to retrace their steps to a point forty or so yards further back and deep in cover. Here they spent the night, watching alternately. Just before dawn, Ncubi shook Buchanan awake and they began to inch their way round the camp and up the gentle slope in the soft early wash of light from the east. They could feel it: they were close, very close, to a very large group of hostiles.

It took them two hours to pick their way to the top, crossing from deep shade to cover and always upward. Once there, they found a sentry asleep, and smiling to each other they began to edge westwards along the wide flat surface of the summit. It was strewn with rock formations, but few rose higher than the acacia trees and the dappled shade was welcome as the heat of the day began to bake the still air about them.

Twice as they moved, they slipped to the edge and, crawling forward, peered down the northern slope. Ahead, a short steep spur cut away to the north and swung back westwards. As hills went they were very insignificant at only two or three hundred feet at their highest point, but on the flat rolling bush they rose with a gentle splendour from the south and dropped quite steeply on this northern face.

Ncubi looked around to get his bearings. "Busy river down there," he whispered, stretching one scarred index finger westward. "Near the water? Against the slope?"

"Yes," said Buchanan, sliding back from the lip of the rise and getting to his feet a few yards back from the edge. He led the rest of the way and, as the sun reached its zenith, Keith Buchanan looked over the crumbling clay edge of the eroded hill – and there below them there sprawled a camp so vast and sprawling that it eclipsed everything else they had seen since the operation began.

Buchanan crawled back a few feet, rolled onto his back and looked at his companion. Then he lifted both thumbs triumphantly, his huge bearded face covered in a beaming smile.

*

The drive back was long and uneasy. No-one said much and the cab was cramped with six men and very hot even with the windows open. Spirits were low, no-one wanting to admit that the search could be over and the three English victims dead. It didn't seem to matter that they may have just earned stage one of the bonus, that of finding proof of death.

Seager displayed everyone's feelings when, after brushing one of the inevitable flies from his face a second time, he angrily squashed it with his hand against the windscreen, smearing its remains across the glass. The others knew him well enough to avoid him when he had that look, especially the Shangaan and Pascoe; both had seen it before with disastrous results.

Seager turned to Pascoe. "Ken, when we get back, I am going to clean up that piece of evidence and photograph it, the lower jaw, for dental record checks. While I do that, I want you to line up the boys. Enough with crossing tracks and just looking. Get an overlay over each subsector. Have each team fill in where they've looked, the places we can discount. What we have left, we'll go into, every cave, every fucking piece of contoured ground, every hut, every kraal line. They are still out there somewhere, I can feel it. We are close. We have walked past them, clear?"

Pascoe nodded. "Ja. Leave it with me," he replied, as the vehicle eased its way over the uneven terrain, picking its way homeward.

Pascoe waved another fly from his face and wiped the grime from his forehead with the back of his hand and hoped Seager was right.

In the back, asleep on the packs, was Tim Sibanda. Pascoe turned and shook him. "Corporal Sibanda."

The sleeping man awoke and looked forward at the eyes peering from under the floppy hat, the crows' feet accentuated by the deep tan and the dust.

"Yes Sah?"

"Well done lad. That was a good piece of work yesterday."

Sibanda's face beamed with pleasure and he stammered a 'thank you' at his officer. Seager also turned back, feeling guilty at his forgetting the efforts and initiative displayed by the pair. "Bonus," he said. "Thousand each Masters and Sibanda."

Easy come easy go, he thought. *Sheik Rashid, of whatever place, can afford it.*

Thanks were murmured from the rear and they fell silent again. They were still hours from base, it was hot and they were tired.

*

Buchanan pulled rank to be the first at the eyepiece of the instrument. Its beautiful white finish was mottled by camouflage cream that kept coming off on their fingers. Looking pious, Buchanan made three fingers and tapped his arm. Ncubi made a long patient look and, curling the fingers and thumb of his right hand, he made the flicking wrist action of the wanking he considered all sergeants do.

Imitating anger, Buchanan bent forwards and slowly and steadily began to swivel the scope that rested on a shirt on the rock. They had not carried the tripod; it was too heavy. He also began to draw a rough plan of the camp on the ground with a twig, picking out lean-tos and rough huts with symbols, pathways and a chicken run and the other varied symbols he had decided on for open areas, clear ground stamped by many feet, lines for drying, washing and the sites of the cooking fires. The wind had been southerly for the last week, hence the reason they had not smelt the smoke of the fires. Once the smoke had cleared the ridge top and been picked up by the breeze it would dissipate very quickly. You would not see the glow except from directly above. It was the perfect place to build the headquarter camp. He handed the scope to Ncubi and began to elaborate his sketchy map, copying it onto the small paper pages of his notebook.

They watched the camp for the next two hours, making detailed notes of the movements of anyone below, hoping for a command structure to become apparent. At one end of the parade ground, as they were to call it, there was a yellow detergent bottle on a piece of rope, and

Buchanan thought this might be a signalling device. A muted bell of sorts possibly.

It was twenty past three when Ncubi, without removing his eye from the scope, tapped Buchanan on the arm. Buchanan looked across quickly, to see Ncubi indicate long hair and breasts and point below. *Oh sweet Jesus*, thought Buchanan, taking the scope. *We have done it. Murungu woman. Has to be the target, has to be, please shit fuck, fuck, focus up too close, there an arm … white!*

He pulled back the scope, too powerful at the shortness of the distance. A girl was now entering the parade ground area carrying washing. Her hair was wet and it hung in curly ringlets. She had a very light complexion. Buchanan tried desperately to remember the photographs. This one had to be the English girl Maggie. Behind her walked a guard with a weapon slung over his shoulder. He trailed lazily, chewing on a grass stem, his jeans tattered and no shoes on his feet. The girl began spreading the clothing on a line. He looked back at her. She was wearing an old T-shirt and khaki trousers that were too big for her. Her feet were bare and dusty.

They've got them working, he thought, *they are alive. Fuck, we have done it.*

They waited another hour to see the second girl. She too appeared from the west through the trees, carrying a pile of pots and pans. She seemed taller and wore clothes that were equally badly fitting, but her long black hair shone and was tied in a pony tail. After dumping the pots, she was ushered back towards the trees and the shadows out of sight.

Ncubi looked over at Buchanan and tapped his arm. The Matabele looked at the sky and then at his watch, and then mimed the radio listening watch that night. Buchanan nodded. They would have to be clear of the hill well before dark and reach somewhere they could call in. They only had another half an hour at most, before having to make their way downhill and past the sentries.

They began to edge backward and were soon moving steadily along the ridge, leapfrogging each other from cover to cover, pleased with the day's work. Both knew without saying that, if the two girls were still alive, they were in no immediate danger of death. Buchanan was, however, concerned that he had seen no evidence of the third member of the party. If they were being used as a work party, then they might have been separated, but if the girls' primary use to their captors was of a sexual nature then the lad might have been killed. He would be of no use whatsoever, difficult to guard and possibly dangerous.

The ancient Celtic blood of Buchanan's Scots forefathers began to simmer when he thought about the way the girls could be abused and he picked up the pace. If he had discovered the camp while on a bush trip he would probably have gone in alone and relied on stealth and the awesome firepower of the pair of cut down pump action shotguns he favoured in thick bush. He had long ago ceased to be surprised by the actions his species were capable of. His philosophy was simple. Stick with the animals and, if he needed to mix with his own kind who did things like that, then do it, and do it first and fast.

On this occasion, however, he was acting in a unit that not only intended to accomplish the same task, but would also be as able as he, multiplied seven times. The girls could wait for a couple of days before being released – and then witness the actions of Seager's team if anyone resisted.

Seager, Pascoe and their colleagues rolled into camp in time to watch the cook going off duty, then called him back and had him stoke the fire and begin cooking again. Seager went straight to his tent and began to clean the skull. It was a nasty job and he was saved by Andre, who suggested boiling it to kill off any of the bacteria that are normally associated with cadavers. Seager handed it over and Andre gingerly received it.

"I'll wait up," he said "Let me have it as soon as it's clean. I don't want it scrubbed or bashed at all. I'll do the teeth myself. They're the only things we have to identify whether its one of ours or not. O.K?"

Andre nodded. "Thanks boet. I know you are tired."

"We all are," Seager finished.

"Yeah," the other said. He smiled and walked away, holding the skull in the bag as though it would explode.

Afterwards, Seager walked to the mess tent and watched the others in the team all clean and scrubbed, poring over the overlays and filling in areas with china graph pencils and marker pens. "If it's bigger than this site we're on and you haven't walked through it, don't mark it. We go back," said Pascoe, marching around the table.

Seager walked over, looking round the tent. "Where are Keith and Ncubi?" he asked.

"That vehicle isn't in yet. They missed the pickup yesterday and called in last night, said they wanted an extra day on the site they are on."

"Why?" asked Seager quickly.

"They didn't elaborate. Just said they wanted their pickup a day later."

"And they missed it?" Seager interrupted.

"Ja, looks that way. The driver called in a few minutes ago."

"O.K. Try again tomorrow, get on the net, make sure they at least receive a message."

"Done," answered Pascoe. Then, cautiously, he said, "They may be onto something."

"Let's hope so," Seager said softly, "let's hope so."

He returned to his tent and began setting up his own AEI Cannon. The Vivitar lens had a macro facility and, up on the mini tripod with the flash and some high resolution film, it would give him film of the dental work, good enough for an expert to establish whether or not it was one of theirs. Seager believed it was. He believed the body was that of Edward Connelly, the shy quietly spoken young man who had accompanied the two girls. He had seen a photo of the boy, he had long brown hair and rimless spectacles. When ferreting around in the cleft, he had looked for the glasses but had been unable to find them. They may have been lost before or stolen from the body, before or after the murder had taken place.

It was after midnight by the time Andre returned with the skull. It was now in two pieces, the lower jaw having separated from the upper skull while in the water. Seager took them and laid out the smaller piece on the black paper he had chosen to back the pictures, and began shooting at different angles, all the teeth with their now clean fillings. The front right incisors had a cap and, when he began on the upper skull, he was careful to make sure that was obvious in the next sequence. He was just finishing when Pirelli and Stockly appeared in the door flap, amusing him slightly by standing waiting for his summons.

"Yeah, come in, come in." He fired the last few frames on the second roll of film and looked up.

"Max, Major Pascoe said that Keith and Ncubi may be onto game?" Pirelli asked.

"Yes, could be. They asked for extra time but they've missed two pickups now. We'll try again tomorrow and the next day. Three days. Then we go in and find them." Seager left it hanging.

"What do you think?" Stockly asked quickly.

"I think they will be O.K., just late."

"Excuse me Sir," interrupted Pirelli. "We *know* they are alright. Buchanan once spent six weeks in Mozambique eating raw meat because he was too close to cook. He was onto something then!"

Seager chuckled, delighted at the faith they all had in each other "Sorry," he said. "I thought you were concerned about them."

"Fuck no Sir, but we could be onto something, possibly be out early. I'm just thinking about all that money and the chicks in Durban. What do you think?"

Seager was non-committal. "Let's wait and see," he said.

Stockly held out his hand to Pirelli. "Twenty bucks," he swore. "I told you he wouldn't commit himself!" Then, swearing, they left.

CHAPTER NINE

Buchanan shook the little radio and held it to his mouth. There was no hiss when the transmit button was pressed and released. "Fucking crap kit," he snarled more to himself than anyone else. It was only then that he looked at the radio and *remembered*. A mile back along the track, he had slid down a rock on his pack and hit the bottom harder than he intended. An ominous crunch had come from the base of the pack where the radio habitually lay, but until now he had thought nothing of it. Now the dead radio in his hand confirmed his worst fears: the kit was unserviceable and that meant that one of them would have to walk back to the base camp.

He rose from his squat.

"Sekuru," said Ncubi, "I will go. I can be there by lunchtime tomorrow."

"No. You found it. You stay here and watch. I broke the radio so I'll go." Buchanan began stripping his gear away and, within minutes, stood with just his water bottle, chest webbing and rifle. "Watch each day and learn the routines. Be here tomorrow night and each night after that. Chiserai."

Buchanan turned and began to jog in the soft moonlight eastwards into the bushveld, toward the base camp some fifty miles away.

Buchanan moved fast all that night, stopping only to change the laces in his training shoes. By 0400 hrs he had blisters on his feet, the lightweight Adidas unsuitable for a forced march, and he broke the run-walk pattern he began with and settled instead into a fast four mile an hour walking pace.

He referred only twice to his compass and, at first light, hit the confluence of the Lutope and Sengwa rivers. Realising he was too far south, he swung north along the river's path, estimating the camp to be ten or twelve miles further up. His hunger growing, he increased his pace. They had not eaten for two days and he wanted time to eat before bringing Pascoe and Stockly and maybe Nya-madze back with him. He knew they would have to do a very thorough recce first, and that would be Nyamadze's job. Nyamadze once lived for two months in the ZIPRA camp in Zambia and had even called himself a Commissar. He had that extraordinary combination of nerve, courage and a lightning fuse all at once. Most of the very brave men were equally cool about everything, but not Nyamadze.

Back at base camp, Seager pinned the last of the acetates over the main map and stepped back to get a better view. "Jesus Ken," he muttered "looks like a patchwork quilt!"

"Yeah it does, but each sector is accurate," he answered. "Shit, I hope so anyway. Has the driver left with the pictures?"

"Just gone. He'll be at the D.H.L. office in Bulawayo in time for it to open tomorrow."

"O.K. Let's look at high ground and water and see what we haven't covered." They began to pore over the acetates, with Stockly's patch first. The sector covered by Buchanan and Ncubi was clear of tracks.

"I'll grab Rob and Nyamadze," Pascoe said, leaving the tent.

It looked like it was going to be a long day.

At the other end of the camp, Masters and Pirelli lay back in the sun, cold beers already in hand.

"Vuarnets. The only way to protect the eye!" said Pirelli. "Cut out the UV light." He replaced his and sighed.

"Bullshit, pizza boy, you just love being trendy. You don't give a damn about UV. You just love designer gear. Don't deny it, you little shit."

Pirelli rose offended and made to make his mock indignations felt, but Masters hadn't finished yet. "Why don't you go to Bangkok, you can get a fake Rolex and pretend you're Max Seager, a sort of short poor man's version!"

Masters chuckled softly as Pirelli lifted his sunglasses and looked at him with disbelief. "You fucking poms are all the same, you wouldn't know a classy bloke if he bit you on the dick."

"If a bloke bit me on the dick he wouldn't have any teeth to do it again," answered Masters, who then sipped his beer.

It was quiet for a moment. Then Masters heard Pirelli move on the sleeping bag.

"Someone's coming," Pirelli whispered. "Tell the boss. I'll go to check it out." Moments later, he disappeared in shorts and bare feet, armed and into the trees at a run.

After he was gone, Masters rolled to his feet and, lifting his weapon, moved back into the main area of the camp at a leisurely jog. Reaching Seager's tent, he swung back the canvas door flap.

"Visitor from the south," he said casually. "On foot. Pirelli gone for a look."

"Thanks Richard," said Seager. "Break out the theodolites and things, Ken. Hide the gats. Cover us from here."

Seager was marching out of the tent when the arrival appeared from the bush walking with Pirelli. "Relax!" he called back. "It's Keith."

Seager watched Buchanan walk into the camp. He looked tired and bruised and his shirt was holed in several places. His beard was matted and filthy but he had a twinkle in his eyes and his walk was jaunty.

"Kanjane Boss," he called out, in full voice for the first time in days. "Radio is buggered," he said, swinging his rifle into his other hand as he took Seager's right hand and shook. "I left Ncubi watching a camp."

Seager stopped. "Get a shower and some graze into you, everything alright?"

His huge blue eyes twinkled. "Ja, better than alright."

"Spit it out Buchanan!" Pascoe wasn't as patient as Seager.

"We're on, Boss! We found the girls alive and well."

"You're sure?" Seager quickly asked.

Buchanan nodded. "Ja, confirmed sighting, matches the description. It's them."

It was quiet for a moment and then all hell broke loose as the men began whooping and cheering and shaking hands with anyone in reach. The local team members ran from their line to see what the fuss was about and they too joined in. It took a few minutes for it all to simmer down and they all turned to Seager awaiting his instructions.

"Keith, well done to you and Ncubi. Bonus five thousand each.

Clear up and graze and be ready to debrief in my tent in half an hour. Major Pascoe, please select a recce team and move out to be on site tonight. Keith, you can sleep on the way back. Masters, put together a short three or four day brush up and select with Major Pascoe who you want in an assault team. Andre, be prepared to break camp on Wednesday night. If we're ready, we'll take 'em back on Thursday. Can you get out and uplift some supplies we'll need? Good. The rest of you will now be under the direct command of Major Pascoe. My role is over. Preliminary briefing at 1400 hours for those left. Let's fucking do it!"

As the men dispersed about their tasks, Buchanan walked forward to Seager. "Max, no sight of the bloke they were with. I reckon they have."

"I think we've found him Keith," Seager replied. "They did it months ago."

"Bastards," Buchanan snarled, adding, "Let's cull these bastards sir?"

Seager looked at him and understood. "Have a shower and something to eat and then come and show me where you found the camp and whatever else you have."

Buchanan nodded.

"Major Pascoe will be there. You did well Keith, you and Ncubi."

Buchanan mumbled something, smiling at the compliment and turned and walked towards the shower apparatus, stripping his gear as he went. As he passed, the men made ribald remarks and rough congratulatory murmurs.

It was day twenty-three and Seager had already decided on day twenty seven for the extraction. Buchanan re-entered the tent twenty minutes later.

"Feeling better?" Seager asked. "Right. What have we got?"

The big man's hair was wet and uncombed, and smelling of the cheap sunlight soap they were using. He had a jam sandwich in his hand and was chewing and nodding all at once. He indicated with his little finger his sector.

"Here Sir." He paused as Pascoe entered, short and wiry and now wearing a beret. Then, nodding, he continued, "At the top end of the Busi. Just here there is a fold in the ground – a hill, small, but enough because on the northern side it drops steeply into a small gutter. A spur runs here –" He indicated again with a jammy finger, "– in between the spur and the hill, there's a triangular basin that drops to the west to the Busi itself. It's there, a camp of maybe sixty men, it's well set out with a parade ground up the top end. Right here is what looks like senior quarters. The girls were walked across the ground with washing and shit. They were under guard." He stopped, licked his fingers rather like a child and then reached into his pocket for his notebook. "I've got heaps of stuff here," he said and then paused and looked at them.

Seager threw him a felt tip marker and indicated the flip chart against the green side wall of the tent. "Go for it. Everything you can remember."

Buchanan began to draw on the map. He had the natural observer's memory for details but lacked the artistic technique. He used big bold strokes and copied directly from the map for his little symbols. When he finished, Seager began a passive interrogation as gently as possible filling in the details.

"How high here?"

"How steep is this face, anyway down it?"

"How many men would sleep in the shelters?"

"What trees are the cover overhead?"

"Any grass in here? How high?"

It went on for the better part of an hour, Buchanan surprising Seager by being able to answer almost everything, and impressing him even more by admitting when he didn't know.

By the full preliminary briefing at 1400 hours, they had absorbed what they needed to know. The men were milling impatiently, awaiting the choice of the recce team, when Pascoe walked into the shaded clearing. He stood, ramrod straight and looked at them his beret squared perfectly on his head.

"Right, listen up. Teams as follows: Buchanan and Ncub." A muffled groan rose up from the men. Pascoe smiled briefly, "Success has its perks, Nyamadze will go in. I will spot with Keith from the ridge. Seager and Chimkuyu will establish three escape routes num-

109

bered by preference in order. Back here, Masters and Pirelli and Stockly will break out the black battle trunk. In it is the arsenal. Sight and choose your kit. Chana, you'll find a MAG in there as well. Leave the Mannlicher for Keith to set up when he gets back. Understood? Right, load up and let's move out."

The vehicle dropped them just before seven that evening. It was dark and the men covered the last two miles on foot to rendezvous with Ncubi. Buchanan covered the point, moving easily in the soft dry grass leading the group from cover to cover. The Matabele was at the correct place and, after a series of soft clicking noises made by his partner, he moved from the inky blackness of a small outcrop of weathered rocks. There were muffled greetings and Buchanan handed him a pack of food. Settling immediately to his haunches, he began to eat the bread and cold steaks and boiled eggs.

Before the others arrived, Buchanan handed him a bottle of beer.

"Hide this in your kit. drink it another time."

Ncubi grinned and, flicking the cap off with his lower teeth, he drank the entire bottle in under ten seconds.

"That is of course an alternative." muttered Buchanan.

As the main body arrived, Buchanan was listening to the events of the last day through mouthfuls of food. Then, Ncubi stood and saluted in the old-fashioned way. Pascoe and Seager conferred briefly, then decided to spend the rest of the night where they were and move into the low hills just before dawn. Hopefully they would spend the next two days overlooking the camp. They were directly east of the formation and Ncubi had found no evidence of any pickets of small guard camps in that direction. Obviously the dissidents felt that the eastern slope was least likely to be a threat. To the east lay hundreds of miles of bush and isolated villages and settlements until the small town of Gokwe and the Empress and Copper Queen Mines.

Excited like a child the night before going on holiday, Seager couldn't sleep. They were sprawled about in the blackness of the rocks in which Ncubi had waited, heads on packs, each awaiting the dawn in their own way. Buchanan and Ncubi slept like the dead now, with the security of Chimkuyu watching the bush for danger. James Nyamadze chatted softly with Seager until he too fell asleep. In the end, it was just Pascoe and Seager awake and tense, wondering what the light would bring. They both felt responsible, Seager for the overall success of the attempt and Pascoe for the 'heavy mob tactics' as Seager had called them.

"We want to bring everyone out, Ken. No casualties, no-one left behind."

Pascoe nodded, and slapped at a mosquito and missed.

"I don't want to teach granny to suck eggs." Seager continued, but Pascoe interrupted. "Then don't. We go in quietly steal them back. No fuss. No-one knows. I have silent weapons, two I threw in the trunk. We'll all come out O.K." He stopped and slapped at the mosquito again. "Anyone rumbles us and they have to go, but quietly. Dawn before anyone knows."

Seager looked, then opened his mouth to speak. Pascoe cut in first, "Max, you aren't paying me fifty thousand dollars because you like my jokes. Trust me, and trust my command. We may look like we're all a bit peculiar. We *are*, but we are also good."

Seager let it ride and they changed the subject to talk of the marina and Svea and Seager's children. Pascoe made Seager an offer for the eighth time for his ketch, and for the eighth time Seager said, "No, build your own boat." It was an old joke and a familiar one, but a comfortably normal remark under the circumstances.

At 0330 hrs, Pascoe rose stiffly to his feet and began shaking the team awake. "Move out in five."

Seager wished he had a cigarette. He stood, pulled his lightweight pack on and checked the load on his rifle. He had fingernail polish on the foresight, and Andre had lightened the action on the trigger. Otherwise it was a standard AK 47. Long ago, someone had carved three notches in the lightwood butt, and there were gouges in several places on the fore grip. He had wondered about the notches several times, if they may have been men he knew or heard of.

"Let's go," he said and together they walked carefully in the funereal darkness, Ncubi on the point and Buchanan walking with them.

Nyamadze came up from the back and whispered to Pascoe, then moved up to where Chimkuyu waited for the party to reach him and past him to the point where he would peel away and enter the camp from the southerly ridge, ahead of the team's arrival. He knew what he had to do once there, and Pascoe had been told by Stockly that part of James Nyamadze's psychological preparation for walking into an enemy camp was to travel the last distance alone, and become like an actor waiting alone in the wings to adopt another character on stage.

Seager noted that Chimkuyu had somehow procured a machete, and it was now slung over his shoulder, lying between his shoulder blades in its canvas sheath. He remembered the last time he had seen the Shangaan adopt less conventional weapons and just how effective he was at close quarters without a gun. Seager was glad he was on their side. They were veterans of this kind of penetration. They moved stealthily and spoke in whispers and never stood still. If they stopped, they sank to one knee and they watched all the time. They leap-frogged each other and moved in a narrow inverted V formation, each man with his own fields of fire and each selecting his own cover as they went. Seager was now much more confident to move among them as an equal and their original distrust of his bushcraft was now a grudging respect for a fast learner. Teamed with the Shangaan they were a formidable pair indeed. By the time soft light from the east filtered over the horizon, they were halfway up the slope and moved into cover to allow Nyamadze to enter the camp and find his niche.

They moved forward at eight that morning, to establish their position on the clay ridge above the camp's southern perimeter. Buchanan moved on his belly, inching towards the edge like and overfed python. He arrived, lifted his great shaggy head, peered over, and then rolled back and made a thumb's-up sign. Pascoe, Seager and finally Chimkuyu moved forward until they lay in a row beneath a jesse bush that struggled to maintain its grip on the edge.

Down below, Nyamadze walked confidently through the first shelters in the basin's entrance area. He was challenged once and said in coarse Sindebele, "Fuck off or I'll kick your Fucking teeth in." Being big, armed and confident, the man who challenged him muttered something about just doing his job and then backed off.

After that, Nyamadze moved easily through the accommodation lines and several things became immediately apparent. These people were as shit scared of their command as they had been during the bush war. Ergo, somewhere round here, there was a command. Several notices pinned to the trees talked of ZIPRA, Nkomo's wartime guerilla army who had waged war on the Rhodesian government during the bush war and persisted to this day – and the early indications were that this was a ZIPRA camp, rather than one full of money hungry dissidents making ends meet.

Nyamadze stopped beside a group in conversation and tried to listen in. The gist was that the boss was away and wasn't it great.

"You!" he commanded. "Who is your section leader and where is your Commissar?"

The speaker rose to his feet respectfully and pointed up the camp.

"Comrade, he is there."

"And who commands this fuck-up? Speak!" snarled Nyamadze.

"Colonel Magnum, eh, Colonel Chabegwa sah!"

"Not the camp, you idiot. I know that. The guard at the entrance. Oh, never mind!" With that he walked away, leaving the young chap shrugging at his friends.

So, Nyamadze thought, Chabegwa commands here. Nyamadze had come across him five years before in Zambia, and had rated him well as ZIPRA half colonels went. He must have been away for this to be so slack. *Taking the two murungu women,* he thought, *will be like taking candy from a baby.* Nyamadze liked the expression and had picked it up from television. He began pacing the distance to the huts, noting the big ones and their relative distances to trees and boulders that could be identified from the ridge. Most of this would be obscured by heavy leafy foliage of the trees overhead.

Ahead he could see a substantial hut with a corrugated iron sheet on wire hinges as a door. *Interesting,* he thought. *Arsenal, food store or jail?* Settling down against a tree, he pulled his hat down over his eyes and watched from forty yards as if dozing against the trunk.

Nothing appeared for an hour so he got to his feet and walked deeper into the camp. A second similar arrangement stood centrally and had a guard at its entrance. *That's it,* he thought. Carefully estimating the distance to the parade ground through the trees and the ridge beyond, he looked for access and escape routes. A group of three armed lads wandered past and he listened to them talk. They were going out to spend a day or two at one of the guard camps. *Better and better,* he thought. He crossed the camp, smiling at some and scowling at others who looked like they wanted conversation, and approached the large guarded hut from the rear. Then he waited for a quiet moment to look in.

Above, as the camp settled into its routine, Pascoe deployed Chimkuyu and Ncubi to guard their backs for the first hours. Seager and Buchanan then took a turn, off duty men making notes and filming the goings-on below.

By lunchtime, they had five full cassettes of material and batteries that needed charging, and as Murphy's Law would have it, that was when Maggie Nolan walked escorted into the parade area with arms full of what looked like clothing from the ridge. Pascoe and Seager were back on watch and silently congratulated each other. Buchanan had, as usual, been right. They were the right people. It wasn't until after four that Layla Rakkafian came into view. She was taller and moved with grace and confidence and hardly seemed to notice her armed shabby nose-picking escort, as she was pushed into the hut and the door locked behind them.

Ten minutes later, Nyamadze moved forwards. Between the eaves of the hut and its thatched roof there was an eight-inch air gap. Rising onto tiptoes, he looked through carefully. In the gloom, two figures sat sewing rough stitches into clothing. As his eyes adjusted he saw they were women and white, both with dark hair. One leant across and held her sewing into a beam of light from a hole in the old thatch. They didn't look up and he melted into the trees again, very pleased with what he had found. For another couple of hours he continued to watch, and then meandered further up the tree line across the parade ground. In a very cocky display that would have unnerved Seager if he had been watching, he waved at the sky like he was stretching, to identify himself to the watchers above.

He was back in time to see the guard changed at the door and the procedure was sloppy. One walked up, took the rifle from the other and the first left. *Better by the minute,* he thought. He turned and walked back through the camp and, as he passed the guard, he nodded patronizingly. Then, halfway to the first guard camp, he stepped right off the track and into the bush westwards to meet the others later. Whistling softly, he walked confidently from one world to another.

Pascoe looked across at Seager and smiled inwardly at the changes already apparent. His eyes were rimmed with pale ochre dust and his hair hung in sweaty rat-tails of the same colour, the moisture having absorbed the dust too. His stubbled chin was smeared with dirt from the back of his hand and his skin beneath the grime was the colour of copper, dry and leathery from the sun. He had lost weight in the last weeks and was now as fit as any of them, and as he raised the telescope to his slate grey eyes, Pascoe could see his jaw muscles working beneath the skin, a steady rhythm like a heart beat, as he clenched his teeth and relaxed over and over. Most men who were asked for continual silence developed mannerisms, and Seager did this when he wanted to smoke and couldn't.

At five, the team moved back from the lip and Seager and Chimkuyu moved away to plan the escape route. All Seager's routes would eventually swing them northeast. He had decided on a pick-up point for the big Bell 212 helicopter that would be reported technical to its prime contractors and owners, and flown at high speeds and low levels across the Zambezi River from the Copperbelt on the Zambian side, by its young Canadian Pilot. The man couldn't be blamed for taking Seager's offer; he hadn't been paid in four months by his company, who in turn hadn't been paid by the mine that was about to declare its deep financial trouble to the world. The man had a son in school in Toronto and the school wouldn't wait for payment. The chopper would come in exactly on a predetermined time at a River Vlei where the Sebungwe River flowed out of the Chizarira National Park. Seager had decided the place because it was easy to find, and only fifty kilometers from Binga and the border where he would once again enlist the help of Silas to get the team clear if the chopper didn't show up. It was also a long way from the rescue site and unlikely to be hostile.

Chimkuyu led them clear down the eastern slope and they swung immediately northwest to scout the track in reality. The route he favoured was direct and they would cross the almost dry Busi riverbed twenty-five kilometers north of the dissident camp and forty from the pickup point. Plenty of miles for Pascoe's team to shake any followers if they were so inclined. Being heavily armed with packs and with the girls – who had had uncertain dietary conditions and were of uncertain levels of fitness – in tow meant that Seager would plan on no more than twenty miles a day. He reminded himself to have Andre raise the chopper pilot and give him a radio frequency and ground identification codes. They didn't have smoke except in bright green, so that would have to do.

They found the two picket camps that side of the hills and skirted them carefully. Seager did a head count at both before moving on so that Ken could ascertain what resistance they might offer after hearing the worst case scenario of gunfire at the camp. There were five men in the first camp and seven in the second. More enemies here than in the Senate, he thought to himself as he slithered back to meet the tireless Chimkuyu.

For the next night and day they zig-zagged across the area, until they were happy with the general layout. They could easily switch escape routes as they willed. By dusk that day, they were back in the rocks east of the hills. Pascoe, Nyamadze and Buchanan were waiting for them quietly, Ncubi asleep beneath a bush. Seager and Chimkuyu bolted down the food that was left and then the six of them began their walk eastwards towards where one of Andre's drivers would be waiting for them at the drop point. They were back at base camp by dawn, the Land Cruiser picking its way over rock and through bush and gullies at a crawl.

At base camp, Masters and Stockly had broken open the arsenal trunk and stripped and checked all the weapons. Pirelli, Chana and Sibanda had rigged heavy tarpaulins a mile from the camp and, between the layers, they had wedged grass, boxes and anything else they could find, into a muffled padded igloo. It would be almost soundproof for the weapons testing and sighting. Weapons fired in the enclosure couldn't be heard more than five hundred yards away, ample for their purposes. They didn't want to attract any attentions with the testing and sighting process essential before any soldier felt comfortable with his prime weapons. By the time the recce team was back they had test fired every firearm and begun making adjustments to their own personal weapons. The Mannlicher they had left for Buchanan, and Chana had already tuned the MAG to his own requirements. He had decided to carry the heavy gun and one of the seven Browning pump action shotguns. Masters had already purloined two of the Brownings and shortened the barrels by four inches on both. He had shortened the stocks to improve the balance, and rigged a harness to carry both weapons on his back. He also chose to keep his AR15. Ever traditional, Pirelli stayed with traditional assault weapons and opted for the F N 7:62. He liked its hitting power, but also prepared one of the batch of Ingrams for his own use, by padding out the handle like a tennis racket with toweling strips to better suit his grip. Once a very gifted armourer, Andre worked trigger mechanisms for those who wished and, by the time the recce team was back, the bulk of the work was done. The next three days were completed at a furious pace. A mock-up of the prison hut was built and Masters' team practiced finding it, attacking it, and defending it.

In the end they opted for plan "B", which was everyone in together. Masters and his team would simply be there in case the dissidents became hostile. This plan meant that a pair, yet to be chosen, would enter the hut, and the shock unit waiting in the shadows would only bite if, as Masters put it, they were 'sussed'. They had practised getting into the hut several times when Seager joined the group.

"I thought you S.A.S guys used shotguns to open doors," he said.

Masters held up a pair of wire cutters and smiled sweetly. "High technology. Cut through the wire! Not as dramatic – but this isn't the Iranian Embassy. It's a hut in the sticks. The Regiment frowns on drama for drama's sake."

Pascoe and Masters sat for hours overlooking a scale model of the camp, planning routes and fields of fire and, most importantly, the way in and the way out.

"There's a slope on the other side, heavily shaded by the bush. If we put a rope down it, then you could pull your way up fairly fast, covering fire from the top if necessary, and lots of diversion at the other end, something to roll their eyes at."

"Sounds alright. Who will be the diversion team?"

"Rob," said Pascoe, "with Tim probably."

Masters nodded. "Chana with the gun above?"

Pascoe nodded.

"Buchanan and Ncubi?"

"The base of the slope during the escape and with you in the assault team. Final members Pirelli and of course, Nyamadze."

"Five is good," Masters agreed. "And you?"

"I'll be at the top with Chana and the comms."

Masters narrowed his eyes. "That leaves going into the hut."

"Seager and his Shangaan," Pascoe finished, grinning. "You disagree?"

"No," said Masters. "That would be my choice too. Seager's good enough at that, but not good enough for my team."

At that precise moment, Seager entered the tent. He was sweating freely having just run a fast two miles with the rest of the team, carrying full kit and, at times, Buchanan's across his shoulders. "Now I know why I didn't want to be a squaddie," he said panting.

Pascoe looked up. "That's why you're going into the hut and leaving the squaddies to do the Roy Rogers bit. O.K?"

Seager smiled through the sweat. "Ja, that's O.K. Chimkuyu comes with me, alright? He's been sharpening his machete especially."

"Wouldn't want to separate you two lovebirds," said Pascoe, pleased with it all.

Seager tried not to show his elation. He had not primed Pascoe nor pulled rank; he had been chosen for the reasons he would have chosen himself. His flippant remark about Chimkuyu sharpening his machete had been to cover his delight. He liked being close to the danger. He liked being there at the kill. He stripped his clothing and walked towards the shower across the clearing in his underpants, wiping the sweat still beading on his forehead. Svea had once accused him of having a death wish, but that wasn't it. He liked to conquer the fear, he liked the elation of the adrenalin and he liked winning.

The next day was spent training again, stripping their weapons and sighting, breaking the door, and the next night moving absolutely silently while Chimkuyu cracked anyone he could hear with a stick. He heard everyone, in fact, but only struck those who had made noises that a mortal man would hear. They spent all night walking through grass and leaves; he showed them how to slide their feet, how to soften their walk. Even Stockly learned new things. They learned the soft muted signals that the Shangaan had taught Seager three years before, the soft blowing noise that was inaudible to the human ear unless you were waiting for it.

That day, at midday, when the sun was at its hottest, Seager walked out of his final debrief with Andre and stood with Pascoe as the squad ran past carrying Nyamadze. They were in full kit with weapons and Nyamadze had Chana's machine gun to add weight. They moved fluidly and like a team. In three days they had honed dry skills and channelled their fitness and experience; they had ceased to become eight individual veterans with varied specialist talents, and had become a team.

"How they doing?" Seager asked.

"They are ready. They would take on and cull any unit under fifty men north of Messina. Here in the bush they are in a league all of their own. Brit S.A.S. would be a problem, but anyone else? These blokes would fucking eat them for breakfast."

Seager laughed loud.

"What's funny?" Pascoe muttered, a little embarrassed at his rhetoric.

"That's what I told the Emir." It seemed a long time ago already, and he walked toward his tent to fine tune plans for the trip home. Now that the moment was near, he was concerned about one thing and one thing alone. The girls were alive and well. Why, he thought, no ransom had been paid? They were under guard, so not willingly staying. They were alive for a reason and the pieces didn't fit. Seager didn't like pieces that didn't fit.

CHAPTER TEN

They went in a day late on Seager's plan. It wasn't important in itself but they did have to advise the chopper operator, who grudgingly agreed to the new schedule. Andre's men broke camp in the morning and left with all the vehicles except the two land cruisers just before noon. The team spent the rest of the day preparing themselves individually. Soldiers always have their own little foibles. They change gear, they break little rules and as they prepare they begin the psychological build-up. Masters cleaned every round for his shotguns, checked each and reloaded two cartridges that were suspect. All the while he hummed the tune Chris De Burgh's 'Lady in Red'. Pirelli, happy with the new grip on his Ingram, spent time shortening fuses on a selection of grenades he had amassed. He had two stun type and three fragmentation and one smoke. He looked at the three fragmentation, walked back to the trunk and changed one for a white phosphorous. He was keen on incendiary devices and loved to indulge his pyromaniac tendencies.

Buchanan, at last satisfied with the Parker Hale and the shotgun, unpacked and checked the only claymore mine in the box. The electrical fuse seemed alright, and he looked over at Stockly who was cleaning an F.N., along with Nyamadze and Sibanda and Ncubi who had similar weapons. He put the heavy mine down, reached into his pocket, pulled his hand clear and uncurled it. The young snake slithered across his palm and, looking at it, he walked into the scrub and released it back to the wild. He was ready for the night's work. They all were.

Pascoe walked from the vehicle where he had stashed his kit and weapon. "Right," he said. "Listen up. We pull out in twenty minutes. You know your jobs. Teams as follows: Zulu One, Seager and Chimkuyu; Zulu Two, Masters' mob; Zulu Three, Rob and Tim; Zulu Four, Chana and myself. One and Two into the camp, Three diversion then meet at Alpha." Alpha was a point three miles from the camp.

"Any Snafu meet at Bravo." Bravo was a further three miles further on along escape route three. It bisected the other two and was the logical place to team up if separated. "Zulu Four, on the ridge with the gun. Now, Max wants a word."

Pascoe stepped back and Seager stepped forward.

"Any of you who saw the movie 'Uncommon Valour' will remember the naff speech at the end." Pirelli and Masters laughed; they had seen the film. "We are going in, we will take them back, have a bit of a wander to the chopper and be in a pub in London within seventy-two hours." Muted cheering came from the team. "Those staying will contact Andre for their money. You all have his number in Bulawayo. Let's cut the crap. I bags not driving."

Turning at the laughter, he walked to the nearest vehicle and swung himself into the front seat beside the driver. The others followed, joking and hefting kit and weapons into the back doors of the land cruisers. The packs were smaller than ever, but heavy still. Ammunition, medical packs, everything would have to be carried, including the heavy steel boxes containing the belt ammunition for the MAG. Pascoe's flawless logistical preparation even included things for the girls, bought weeks before in London, assuming that they would be found. They were little things, toothpaste and creams, hairbrushes each, tampons, shampoo and a few items of clothing that he hoped fitted. Andre would carry them to the landing site and leave them there before crossing the border at Victoria Falls and making preparations for the team's arrival in Zambia. Passports, original and new, from the Emirate were awaiting them all. They even had Zambian entry stamps.

Everything was ready. The last door slammed shut and the last two vehicles left the now spotless site cleared of all equipment, litter and people. That was something Seager was most pedantic about. *Leave nothing but footprints, take nothing but memories.* He looked back at the now deserted camp site as they drove away for the last time.

It was on.

The team split up three miles away from the hills. Stockly and Sibanda broke left to swing south where they would attack the two guard camps at the head of the basin. They would be in position to do so under

Pascoe's orders from just after midnight. The timing was important. There were two factors to consider. An early attack would risk being compromised by people moving in the camp prior to sleeping, but give them more hours of darkness to clear the area before any efforts to follow might be mounted. The second alternative was to wait for that time just before dawn when people sleep deepest and the night is darkest. There would be less chance of being caught in the act, but less time to get clear before first light. Pascoe chose the first option. He reasoned they would be pursued anyway for some distance after first light, so the further away the better. After hours with Nyamadze, he and Stockly had estimated the camp to contain between eighty and a hundred men. That number asleep in solid buildings would not be a problem for four-man killing teams moving from building to building under the suppressing fire of automatic guns. But they didn't want to start a war – and men scattered in flimsy shelters over a large area couldn't be contained and killed with fragmentation and stun grenades followed by small arms. They were a problem, so it was best to avoid them and be well clear before dawn.

The main team moved up the slope in the darkness and reached the peak by ten. Shuffling forward, they began deploying at the head of the steep slope. Nyamadze and Buchanan lay and watched the camp below. It was quiet but that was not unusual. Most bush camps sleep early irrespective of the occupants. The lack of electricity to run the lights, radios, and televisions that keep Europeans awake had no part here. The evening fires would burn down by eight or nine, eyes would become drowsy and people would go to their shelters and be asleep soon.

They had only seen five women in the camp other than the two captives. Wives of senior men maybe, or genuine dissidents, believers in the ZIPRA cause, they didn't know. What they did know was that there were insufficient women in the area to keep more than half a dozen men awake until now. That only left the guards and, down the slope at the back, the only real problem would be the guard on the door of the prison hut.

Behind Buchanan, Seager and Chimkuyu were unrolling the lightweight nylon line they would run down the slope to assist the escape. Pascoe had produced tins of green camouflage cream and handed them about without comment, for the men to cover all exposed white skin. Pirelli pulled his battle knife clear of its sheath and covered it in cream, then pushed it into the sheath clipped to the webbing over his heart. Pascoe crawled quietly over to where Chana was setting up his gun, and carefully checked the preparations. It was unnecessary; Chana had laid out a spare barrel and three full belts of rounds. Pascoe hoped they would never need the gun, let alone three full belts of ammunition.

"Confirm hapana tracer," he whispered. *Confirm no tracer.* He didn't want the position visible from below if possible.

"Roger," Chana whispered. He had expected the question.

Pascoe handed him the welder's gloves that would be required to handle the hot barrel if changing became necessary and crawled back to where the others were checking each other's kit, rather like divers.

"O.K.," he whispered. "If it starts, I'll let Rob and Tim loose. Cut back across the parade ground, I'll let a flare go, and Chana will suppress anyone following. Richard is in command down there. Max, just don't argue with him O.K?"

Pascoe grinned widely in the dark and Seager could sense the excitement growing. *Soldiers like proving their skills,* he thought. *I wonder if the others are scared like me.* He looked over at Chimkuyu, who squatted with his back to a rock impassively and relaxed. He was carrying one of the shotguns in one hand and his machete in the other, balanced point down on the hard clay.

"Let's go," he replied softly. Now they were here, now they were ready, he wanted to do it and get it over with.

"No. We wait until midnight as planned. Relax for a few minutes." Pascoe turned to Buchanan. "Got a Flakey?"

Buchanan smiled and shook his head. "Aziko." *None,* he replied.

Seager smiled. Pascoe was a master at diffusing tension. They all recognised the ploy and all appreciated it. The mere fact it was so obvious amused them all, like the legendary Colonel Frost at the bridge of Arnheim who walked through the gunfire with his umbrella twirling. His men adored him and followed him anywhere. Pascoe would, in time, develop the same kind of respect from any unit he commanded, but this team had been together too short a time and were too experienced. They themselves had all used the same techniques.

Masters leant forwards. "Ken?" he whispered.

Pascoe looked over. "Give us a kiss?" he said. Seager and Buchanan started giggling at the farce.

"Bring those girls up safely and you can ream my arsehole," Pascoe countered. Even Pirelli began to chuckle then.

Pascoe looked down at his watch and peeled the fabric cover back to expose the luminous dial. "O.K.." he said. "Move in."

Ncubi was the first down the slope, sliding as quietly as he could holding the rope. Nyamadze followed him, with Masters and Pirelli close behind. They arrived in the heavy growth at the base of the slope and looked back upward. Masters signaled and they fanned out, settling to watch the dark shadows as Seager and Chimkuyu slithered down the incline. Seager moved forward, his rifle butt to his shoulder like the instructors all said to do. The Shangaan melted into the trees and Masters nodded to Ncubi, as Buchanan arrived at the basin floor. He would be tail-end charlie, until the return route.

Ncubi and Nyamadze moved forward confidently through the sparse bush and into the camp lines, then began to edge closer to the slope to avoid crossing the parade ground. Masters and Pirelli moved abreast of each other in their wake, with Seager immediately behind them.

They had gone thirty or forty yards when Nyamadze froze close to a tree. Everyone stopped, settled down into cover and watched. Eventually Nyamadze made a wide sweep of his arm and pointed to the tree. Masters nodded and moved up. Seager followed until he saw the reason for Nyamadze's halt. A figure lay rolled in the dust a few feet the other side of the tree. Ncubi moved up and loomed over the prone form, as everyone moved past. They were now entering the camp proper and carefully picked their way through the huts and shelters, stopping and listening and moving forward only when all was quiet. It took twenty minutes to get to the prison hut – and there, in the heart of the camp, they could hear the odd voice talking away in the night. At one point another cut in and said "Shut up!", and Seager wiped the sweat from his hands on his shorts. Meanwhile, Pirelli put his gun down, pulled his knife clear and walked like a cat round the side of the hut. Buchanan moved to the other side, and Masters followed with Nyamadze on a wider half circle to cover the approaches from the western end of the camp, where the main concentration of sleeping men lay.

This is it, thought Seager. *This is what the Emir of Ras Al Qaleem is paying a million dollars for.* He slung his rifle and pulled a small torch from his pocket. Its lens was all but covered with black insulation tape, leaving only a sharp sliver of light when turned on. He pulled the wire cutters from his other pocket and waited. Pirelli edged round the side wall of the hut at a crouch and pulled the woollen tea cosy hat down over his head. He watched the guard amble back and forth and tried to estimate the extent of his beat. The man stopped and, slinging his weapon over his shoulder, pulled a packet of cigarettes from his trouser pocket and with great display pulled one clear and struck a match.

As the magnesium flared in the darkness, Pirelli moved across the ground like a leopard and, with one hand clamped over the man's cigarette, mouth and nose, he drove the sharpened point of the battle knife into the man's throat from the side. In one short vicious stroke, he severed the man's carotid arteries, windpipe and vocal cords. The man gave a great shudder and a fountain of blood spewed from the almost severed neck.

As Pirelli pulled backwards into the shadows, supporting the twitching corpse, Masters clicked his tongue twice and Seager moved forward to the corrugated iron door. As he felt for the wire hinges and cut the first one, Chimkuyu took the weight of the door in two hands. Seager bent the other hinge and, as the cutters separated the soft wire, the Shangaan lifted the door clear to the right.

Seager pocketed the pliers and, scooping up the torch, entered the blackness of the hut's interior. The way was clear, except for a half-gallon petrol tin that contained water.

Two figures lay at the far end asleep. *Fuck*, thought Seager, *it better be them. There's a dead man outside with a hundred pissed off mates. It better be them.*

125

He moved forward and knelt beside the first figure. The Shangaan crossed to the second and, as Seager dropped his hand over the first girl's sleeping mouth, Chimkuyu did the same to the other. He felt the person awake and stiffen in fear.

"Layla Rakkafian I presume?" he said. "Don't worry, we've come to take you home." He felt the figure relax, her mouth working as he lifted his hand. She said nothing, just stared up. He could feel her stare in the dark.

"Layla?" he asked, fearing for a second there had been some terrible mistake.

"No. Maggie." Then she began to cry.

The Shangaan lifted his hand from the struggling form on the other side. "I am Layla Rakkafian." The voice was strong and proud.

"Let's go," Seager said. "Very quietly please. There are only five of us. Let's not wake up the tribe."

Seager was elated; the success, however tenuous, was tangible. He pulled Maggie to her feet – she felt incredibly light – and led the way to the door and the soft moonwash of the outside.

That was when things began to go wrong.

As Seager arrived at the door, Nyamadze's hand swung onto his chest from the right, stopping him going any further. He looked across the area in front of the hut and he could see Masters and Pirelli sink to their knees behind a sparse little Jesse bush, one of many round the camp. Someone was coming.

CHAPTER ELEVEN

The problem lay with the weak bladder and the natural rebellion of a drunk.

Johnny Walker, as he was known, had drunk five large mugs of Katchase. The illicit brew was banned all over the continent because a bad batch could send men mad or blind or both. There was no proper alcohol out here, so if the men wanted to drink they had to brew their own. He was careful as drinkers of Katchase went and didn't overdo it, but he was drunk and he did want to urinate. He rolled clear of his filthy blanket lying, rose carefully to his feet and walked unsteadily towards the opening of the crude shelter. On the way he kicked his sleeping companion, but the form didn't stir. Muttering abuse under his breath, he walked into the soft light and headed towards the latrine. It wasn't a proper latrine by any means, just an area designated for the purpose. He remembered the last time he had been there at night. He had stepped in a pile of shit. He muttered to himself and slung his rifle more carefully over his shoulder. He never went anywhere without it. As he weaved his way through the shelters he thought about the shit he had stepped in. Pigfucking commissar who made the rules never had to go in there. *Well, fuck him. I will piss where I want.* Ahead was bush, only yards from the commissar's shelter. *Just because he has a card, just because he was in ZIPRA from the old days, gets his own shelter. Well I will piss right by it,* he thought.

He staggered towards the bush, the bush that contained something he had nightmares about. Many ZIPRA cadres had nightmares when they thought about the S.A.S. or the Selous Scouts. This bush had one of each, but he didn't know, so he pulled his penis clear of his jeans and, staggering to a halt, began to direct an unsteady stream into the undergrowth.

Pirelli remained absolutely still as the man urinated on his right knee every few seconds. He had his Ingram in one hand and his knife in the other, both options open. Inwardly, he blessed Pascoe's little silencer;

it had increased the weapon's length by seven inches, but allowed it to kill in almost complete inaudibility. Masters, three feet to his left, was pointing his shotgun at the man's chest, dead centre and waiting for something to happen.

Buchanan watched from the rear of the hut, his gun to his shoulder, and aimed at the man's head. He couldn't fire, not from this position. He was thirty feet away and the spread from his fire would hit Pirelli if he moved even a few inches upward. In the door, Seager could see nothing – but, leaning against the door's mukwa jam, looking like the now dead guard, Nyamadze could see everything.

Ncubi was standing stock still in the shadows beneath the eaves of the hut's thatched roof, just forward of Buchanan. Slowly, he edged his weapon to bear. He *could* fire. Even fired over open sights in the dark, his rifle – the 7:62 FN – could put a round into the urinating man's head if required. He could imagine Pirelli's fingers tightening on the trigger of the Ingram.

Buchanan's hand touched his shoulder and pointed. Ncubi nodded, brought his rifle to shoulder height and made ready to fire.

Then everything began to happen at once. The man concentrating on his stream of urine overbalanced and began to fall forward towards the now wet-legged Selous Scout with death in his eyes. Pirelli didn't wait for the man to reach him; he swung the battle knife up and rose in one lightning movement, driving the knife into the man's throat and aiming for the spinal cord at the back. He missed by a fraction, knew it instantly and twisted the blade as the dying man fell backward. Following, he tried to catch the falling body without releasing the Ingram, afraid of an accidental discharge. The irony was that that was exactly what happened next. Not his weapon, but the man he had killed. The AKM dropped from the flailing arm and, hitting the ground, discharged one round harmlessly into the night. The noise would have woken up the dead, and the crash echoed round the narrow basin.

Masters burst from cover as Ncubi dropped to one knee and peered into the darkness of the camp, awaiting whatever came.

"Move!" Masters barked.

Seager burst from the door, Maggie's hand in his and Layla following close behind. The Shangaan followed, inches behind her, through the narrow door. They began to run towards the escape rope. They had gone only a few feet when the sacking cover over the door of one hut was thrown back. Buchanan blasted at the figure, the roar of his shotgun awesome as its muzzle flashed. As Buchanan's ears stopped ringing, he heard the more distant roll of gunfire from Stockly's attack at the other end of the basin, and Pirelli zigzagged past him with Masters. Nyamadze fired two rounds at a running figure and he fell. Above, Pascoe swore bitterly, reached for his flare and tapped Chana on the shoulder. Chana cocked the action on the MAG, looking down over the barrel as a group of figures broke into the moonlight parade ground. He saw one man stop and throw something back and, a few seconds later, he heard the familiar flat crack of a phosphorous grenade. Its burning shards lit up whichever of the hut's custodians were unfortunate enough to be that close to the blast. Behind him, Pascoe fired the flare and, as the area lit up, he began to fire slow methodical bursts into the camp.

Maggie tripped and, as she stumbled, Seager scooped her up by the collar. "Run!" he cried out. "Watch the ground, and run!"

He still had no weapon and, as they reached the dark pool, Chimkuyu surged past him. A figure had appeared from the huts at the north end. The Shangaan kept running; perhaps the figure didn't see him or didn't recognise the threat – and, as Chimkuyu swung the machete, Pirelli grabbed Layla's arm. The man's head dropped back, held by tendons at the back of the neck, and blood pumped upwards in a scarlet flume.

Pirelli's Ingram stuttered briefly and a second man stumbled and fell. He looked over at Layla. Her eyes were wide with fear and horror.

Up ahead, Chimkuyu swung his shotgun and blasted at a movement in the trees. All around the camp men were running and voices shouted orders. Above that, the machine gun fired its ceaseless and regular tattoo across the open ground wherever figures ran.

Seager reached the rope, and without stopping pulled Maggie over his shoulder. In hugely powerful strides, he began to climb the slippery slope. Without a weapon he felt vulnerable and open, and his fear drove him upward like a man possessed.

Below him, Masters' team formed up in a defensive group and

ceased firing, hoping the confusion would allow the firefight to roll over them. Buchanan, following Seager's example, grabbed Layla and began to climb the slope. His extraordinary fitness and strength were immediately obvious.

Pirelli adjusted his load and flicked a look upward. Ncubi fitted a second magazine and Masters chambered three fresh rounds. Above, Pascoe spoke into his radio. "Zulu Three Zulu Three!" There was a pause and the radio crackled back. He could hear the gunfire as part of the transition.

"Zulu Three."

"Sunray, give it another two minutes then take the gaps!" Pascoe shouted into the mouth piece.

"Say again?" came back, the weapons fire loud. Stockly obviously couldn't hear a thing.

"Two minutes repeat two minutes!"

"Roger that. It's getting hairy ova."

Down in the camp, frightened men were shooting at shadows and fleeing figures, their own men. Some were trying to break out, thinking the camp under attack by government forces. One group of three ran towards Masters' team and into their deaths as Nyamadze and Ncubi joined Pirelli's stuttering silent Ingram and opened fire. Two seconds later all three were dead or dying.

At the top, Seager's lungs were bursting. He dropped Maggie Nolan on her feet.

"Fuck that was steep!" he said in panting bursts.

Pascoe, just reaching the top, looked at the girl. "Stay down. We leave in a couple of minutes down the hill the other side."

She nodded, confused but hearing him.

"Where's Edward?" Seager asked, bending over like an athlete, breathing deeply.

Chimkuyu arrived at the top and moved to rest at the gun.

"He's dead. They killed him on the third day," Maggie said.

"I thought so. We found his body." Seager stood. "Where's a gun?"

"Use this–" Pascoe handed him Buchanan's Mannlicher, "–until yours is back." Its shiny stock gleamed in the moonlight.

"Who are you all?" Maggie asked, rising to her feet.

At that moment, Buchanan came pounding up the last few feet and dumped Layla like a sack of potatoes. Grabbing Mannlicher from Seager, he closed the bolt home and went immediately to the edge, where Chana had stopped firing, and looked over breathing hard.

"Friends," said Seager. "Don't worry, you're amongst friends. I saw your Mum only three weeks ago. She's looking forward to having you home for Christmas."

Then Layla spoke. "Are you mercenaries or what?" Her voice was low, her accent faintly Middle Eastern.

"Sort of," said Seager as Ncubi reached the top and threw Seager his rifle. Chana had started firing again. "We'll talk later," he said and moved forward to cover the retreat of Masters, Pirelli and Nyamadze.

Their retreat was about to become difficult. Nyamadze had begun his climb up the slope with the other two covering his escape. A large group of seven or eight heavily armed men had been rallied by a superior and were moving fast through the confusion on the edge of the camp. They had obviously pinpointed the probable site of the gun and were trying to silence it and that would mean the slope that Masters and Pirelli were guarding.

From above, Buchanan could see nothing in the dark undergrowth. He swore and peered through the scope on his rifle.

"Shall I get a flare?" Seager asked.

"No. Fuck up their night sight," Buchanan answered. "Once those bastards get in that scrub they'll be dead, unless they catch our blokes with a stray shot. We don't want to do anything to alter the conditions."

It was the most Seager had ever heard him say in one go. Chana's gun fired again, and Pascoe's hand touched his shoulder.

"Max, take the girls down the back slope. Ncubi will go with you."

"No!" Seager replied, loudly over the roar of the gun. "I want to help here!"

"ON YOUR FUCKING FEET!" Pascoe roared. "This is now getting critical. YOU take the girls. That's *your* job. Leave the heavy stuff to us. COPY ME?"

Seager rolled back onto his side and looked up at Pascoe. "Fuck off!"

"I thought you would say that," Pascoe grinned. "Please?"

"O.K.," replied Seager congenially.

Layla and Maggie looked on at the banter, amazed at the good-humoured delivery in the midst of the shooting and noise. Then the big man rose and, collecting his pack from the ground, looked at them. "Let's go down the hill. Chimkuyu, let's go."

Seager set off down the hill, weapon raised. He stopped and looked back, the girls hurrying in his wake.

Layla reached him first. "Who are you people? Who sent you?" she asked, pleased to be escaping the noise. "Was it my father? Please answer me. Who are you?"

"Later," Seager said. "Be quiet now." He stopped and let Ncubi take the point.

"Stay close. We're almost home and dry."

Chimkuyu followed closely, machete sheathed and his bloodlust cooled.

At the base of the slope, Masters pulled his second shot gun clear of the scabbard, pumped a round into the breach and pushed it back. He looked at Pirelli and nodded to the left. Pirelli nodded back. They were about to engage in the most frightening kind of firefight: outnumbered, moving fast, and in complete darkness. The only way to win was to move rapidly and shoot before they did.

Something moved to Masters' right. He blasted two rounds into the foliage and charged in. Pirelli heard his shotgun roar again and a man screamed in the dark. He saw movement to his front and fired a short burst. Masters wouldn't be that far left, so Pirelli ran into the front left quadrant of his previous vision sphere. He fired again, ran into the darkness ahead, rolled and fired again at a figure. He heard Masters shotgun again, one round and then a second. *Change guns Richard,* he said to himself. *Where are you you fucker?*

There was movement. His eyes flickered left. Pressure on the trigger, the slide working. A burst of fire from the man he had hit. He fired again, changed mags on the Ingram, and then he was up and moving into them. *Move and fire, move and fire.*

The camp shuddered as each round was discharged with devastating accuracy. A dark figure writhed in agony on the ground. He heard two more rounds up close, stopped and listened. It was Masters' gun again. Pirelli turned and ran back to his starting point. Seconds later, Masters appeared. He looked alright.

They had killed seven men in twenty seconds.

"Let's go," he said and they ran up the slope together.

Fires burned brightly and ammunition began to explode somewhere in the centre of camp. It was complete mayhem, exactly as Pascoe had intended. Now they could leave the scene and make distance before the dawn, it gave them confidence.

Above them, Chana fired one long burst and sat back, his belt finished and a beaming smile on his face. He did like the GPMG, even if it was heavy to carry. He was careful not to burn himself on the barrel, hefted the gun and slung it over his shoulder.

Buchanan took the tripod as Pascoe laid out Masters and Pirelli's packs. Nyamadze looked to the right and listened for the whistle. It came. Pascoe smiled.

Seager moved forward to halt Ncubi, and then came back down the way he had come.

"O.K. girls, let's halt here and wait for the others."

They sat wearily where they stopped and Chimkuyu moved away into the darkness. After he was gone, Seager dropped to his haunches, his rifle between his knees, butt down in the thin grass.

"Can we talk now?" Layla asked. She had lost her hair band and her hair lay across her shoulder like a shawl.

"As long as you whisper." He smiled suddenly. "Sound carries at night."

"Who sent you?" Layla asked. "Who are you? Who is paying you? My father?"

"No. A friend of his who wanted to give you back as a gift, alive and well." Seager didn't say *dead would have done*. "The Emir of Ras Al Qualeem is your benefactor."

Layla's head dropped in the moonlight, pleased and disappointed all at once.

"Uncle Rashid," she said, covering something else.

"You said you saw my mother," Maggie cut in. "How is she?"

"Very persuasive and missing you lots."

Her bouncy permed hair had grown out somewhat and needed brushing, but he could see the likeness to the photo of the girl waiting to go out for the evening.

"I can't wait to see her," she said softly. "Oh Layla, we're out. We are free. We are going home."

"No thanks to my father," she said bitterly in reply. Seager looked back at her quickly. "We were never very close, but I thought he might at least try." She began to cry very softly and to herself.

"Not everyone has access to people like us. We had to be talked into this. The chances were very slim that anyone would find you, let alone alive. Don't be hard on him."

She looked up at him. Her face was clear in the moonlight. The tears had dried and something else was there, anger and a hopelessness that gave strength to her next statement. "He knew we were alive. There were three demands for ransom. My father," she spat the word, "is a very wealthy man. The ransom was pathetically small."

Seager thought quickly. "I'm sure he never got them," he said, not believing it himself. *So that's why they were still alive.*

"I addressed the envelopes myself. He doesn't care a damn about me."

Seager's eyes glittered in the moonlight. *Bastard.*

CHAPTER TWELVE

Stockly watched the mayhem from the other end of the camp. It was distant compared to the firefight going on where he was, but impressive all the same. The gunfire and glow from the flames provided an eerie backdrop to their more immediate role. He looked across at Tim and watched the young man coolly firing into the camp where return fire arced skywards from the dissidents. Stockly found another blank round, fed it into the chamber of his rifle and attached a rifle grenade to the business end of the barrel. Then he fired it into the camp. It landed behind but still served its purpose: noise, confusion and fear. He wasn't sure if they had actually killed anyone, but that wasn't important. He watched a group of men running away from the main camp, their bobbing figures silhouetted against the fires that Pascoe and the boys had thankfully provided.

"Tim. Tim!" he called.

"Sah?" Sibanda replied, firing again. He was having fun.

"Time to go. *Kurumidza!*" he cried. *Hurry up!*

Together they zigzagged back into the thicker bush behind them and immediately swung north, leaving nice big tracks as Seager had asked. He wanted them to be easy to follow as far as the first rendezvous, because it was here that Pirelli had something really nasty planned. Something that expanded rapidly and was triggered by a trip wire. A grenade booby trap or two, just to slow up the followers and dampen their enthusiasm.

Sibanda set off at a run through the darkness, the soft moon breaking through every now and then, illuminating the grass and rocks and trees like a monochrome picture on an old television.

On top of the ridge, the last members of the team were about to clear the area, scooping up packs and jamming rounds into magazines. Masters, the last man up, heaved his pack on and, with a handful of rounds for his shotguns, grabbed his AR15 from the ground.

"Okey dokey, let's take the high road," he said.

"Glad you're ready" said Pascoe dryly. "Nyamadze has point, Buchanan and Chanah tail end. Let's move, and don't shoot Max. He'll be really pissed off."

They moved off quickly. Some time later, they joined up with Seager, Ncubi, Chimkuyu and the girls, moving northwards away from the slope. Ncubi settled down beside Seager.

"They're coming," Ncubi said. "I can hear them."

Seager cocked an ear; he could hear nothing.

"O.K. girls, let's move out."

The enlarged party stopped at the Alpha One point to wait for Stockly and Sibanda, and broke open the light ration packs to eat. Everything was on schedule and Pirelli began to prepare his booby traps as the sun crept over the eastern horizon, whistling to himself. It was Masters' tune, "Lady in Red", but he had the notes all wrong.

Seager ate ravenously from a tin of baked beans and frankfurters and washed it all back with long drinks from his bottle. Though he was watching Pirelli setting up his traps, his mind was elsewhere, brooding on what Layla had said.

Bearlike, but gentle as a lamb, Buchanan opened a second tin of something for Maggie, a silly grin on his face. She smiled like an angel and took the proffered tin as if it was caviar.

"Five minutes," said Pascoe. "Seager? Wanna sell your boat?"

Seager broke from his trance and looked up. "Build your own fucking boat" he said and lifted his rifle.

Pascoe had noted the mood. The others were pleased and confident of the outcome so close to the pick-up. Seager was dark and, for a moment there, his eyes had that glitter, the same Pascoe remembered as in Johannesburg three years ago when a man died in a hotel room, shot by Seager who looked him in the eyes while he was doing it.

Seager was looking now at Layla, the stunning Arab girl and he had that same look in his eye. It bade no good for someone.

"Can we go?" Layla said. "I like Africa, but this trip has gone on long enough."

Seager smiled, pleased that she had bounced back. Then they moved up the track and waited for Pirelli to set his wires. Chimkuyu would remain behind to watch the outcome from nearby and report to the main party who would wait at Alpha Two – or, as Chimkuyu knew it, the big Marula tree at the bend in the river.

On the track the realisation they were free finally sank into the girls. Maggie began to cry again and confused Buchanan because she was smiling at the same time. She then began to ask dozens of questions: political questions, social questions, news story questions; had there been another royal wedding, and was Mrs Thatcher still in power? Pirelli told her about Bob Geldof's 'Live Aid' and she regaled him with stories of a Boomtown Rats concert she had seen. Eventually Pascoe swung back and apologetically asked them to 'quieten down'. Aloof and beautiful, Layla walked quietly.

Back at the Alpa stop, Chimyuku watched the traps that Pirelli had set and, with his natural hunter's eye, more recently tuned to the habits of men, he silently applauded the wily little murungu's choice of place-ment. The two devices were very close: one wire across the path where they had been walking just after a large boulder on the right; the other across the path on the left. With a growing sense of expectation, he waited for their trackers to arrive. When the lead man set off the first wire across the track and detonated the fragmentation grenade, his comrades would instinctively break for the cover of the bush to the left. To the right was the boulder. Once in the cover they would set off the second grenade. It would, with luck, incapacitate several of the party, meaning delays while they were treated and carried back to the camp. From that moment on, if they pursued the chase at all, they would be very slow, expecting more traps at any time.

Chimyuku lay on a shallow rise on his stomach fifty yards from the boulder and watched. At this range the chances of being hit by a piece of shrapnel were remote, particularly considering that there were only eight or nine inches of exposed flesh, so he decided to actually watch them as they approached the trip wire. He waited for just over three hours to see the first figures bobbing along the spoor below him. It was a large group of seventeen or twenty, moving tightly packed and confidently on the tracks of a group half that size.

One very optimistically carried an RPG tube over his shoulder and the rest had a variety of small arms. A few wore brightly coloured shirts and at least three sported long Rasta dreadlocks and 'Bob Marley' woolly hats. The Shangaan watched the lead man only ten or twelve feet ahead of the rest moving into the trip wire. There was a flat whiplash like a crack of a blast and Chimkuyu thought he saw a puff of white smoke. Two men were actually hit by something and the rest dived for cover, some going immediately to ground, others running into the bush, one dropping his weapon and running the way they had come, terrified they had walked into an ambush. Then came the second blast, closer and louder, and the screams from those who had been hit rose into the night.

It was a few minutes before a few heads started appearing from the grass and recriminations were hurled at others. Gingerly, they began probing the grass for more devices and five were helped limping back onto the track from which they had arrived. Two bodies were left in the grass for the ants, the jackals and the big blue flies and their maggot offspring.

Chimyuku crept back over the shallow rise, rose to his feet and began to jog northwards at a steady pace, his weapon in one hand and a walking stick in the other.

Seager moved up beside Layla. The girl had not spoken since the first stop before dawn that morning. The others had put it down to that particular type of re-adjustment that hostages require after release from long captivity under threat of death. For many, it changes their lives. They seek comfort from their gods, they often blame themselves and self-recrimination is common. Many fall to the cause that has taken them, the best example being that of Patty Hearst, the American billionaire's daughter, who during her confinement actually became an active member of the cadre that held her. For all, there is a period of re-adjustment to the prospect of re-entering society after an experience that may have altered their priorities and their beliefs. And yet – Seager knew that wasn't the case with this girl. Her silence was more anger and resentment in her belief that her father had finally let her down, finally sold her out. Walked away from her when she needed him.

"Layla, do you get along with your old man? You seem convinced that he knew of your predicament and decided to ignore the ransom requests. You say you personally addressed them?"

He spoke softly. Her skin was a dusky golden colour and her hair a rich thick black beneath the dust. A slight widow's peak dropped perfectly to accentuate her fine chiseled nose and her eyes were large, dark and moist over high cheek bones. She was startlingly beautiful, and the photographs Seager had seen did not do her justice.

She looked across at him, walking steadily, then back away at the horizon. "Even when I was little he was distant, always busy, always working."

Good answer, he thought, *defensive as only a daughter can be about her father.* He decided to change tack for the moment.

"Tell me about the beginning, the day you were on the road."

She looked across at him again. Her dark eyes deepened for a moment and she began to talk.

"They stepped onto the road, five of them. There was a bus stopped and, as we slowed down, the bus drove away. Our driver was saying we better stop or they would shoot. I thought they would just take some money. Edward said no, drive on. But we stopped. The driver was terrified. They pulled us from the car. Edward offered money and they took it. Then they started arguing amongst themselves. I am woman enough to know what the small one wanted. The leader, I think, wanted to let us go, but they continued arguing. Then another car came along and we were pushed into the bushes at the side of the road. As the car came closer our driver tried to run out into the road. They stabbed him. He fell over. That was when they were committed, I think. They just pushed us deeper into the bush. It was a couple of days later that Edward started getting stroppy. Maggie and I told him to keep cool, but he refused. He was full of righteous indignation. He even tried the 'I've got a British Passport you can't do this to me' bit. Then he tried, 'Let them go, keep me.' Finally, the short one just turned round and began stabbing him with a bayonet, shouting and screaming at him. Edward fell over, clutching his stomach. God, it was awful. Maggie started screaming, and then the leader began hitting the small one. I bent down to try to help Edward. There was blood everywhere. He had a sort of 'this can't be happening to me look.' Then someone pulled me

139

away and they shot him as he lay there. The leader was still shouting at the little one, and then they threw Ed's body in some rocks."

"We found it," said Seager. Layla had begun to cry, great slow tears that rolled down her angry cheeks. *Come on girl,* he thought, *get it all out. Cry for Edward, the blood, the horror and the months in a locked room.*

She began talking again without prompting, so he let her carry on. "Syphilis," she said.

"Sorry?" Seager queried.

"Syphilis. I'm sure the little sadist was syphilitic. The leader apologised that night. We seemed to walk for days. It was awful. Maggie came on, and our handbags were in the car. Eventually we arrived at the camp and were brought before boss there. Chabegwa is his name. He thought of the ransom and I jumped at it. Pitiful really. He wanted two hundred thousand for us both."

"How long before they put you to work?" asked Seager.

"That was my idea. I thought, if we were useful, then we would last longer, at least until the ransom was paid. Chabegwa wasn't unpleasant." She looked at Seager, the tears drying and the anger back. "And, yes, I suggested *that* too. It kept them away from Maggs. She couldn't have coped with that. I became Chabegwa's whore, and that's how we survived."

"I'm sorry it came to that," said Seager.

"Don't be," she replied bitterly. "I will survive, ransom or no ransom, Chabegwa or no Chabegwa!"

For a time, Seager said nothing and just walked beside her. Eventually she spoke again, the fire in her eyes gone. "Thanks for coming in and finding us. Even if Uncle Rashid paid you to come, thanks anyway."

"You're welcome."

Layla looked across at him and squeezed his hand. Then they lapsed into silence and Layla moved forward to put her arm around Maggie. Both girls were sweating freely as they walked in the sun. Maggie was wearing a floppy hat that someone had given her, her curly hair hanging below and adding a strangely feminine touch to the khaki shirt given to her by Pirelli.

They didn't hear the grenades detonating – they were too far away – and it was Chimkuyu's arrival back at the rear of the line that brought them the first news of success. Buchanan saw him first and whistled to Seager. Seager turned and walked back to Buchanan.

"Chimkuyu," he said, "coming up the track."

"Thanks Keith. Tell Major Pascoe please."

Buchanan hurried up the track and Seager squatted on his haunches to wait for his friend. He didn't wait long. The rangy figure came into view, jogging steadily. He was still with weapon and stick, but now he had a healthy sheen of sweat and was breathing hard. Not surprising, he had run the entire distance from the booby trap, a full fifteen miles.

He stopped by Seager and stood, breathing through his nose.

"You saw?" Seager asked.

"I saw," Chimyuku answered.

"Good. Wait for the Major. Rest. Then tell us what happened."

Pascoe arrived moments later, jogging down the track to where the two men waited.

"Chimkuyu kanjane?"

The Shangaan nodded at Pascoe. "Small Feather."

"Well?"

"They came, the bombs went off, they carried five away and left two dead. They have not followed since, but may come again with more men, and slower."

"Good! How many in the group?" Pascoe asked.

The Shangaan had never learned to count in a conventional manner, but instead had a memory system that relied on total recall and then holding up a finger for each man remembered. As the fingers rolled out from clenched palms, Seager counted.

"Eighteen," Seager said.

"You're sure?" Pascoe asked.

"He's sure," Seager said half defensively and half in admiration, standing up and hefting his rifle. He turned to Chimkuyu, holding his bottle. "Move behind and cover our spoor," he said.

The Shangaan nodded and took the proffered water bottle, sipped twice and then nodded. "I will, but they will not catch us now, they have no heart for the chase. I should go to the point. That is where I am best."

Seager nodded. "We have good men there and to the south are those who are pissed off." The Sindebele and English mixture fell naturally from Seager's tongue, and the Shangaan chuckled.

"They are like bees when their hive has been disturbed."

The Shangaan was right. The point was the place he should have been.

CHAPTER THIRTEEN

Sibanda ranged ahead of the main party, scouting the area ahead. As scout, he moved both left and right on the more central path the others would follow. If necessary he could change their direction to move around any danger, slow-going terrain, or kraal lines that might be in their path. As point, Nyamadze had a different role: to establish the imminent presence of any danger in time to warn the main party to his rear. Sibanda was moving east again to bisect the route that would be taken by the rest. He wanted to have a look at a drop in the ground to the east that should have been the Busi River again. That would have put them half way approximately and, once across the river's dry bed, he would wait for Nyamadze.

Ahead, a low hill rose where the river bent round and headed eastwards for a bit before swinging again for the Sebgwa. He dropped down the slope, crossed the riverbed, climbed up the other side and moved along the middle ground below the slope of the hill. He was walking steadily with his rifle butt to his shoulder ready to react, his eyes flicking left to right. Behind him, Nyamadze would only be forty or fifty yards back. He would walk the track for a short way, then cross the high ground and look at a thick patch of bush he could see ahead and to the right.

The three dissidents were the point for a party returning to their camp after a successful trip north to fly the party flag near Binga. They were near home and were not anticipating problems with police or security forces, 'National Army' as they were now called. Their main group were resting atop the small hill and they had walked down three minutes previously to lead the group back the last few miles. Then everything changed.

They saw Tim Sibanda before he saw them, but there were only milliseconds in it. He was directly ahead in the waist high scrub when they walked into the area directly to his right. For him it was a fleeting

143

impression in his peripheral vision. To the three lead men of Chabegwa's returning party, he was the enemy. They recognised from the way he carried his rifle, the way he moved, the way he wore his webbing that this was not one of the masses, not one of the cadre. They fired and, at forty yards range, the three rifles were effective. Already falling and swinging his weapon, Sibanda jerked as the bullets hit him. He returned fire immediately, but the three men split up. Knowing that his vision was limited in the scrub, that they outnumbered him three to one, and aware he was hit, they moved forward bravely.

Nyamadze began to run. The only person to his front was Tim, a comrade in arms, and he was in trouble. He remembered that Sibanda was using an AK so there was no telling the weapons apart by sound. Bursting into the scrub from the tree, he saw three men standing over something and opened fire. His FN made a deeper note than the earlier reports, ripping across the clearing. All three men fell. He moved fast, broke left and circled – and then all hell seemed to break loose from the hill behind him. He kept moving and rolled into cover behind an anthill.

From here he could see the wounded Sibanda, who the dissidents hadn't yet finished off. Nyamadze crawled through the fire to his side and, grabbing his webbing, pulled him back into the cover of the anthill. Then he reached for his handheld radio.

A short distance down the track, the team went to ground, beside a smaller kopje, the brother of the larger hill directly ahead. Pascoe pulled his radio from his pocket, as Buchanan and Stockly arrived to his rear, followed by Masters and Pirelli from the front. Chana lay where he was and cleared the belt into the gun, quickly going through his checks.

Seager pulled the two girls down. "Stay here!" he barked and crawled to Pascoe.

Chimkuyu ran from the rear and dropped to his knees by Seager, awaiting orders. His eyes flicked around, the bloodlust rising.

Pascoe's radio crackled. "Sunray go," he said in a calm voice.

"Sibanda's down, fire from the hill, three o'clock towards the top."

"Roger, stand by. Can you move?"

"Negative Sunray. Pinned behind an anthill. Three here are down."

"Roger that. Sit tight." Pascoe looked up at Seager. "Right, what's ahead?"

Seager and Chimkuyu had walked the area when looking for their escape route. The noise of the battle was fearful and, when Chimkuyu spoke, drawing in the dust, he spoke loudly. "Here river bed, dry. Hill like this. River bed is over there, fifty paces or so. We could come from the back?"

"Good. Masters, Pirelli. Ncubi, Stockly, into the river, round the back of that kopje. Pour in fire from the northeast slope and force them into the river bed. We'll be there waiting. Keith, you wait here up that slope and start, keeping head down with your rifle. Give Seager the claymore. Chana –" Chana looked back at him, "– you come with me. Understand?" They all nodded. "Layla, Maggie stay with Keith. Move out."

The river bed would round the back of the small hill. The first team would attack the hill and force the others into the river bed as an escape route, where Pascoe and his team would be waiting. As Seager pulled the heavy claymore mine from Buchanan's pack, the big man pulled the electro trigger mechanism from his pocket. It was a simple small transmitter that would broadcast a VHF signal and detonate the device upon command.

"O.K. River bed, got it." Seager lifted the mine gingerly and put it on the ground.

"You girls, up the slope from the back."

Buchanan indicated the kopje to their left, then picked up the mine and, turning to Seager, lowered it into his pack and dropped the detonating transmitter in on top. "Move!" he snapped at them.

"What are you doing?" Maggie asked.

"I'm gonna make a stand at the top, let's go!"

Buchanan pulled the Mannlicher from its scabbard, and led them back down the track to climb from the rear.

Seager looked at Pascoe, who was watching Masters and his team race into the river bed. Pascoe turned. "You ready?"

They heard Nyamadze's FN raking the hill.

"Yeah," said Seager. He recocked his weapon and a round flew from the breech. It was already cocked. He looked embarrassed. "Nice one. Audey Murphy did that every now and then too," said Pascoe.

"Fuck off," said Seager picking up the round.

"Leave it," Pascoe replied. Then, "Let's go," he said, business-like again.

A few rounds buzzed overhead. No-one was alarmed; they were too high to have been aimed and everyone knew it. They were wildly aimed by someone who was keeping their head down. Nyamadze's return fire from behind the anthill and his accuracy obviously worried the men on the slopes.

Chana lead them down into the river bed. They had to cover only sixty to seventy yards to reach the bend, running close to the left bank under the steep sides of clay. The battle was now closer, gaining in ferocity as the attackers above then realised that there was only one rifle below and it was only a matter of time. Nyamadze had already betrayed his training; he had not broken or run, that made him special and worth killing.

Chana dropped to one knee and waited for someone to pull his heavy tripod clear of his pack. Pascoe stopped, pulled the gear clear and dropped it in the sand beside the man. "Max!" he said quickly. "The mine. Hurry! Keith will open fire any minute, and Richards team will be on the west slope by now."

Seager slung his pack to the ground and lowered his rifle to the sand, careful to keep the workings clear of the tiny damaging grains. He lifted the mine and looked at Pascoe.

"Dig it into the bank facing the bend. Pack it well in, about eighteen inches above the sand." Pascoe pulled a belt clear from his pack. Then he passed it the Chana, who was piling up sand in a small ridge in front of his position twelve feet out into the dry sandy bed. "Here, like this," said Pascoe. He crossed to Seager and began scooping clay clear in a shelf arrangement. Lifting the mine, he armed the switch at the side. "Don't handle the trigger from now on, this little number is armed." Bending forward, he pushed it back into the shelf, looked at the angle and adjusted it by scraping some clay from beneath, so that its blast angle was lowered. "Right. There's several thousand dollars of your

146

money about to go with a bang. O.K. Max, up the bank, take my F.N. Cover the area this side. If they break your way shoot like shit, force them back into the river for Chana and me. O.K?"

Seager nodded and, taking Pascoe's rifle, clambered up the bank and found himself a rock to shoot from. As he arrived, he heard the blast of Buchanan's Mannlicher echo between the hills. A few moments later, he heard Masters' team open fire, a softer, more muted sound that seemed to come from everywhere.

He checked the sights on the rifle and wiped some sweat from his eyes and tried to regulate his breathing. The Mannlicher boomed again, and rapidly a second time. *Tim's down. Fuck them! They should have just let us go. Enough killing already. Fuck them, if they want a fight they have fucking got one now.* He sighted down the barrel and tried to pick a hundred yard marker. That done, he looked up at the kopje. The fire from the other side was intense and he knew that it wouldn't be long before the dissidents broke and ran. They didn't like pitched battles unless they were going to win, which was sensible enough, Seager thought. *Not like us crazy whiteys.* He kept watching and, a moment later, he saw figures moving on the slope, at first moving from cover to cover, then running quicker as they thought it safe.

They were moving this way.

He looked through the sight and, without re-setting them, he selected 'manual' and opened fire at the slope, raking it bottom to top and making it obvious from which direction he was firing. He wanted them to know that, and run into the river bed to the waiting MAG and Claymore mine.

On the other side of the hill, Nyamadze ceased firing as the dissidents disappeared from view and, checking that the barely alive Sibanda was till breathing, he got to his feet and jinked his way towards where he knew they were going. He wasn't out of the battle yet, and his comrade was dying.

High on the opposite hills, Buchanan was following the fleeing men with his thirty power telescopic sight. He zeroed a man who stopped to catch his breath, and fired. The heavy bullet slammed into the figure and threw him back against the slope, dead when the bullet severed his spinal column. Spurred on by the realisation that they weren't safe on that slope, his colleagues ran helter-skelter for the comparative safety of the river bed and its protective walls.

From his position, Seager fired again, single shots in their direction until two men turned and ran his way. Seager never knew if they had realised they were running into an ambush or not, but something had spooked them and they were moving his way, prepared to risk his rifle to get clear. *So be it,* he thought. *Tim's down. Fuck 'em.* He sighted the first man and fired low, aiming at his legs. The shot went high and the second round hit the running figure in the chest. The second man fell, shot from the side. Seager swung his rifle at the threat and recognised Nyamadze just in time as he burst into the grass from the trees.

Standing up, Seager pointed to the river and Nyamadze kept running, straight over the body of the man he had just shot. Seager followed close behind. From somewhere out there, they heard Chana open fire with the machine gun, and almost immediately the ground shook. Seager's ears recoiled as the claymore mine exploded across the river bed below them.

Pascoe, meanwhile, had watched them running towards him, eleven or twelve men. He dropped and jogged back to Chana. "Thirty seconds," he said, scooped up Seager's short barrelled A.K. and, dropping to the ground beside Chana, peered over the nail-polished foresight.

"I hear them," Chana said – and, lowering his eyes over the sights, he swung the heavy gun side to side on the tripod to check there were no snags.

Pascoe pulled the command detonator from his pocket and armed the switch. They were behind the mine and fifteen yards to the right. It would blast a swathe ahead of them and kill everything in the river bed for seventy yards. Between that range and one hundred and forty yards, it was less effective as the shot spread, but hopefully the men would drop well within the seventy yard killing zone.

They could now hear clearly the running footsteps of the fleeing men, and beyond that the fire from Masters and his team, forcing the contact their way.

Suddenly the first man dropped the seven feet to the bottom of the bank and scrambled to his feet, followed by others.

"Wait for it!" Pasco muttered to Chana. More men dropped down the bank and together they began to jog to the far side, one looking back over his shoulder.

"Now! Fire!"

They opened up together, the big machine gun on its stepped cyclic rate of one thousand rounds per minute merciless on the dry flat sand. Pascoe stopped firing at the milling figures and pressed the detonator. The mine, made in West Germany, packed the same explosive charge as an anti-vehicle mine, and literally made the ground shake as it blasted six thousand ball bearings outwards, cutting through the figures like chaff under a scythe. Suddenly nothing moved except the sand kicked up by the rounds down the riverbed beyond the killing zone.

"Cease fire!" called Pascoe. He looked up at the bank. There came the sound of more footsteps; then a voice called out. "It's Seager."

The ambush had been completely successful. Nothing was left alive out on the hot sand.

A man lay propped on his side by Ncubi, his eyes full of pain and shock, his legs quivering and one hand twitching ominously. His breathing was harsh, shallow and quick and he had blood in his mouth. Seager looked. There were two entry wounds just to the right of his sternum and low into his rib cage. The wound sucked air between Ncubi's fingers as he vainly trying to seal the holes, holding the man and willing him to live. The third wound was high in his left thigh and was bleeding dark blood heavily through a dressing someone had placed.

"Get a drip into him," ordered Pascoe. Stockly dropped his pack, delved into it and produced the life-saving saline drip and feeder hose. He gently rolled the man's twitching arm and firmly pushed the needle into a vein. Already his skin had lost its healthy black sheen and was grey and pallid. Ncubi was still holding the chest wounds while Stockly prepared one of the plastic airtight dressings that the Swiss issued to their troops and sold the world over.

Layla settled onto her knees beside Seager and, recognising the man, she put her hand to her face. "Chabegwa. It's Chabegwa."

"He just learned life's lesson, but a little too late," said Seager.

"What's that?" she asked bitterly. "Live by the sword?"

"No. There's the quick and the dead. He chose to play with the big boys and now he pays the price like a big boy."

She looked at him angrily, her eyes flashing. "You Africans are all the same. Violent and cruel."

"Don't be so fucking pious. You can't talk! Your own country has the most senseless armed conflict and slaughter ever! They are the same. That man –" he pointed at the dying Chabegwa, "– and young militiamen in Beirut, the gun is all they know. He's been out here since he was about fourteen. He had no other way to earn money. He is unemployed in a country where most of the people are subsistence farmers. The gun is his livelihood, just like your boys in Beirut, except one thing. These people do it to eat. They are not financed by Libya, Syria or Iran. They are not paid killers. They are just the strong, where the strong survive. He just came across someone stronger, that's all." Seager finished his tirade; but Layla said nothing, just gazing off into the bush.

Chabegwa spoke, his voice weak. "I couldn't kill you." He was looking at Layla.

Seager looked at Ncubi. "How long?"

The wily Matabele shrugged and replied in English. "A few minutes, maybe half an hour."

Pascoe looked around. "Where's Tim?"

"He's dead," answered Ncubi and, as he said it, Nyamadze walked through the brown grass, Tim Sibanda's body in his arms.

Oh Jesus, thought Seager. *I wanted to do this without losing anyone. They knew we were good, why did they follow? We must have killed fourteen or fifteen of theirs. They fucking knew they weren't a match for this unit.*

Nyamadze knelt on one knee and gently lowered his comrade's body to the ground. Ncubi and Seager walked over and Seager closed the dead man's eyes by running his hand over his face. "Had he children?"

"Yes. Three. Now they are mine," said Ncubi sadly.

"And so is his share," said Seager. "See they are schooled and fed."

Ncubi nodded, "It shall be done." He paused and looked at Seager. "He was a Christian, can you say the words?"

Maggie Nolan stepped forward. She had heard the word 'Christian' and understood the context of the Matabele statement.

"I shall say the words if you like. He died for me, as did Jesus who he believed in."

The stocky man nodded. It was appropriate, and he felt no resentment and the truth of the statement. His friend had died to free this girl. He understood the risk was there. He was a soldier. They scraped a shallow grave from the hard clay and gently lowered Sibanda's poncho-shrouded body down into the dampness. Ncubi leant forward, and in an almost pagan gesture placed a fully cocked Kalashnikov alongside the inert form. He then unclipped his canteen and placed that and a tin of braised steak on the opposite side.

He looked up at Maggie. "Say the words. He is ready for his journey."

The Matabele traditionally buried their dead with food, weapons and valuables for the next life. Those of noble blood would often have cattle slaughtered and buried with them. Even ninety years of Christianity hadn't completely erased the concept and, for Ncubi to give his friend these things and then stand and hear a Christian prayer, it was the old and the new and quite appropriate.

Buchanan moved forward and, unclipping his sheath knife, placed it in the grave. Pirelli and Stockly each placed some small item, and finally Chana dug beneath his shirt and removed a small tarnished crucifix and a chain from around his neck, surprising Seager who wasn't aware that he ever had one. Chana placed the tiny cross on the shrouded head. "Let's finish this," he said, momentarily embarrassed at his display of emotion.

Moments later, Nyamadze arrived at the grave, looked at Seager and shook his head. Chabegwa had died.

Maggie had almost finished her prayer when Chimkuyu walked quickly into the clearing. He ignored the proceedings and crossed to Seager and Pascoe standing together. He had followed the few who had survived. "They ran the course of the river and then swung towards east."

Seager nodded – but it was Pascoe who spoke, breaking his chain of thought. "We've stopped too long already."

"O.K. Let's move it up," replied Seager.

Pascoe waited until they had scraped the grave hill of soil and dumped a few large rocks on top to stop the scavengers, and scatter grass and leaves over the soil. Then he squared his hat and spoke. "Buchanan, Ncubi, scout end point, Stockly the rear. Let's famba."

"No," said Seager. "Chimkuyu scout."

They moved immediately, the spell broken with Chana again hefting the M.A.G. and Pirelli a few yards behind with spare barrels and belt ammunition. Masters left his AR 15 slung over his shoulder and walked carrying his shotgun, resting on his webbing only inches from his shoulder, his eyes sweeping the bush to his right. He knew that Pirelli would watch the left and, with the automatic gun to the centre, the firepower of the main group was substantial. That was without even considering Seager and Pascoe with the girls at ten yards to the rear and Nyamadze and Stockly twenty yards behind the main group, walking backwards and anti-tracking.

Seager's unspoken decision not to bury Chabegwa or his comrades was obvious to all in its reasoning. Anyone who ventured along or heard the gunfire would assume that two rival gangs had met and fought. There was no evidence, other than the disguised grave, to indicate that anyone else had been involved. The survivors of the gang would certainly not report the incident to the authorities – there were none out here, even if they suddenly felt law-abiding, but there was always the danger that, with sufficient reinforcements, they might try to regain some of their damaged pride with a second ambush.

Chimkuyu appeared from the bush ahead of Buchanan, and whistled as he ran the length of their line. He stopped by Seager and gave him an old boy's cap. "Path ahead, some new spoor going," he said, indicating eastwards. "Otherwise nothing disturbs the birds."

"Thank you Chimkuyu," said Seager as the man disappeared into the trees again.

Ranging far ahead, the Shangaan would now ensure no ambush took place that they didn't know about. Seager had lost one man and he didn't mean to lose another.

CHAPTER FOURTEEN

Andre's land cruiser sat parked beneath the trees deep in shade. When Buchanan walked into the clearing below, he put down his paperback, climbed from the cab and whistled. The big man below looked up, waved and walked his way. A few minutes later, the others walked into the clearing and Andre drove down to meet them all. He was there to relieve them of their weapons and hand over passports and Zambian cash, Seager's credit cards and some luggage for everyone, including the things Pascoe had purchased for the girls weeks before. He was also to drive out those men remaining. He had an envelope for each man, containing his pay-slip and bonus details. As the men lined up, his eyes swept the group. He knew better than to ask where Chimkuyu was. He had probably been watching the land cruiser for the last hour. Only Tim Sibanda was missing. He saw the lightness of the loads; the mine was gone and that dragged a pack down. They had contacted and not come out unscathed.

They spoke briefly, then Seager took the envelopes and began to walk amongst them. He stopped at Chana first. "Thank you Chana. In here is your cheque. Bury the gun, we may need it again one day."

"Thank you, Sah. It was a pleasure."

"Ncubi," he said. "Two cheques. Take care of Tim's children." Then he turned to Nyamadze. "James, it was a good fight." He handed over an envelope. "Thank you."

The man smiled shyly. "It was good to fight again, even better for this." He held up the cheque.

"Andre will drop you all in Wankie. You can take buses from there home. In the envelopes are some cash for this. Thank you all again."

Seager turned to Chimkuyu as he heard the helicopter begin its approach. "And you, old one? Will you take money?"

The Shangaan smiled. "Would you, if I asked you for help?"

"No. But I would look at something else that came later," he replied.

"Then I shall too. Walk slowly, he who talks to the spirits, and watch around you. You move among men who care nothing and they will seek to harm you."

"Who speaks of such thing?" Seager asked softly.

"When your eyes shine like the leopard, such men fear you and he who fears cares nothing."

"I shall walk slowly," Seager replied.

The Bell 212 came in fast over the trees. Stockly took Pirelli's extra smoke, pulled the pin and threw it into the grass.

Seager had made arrangements with Andre for fifty prime head of cattle to be given to the Shangaan, for him to watch as the years turned his hair grey and his joints slowed. They shook hands as the helicopter clawed at the sky and settled onto the grass upwind of the smoke. Seager then shook hands with Andre, and they collected their new kit, swept up Maggie – who was brushing her teeth with toothpaste, delighted with her items of toiletries – and began to climb into the open side door. Andre collected weapons as they boarded and, two minutes later, the Canadian looked back at Seager. He nodded, the pilot returned to the controls and the chopper lifted. Then, with gathering speed, it seared across the treetops towards the Zambezi river and the Zambian border.

The helicopter dropped them at a lonely farm nine miles out of the main Lusaka to Livingstone road, and without shutting down unloaded and returned to its base at Ndola. The farm's owners, a Scots couple, were away, but had arranged to make it available to Andre's friends for a night, exhibiting the hospitality that has made the Scots famous the world over. It was an old traditional farmhouse with five bedrooms and a sprawling verandah of polished concrete shaded by an ancient wild fig tree.

The girls were given one room, Buchanan and Pirelli shared another, Stockly and Masters yet another, while Seager and Pascoe – in deference to rank – occupied the remaining two bedrooms. All the men had opted to return to London with Seager and the girls before splitting up. Seager had made the offer attractive, expenses on him for a week and return tickets paid to the point of recruitment. The servants at the house turned on the hot water and fired up the old wood stove for a meal, and finally laid out a drinks tray on a verandah table surrounded by old, but still solid ironwood chairs.

Maggie and Layla had bathed for what Pirelli said was three hours, before dressing in front of a mirror and using the new hairbrushes as well as the basic toiletries. Maggie dropped to the bed and lay smiling at the ceiling, her curly hair spread over the soft white pillows. Meanwhile, Layla finished at the dressing table and walked from the room down the dark passage. She could hear Pirelli's infectious laughter from one room and smiled as she passed it, heading towards Seager's.

Seager was sitting at the desk by the window when she walked towards his open door. She paused at the threshold and knocked softly. He turned from his papers and smiled at her.

"Feeling better?" he asked.

"Yes thank you," she said, returning his smile as she entered the room.

"Your new passport," he said and held up the red and gold document.

"Ras Al Qaleem," she said softly. "It could have been Irish, I was born there."

"Oh," Seager said, "your mum Irish?"

"No, she was Lebanese. She is dead now. Died when I was a baby. There was an accident." She held up the passport. "Uncle Rashid was there. His wife and baby died in the same accident too. The car hit a tractor." She paused and walked to the window. "I wish I had known her," she finished. Seager said nothing and let her talk, but she turned and smiled. "Where are your parents? Still in Zimbabwe?"

"They're dead now," Seager answered. "A T.M. 57 landmine saw to that but we won't go into that. You're right Layla, this is a violent land."

"But you knew them, you knew your mother?" she persisted.

Seager thought about the farm and the smell of bread baking and the sound of the rain on the roof, and the gun-oil and doggy smells that were his father's study, his mother walking through the large garden with a pair of shears in her hands and the constant fresh flowers in the living room on the ironwood table. The huge gum trees that shaded the house and the ritual tea in the afternoons on the verandah, the listening to the shortwave at his father's feet, as the lamps hissed and his father sucked at his pipe.

"Yes I knew them," he said, thinking enough of this. "Will you do something for me?" he asked.

"Of course" she replied.

"Phone B-Cal in Lusaka, get us all on tomorrow night's flight to London."

"I will be delighted to! Sorry about being cranky yesterday."

Seager said nothing but winked hugely and turned back to the desk. If she had looked over his shoulder, she would have seen the doodles on the pad, her name and Vickery's, arrows, the Emir's name and her father's where the pencil nib had snapped under pressure, by the question mark.

Dusk settled along with the level in the gin bottle and Seager eventually joined the group on the verandah.

"Hang on boss, I'll get some more ice," Masters said as he leant forward and rang the little bell. An ageing servant shuffled from the main door and, without being asked, collected the ice bucket and shuffled off. Seager sat in the last chair and let the happy chitchat wash over him. The night was warm and, over the noise, Seager could hear the crickets out in the dark garden.

They moved through to eat an hour later, the food plentiful and the wine making their eyes drowsy. Eventually, only Seager and Pascoe returned to the verandah, carrying coffee and brandy, the heady smell of some flower on the air. They sat there a while, Seager brooding and deep in thought, sipping his brandy and staring into the night.

Pascoe eventually spoke. "What's up?"

It was a full minute before Seager replied. "Something smells, Ken."

"Like what?"

"Three ransoms asked for, yet we weren't told. Would have been cheaper to pay than to hire us."

"Maybe Vickery didn't know" Pascoe countered.

"I'm sure he didn't, and that means the Emir didn't either."

"That makes her old man sound."

"Like a prize prick," Seager concluded.

156

"Maybe he doesn't want her back," Pascoe mused. "And that's why you want my guerillas in London."

"Yeah," said Seager. "Keep an eye on the girls while I do some checking."

Pascoe smiled to himself; he could almost see Seager's eyes glitter as he said it, the eyes that said everything if you knew when to look. "Wanna sell your boat?" he asked, chuckling.

Seager laughed suddenly and loudly. "Build your own boat!" he replied.

Out in the dark, the crickets chirped and a Siamese cat jumped onto a low wall from the flowerbeds on the other side. It stretched and, bright-eyed, it walked along the wall and jumped onto Seager's lap. He stroked it with a large scarred hand and it began to purr.

Seager thought about Sarah and Fudge and reminded himself to send some flowers to Svea at the first opportunity. It was Maggie who disturbed his thoughts. She was wearing one of Buchanan's T-shirts as a nightie and it came to her knees. "I was just thinking," she said, "can I phone my Mum? You know, let her know that I'm O.K." She smiled at Seager and bit her lip.

"I am sorry sweetie, not yet," he replied.

"Why?" She looked as though she might cry. Seager wondered what to say for a moment and finally she answered her own question, "Is it because Layla's Dad didn't pay the ransom?"

"Ja. It is. I want to find out why first. You aren't really safe until then, or Layla isn't at least."

"I wondered about that," she said. "Layla's been eaten up over it, she thinks she let me down or her Dad did."

"It hasn't been easy for either of you. Now, off to bed with you. Sweet dreams and God bless."

Her hair, now clean, was a mass of curls framing a creamy soft face with strong laughing blue eyes. Freckles ran across a gently upturned nose and her full lips, smiling all the way from her heart, put dimples in her cheeks. He tried to picture her with her hair up ready to go out for the evening but couldn't. She only looked sixteen. "Do you say that to your daughter?" she asked.

"Yes. She is only six, but she does what she is told."

Maggie walked across and planted a kiss on his cheek, then did the same to Pascoe. "Thanks for coming to get us."

After she was gone, they sat quietly again, listening to the crickets and the cat and the sounds of the night. At one point something moved in the dark and Pascoe silently disappeared over the wall. He was back a minute later and sat down again without speaking, tucking a Browning Hi-Power back into his waist band.

Seager looked at him.

"It's my stock in trade and we are not clear yet," Pascoe said defensively. Then, if only to change the subject, he said, "I think Keith is keen on Maggie."

"They all are. She's a nice girl," Seager answered. "The other is a bit too good looking. Hard too. Real rich bitch."

"Naa, it's all a front," Pascoe said. "She's fiery, but she's soft. Anyway, after what her old man has done, she has a right to be hard. Good body, though. Wonder what she's like in ..." He withered under Seager's glare. "Sorry."

Finally, Seager smiled. "Probably bloody good," he answered, "but we are married men and she is morally under my care. Anyway, she would have your nuts off if you tried."

They lapsed back into silence, and eventually Pascoe stood and stretched. "Right I'm off to bed. Check you in the morning."

They were up early and all sat at the huge scrubbed kitchen table while the cook served breakfast. Soon after, they packed their gear, and were on the road in a minibus that Andre had organised by nine.

The trip was uneventful and Pirelli and Maggie at one point played 'I Spy' like a couple of children. They were in Lusaka by four. Layla and Maggie took Seager's American Express card, Vickery's account for payment, and went shopping, and came back to the pair of rooms Seager had taken in the hotel with things for everyone. Layla had also collected the tickets for that night's flight. Seager was amused when he saw they were all first class. "Vickery's card takes another hammering," said Pascoe.

"Yeah." He turned to Layla. "How did you get all first class, there are only about nine or ten aren't there?"

"Twelve. I had to threaten the man with all sorts of things. There's some Cabinet Minister going out tonight, but they bumped someone else."

"What did you threaten him with?" asked Seager, delighted with her initiative.

"I showed him my nice new Diplomatic Passport and said that, not only were we supplying aid to his country, but his station manager was my brother-in-law, and my brother's cargo company would cease giving his airline any business. I think I about covered it," she said, smiling.

"You forgot to tell him you had shares in the company!" said Pascoe.

Layla turned and looked pityingly. "British Caledonian is a family company, anyone holding large blocks of shares is likely to be British, and not holding a Ras Al Qaleem diplomatic passport."

"Sorry," muttered Pascoe, and as she walked away with her parcels for the boys, Pascoe muttered, "Fucksakes she is bouncing back fast!"

"Isn't she lovely?" Seager said. She would need to be strong and he was beginning to like her.

CHAPTER FIFTEEN

The flight home was three mammoth games of Trivial Pursuit. They played in the centre two seats of the first class configuration, empty after a double booking hadn't shown up for the flight. Buchanan and Maggie teamed up together, Layla with Masters, Seager with Pirelli, and Pascoe surprisingly commandeered the astonishing ability of the Zambian Cabinet Minister, who was the man to beat. Every time he got a pie, Pascoe muttered, "That's the way pal, cull the buggers."

It soon became apparent that Pascoe was worse for wear. They had demolished the entire stock of champagne in First Class and had the stewardesses going into the nether regions of the aircraft for more. Leaning over his seat, Stockly was shouting red herring answers to anyone foolish enough to listen. Buchanan surprised Seager with the broad base of his general knowledge, and when Maggie linked her arm though his after one success, he smiled shyly at her. Two Greek businessmen at the front complained to the stewardess about the noise, and the Cabinet Minister's two aides went forward and spoke to the men, advising them that their contract to supply engineers to a railway project would go out the window unless they were more congenial. They were, and when they disembarked at London's Gatwick Airport, they smiled sheepishly at Seager's party.

Without British Passports, they were all obliged to go through the slower channel at immigration, and it was only then that Seager looked at Pascoe. "What have you done with the gun?" he asked, sotto voice.

Pascoe looked at him. "Left it behind in a toilet at the airport. Shame that." Seager relaxed and walked ahead, relieved.

When they cleared the airport building, Seager hired two cars. Maggie stood in the rain and looked at the buses, the green, green grass and the advertising hoardings, very pleased that she was home at last. Seager made a call from the hire car office to the Emirates Embassy in London, asking Vickery to call them at the Skyline Sheraton. The cars were different, one a large BMW and the other far more nonde-script, a white Sierra.

"Ken, you and the girls with me in the BMW, you blokes follow us." He paused briefly. "I might need you all for a few days. Keep a low profile. I don't want this in the papers. Not yet."

He climbed into the car and, as they drove away, he half turned to Maggie.

"I'm going to drop you home, Maggie. I will go in and see your Mum first, make sure she is alone. Once inside you must stay there. I don't want the neighbours to know you're home just yet, nor your friends. O.K?"

"We will need some milk and things," she answered sensibly.

"Rob Stockly will be staying with you. I believe you call it a 'Minder'"

"I think Keith had that job in mind," said Layla, smiling quickly.

She lit a cigarette nervously, Seager watching her in the mirror. *She's too quiet*, he thought with a worried frown. "That's precisely why he's not being given the job. I want someone alert, not following Maggie around mooning over her."

Maggie blushed brightly and indignantly replied, "He doesn't moon! He is sweet. How long will Rob have to stay?"

"Just until I've made a few enquiries, a week perhaps. Just a pre-caution," he said casually.

They drove for a few minutes longer and, when the girls began to talk in the back, he put the radio on and spoke softly to Pascoe. "Give me a list of things you want for an urban protection job. Get something for Rob straight away. Pirelli can watch Layla."

Pascoe nodded and, a moment later, they turned onto the M23 north-bound, the Sierra following behind.

The rain had started falling when they arrived outside the red brick Edwardian building where Maggie Nolan lived with her mother. Seager parked the BMW as close as he could. It was the Battersea Park side of the road but almost directly opposite.

"O.K. Maggs, wait here till I signal you to cross."

With that, he climbed from the car as the Sierra double parked further up. Seager walked to the car and looked in the window. "Rob, you will be staying here with the Nolans. Keep an eye on them. Ken will bring you a weapon over later. Get your kit and come over in about five minutes."

"Whom am I looking out for?" Stockly asked.

"Dunno yet, but something stinks. Someone didn't want these girls back. It's Layla who is directly at risk I think, but keep an eye on 'em anyway."

"Confirm no-one knows we're back?"

"Ja. I'll make a couple of calls this morning, but should be secure enough."

Seager crossed the road and rang the bell. It was a full minute before the door was answered by way of the speakerphone.

"Who is there?"

"It's Max Seager, Mrs. Nolan."

"Oooh, yes come in."

The door buzzed and, as Seager entered the building, Mrs Nolan came to meet him, wiping her hands on a tea towel. "Have you some news, Mr. Seager? You look even browner than last time. Have you been out there yet?" She rubbed her hands nervously, dreading what he was about to day. She had aged in the past weeks and her hair was noticeably greyer.

"Yes, I have been there Mrs. Nolan," he said gently. "Maggie is safe and sound."

She dropped the tea towel and threw her hands to her face, her eyes wide, the tears welling up.

"Are you alone here? I will bring her over but no-one must know she is home. Not yet. Alright?"

Mrs. Nolan nodded quickly and ran to the door to the street. Across the road, a hand waved from a silver car.

Seager beckoned at the car and moments later, Pascoe and Maggie jogged across the road. Then they were hugging each other and crying. Pascoe smiled and walked back to the car as Maggie said, "Mum don't cry, you'll make me cry too."

She already was. Mrs. Nolan let her go and pushed her back, wiping her eyes with her apron. "Let me look at you. Thank God you're safe!" she said through her tears and hugged her daughter again.

Seager left them alone for a minute, then walked back. "Mrs Nolan. I want to leave one of my men here for a few days. Do you have a spare room?"

Without letting go, she nodded quickly.

"Maggie will explain why. I'd better go. I will phone later." Walking back to the door, he gestured to Stockly who walked across from the car carrying his hold-all.

"Mr. Seager," Mrs. Nolan said. He turned back to her. "Thank you for my daughter. Thank you for bringing her home."

"A pleasure Mrs. Nolan, only a pleasure." He grinned widely at them both and walked across the road as Stockly arrived. "Keep an eye Rob, they are good people."

Stockly nodded. "I'd like a Hi-power if you can get one." His quick brown eyes said he didn't think he would use it, but better safe than sorry.

Seager took a large suite at the Sheraton that he and Layla shared. The rest of the team took rooms across the hall and either side – not as security, Seager insisted, but only so that he could keep his party together. Later that night, the phone in Seager's suite rang, and Buchanan took Layla down to the ground floor to get her hair done, if only to keep her from overhearing.

It was Vickery on the end of the line. "Hello Max how's things? No luck with my order?"

"Yes, I can fill it, but I'm not sure about the after sales service."

"Can you be more specific? Is the item damaged? I have a report on the spare you sent up. It was the model you asked about." Vickery was now being very oblique.

"The items were offered for sale three times prior to my offer at a give-away price. I have two intact by the way, but as the first three offers were not accepted, I now have reason to believe the original buyer does not, repeat, does not want the merchandise."

There was a pause before Vickery spoke. "Are you sure the offer was received Max?"

"Confirm that is the case. Yes."

"O.K. Tell no-one that we now hold the items. This is all very strange, so I think I should come up and view."

"Delighted to see you, but I suggest you don't advise anyone of the reason for your visit. Could create a demand I don't want to supply."

"Should that demand arise, do you have the means to secure the items?"

"Yes and no. I have some useful people, but without any specialised equipment. Can you organise that?"

"Within reason yes. Anything else?"

"The name of a very good inquiry agent. Not some divorce case wanker, some guy who can get into the right places, shares, records, official stuff. I would do it myself but I will have other things."

"I will call you back on that. One thing. Does this affect our employer in any way you can see?" Vickery was being careful now.

"I don't know yet. I don't think he would have known, and then employed me, do you?"

"Certainly not. But it does throw a new light on the relationship between the first and second buyers. You realise that you will need conclusive proof? I suggest you don't return it to its previous owner yet."

"Done already, someone useful there."

"You shouldn't have done that. Not yet."

Seager snarled into the phone. "Fuck you Vickery! You don't have kids, you don't know what it's like, so fuck you!"

Vickery came back smooth and urbane. "Relax. I understand. I'm coming up tonight."

"O.K. but you keep clear of my people and my enquiry. You help, that's all."

"Not when I'm paying the bill. I will run this my way."

"No. I mean it, Richard. There are dead men out there in the sun. One of them was mine. This is my scene. You help when I need it or stay out. This could get very nasty. I started this job and I will finish it."

Seager's voice was low and menacing. There was a pause as Vickery considered. "Alright. I will help any way I can, otherwise not interfere." With all his years running men, Vickery had said the perfect thing to effectively run Seager, and he knew it. "You will get a call in a few minutes. He will ask what you need in the way of gear and he will give you the names of a couple of good enquiry agents."

"O.K.," said Seager. "I'll have someone meet you at the airport. What flight?"

"B.A. about seven or something," Vickery answered.

"O.K. cheers." Seager hung up, crossed to the window and looked at the view, black and chilly.

The rain fell in relentless misery from the leaden skies and the cold seemed to seep through the glass. He thought about the blood red sunsets and clear African nights, the stars like great fairy lights that you could reach up and touch. He thought about the crickets, the doves, the heat, the silence, the dry bush, the glow of a fire at night, the dust rising up from the flanks of the elephants as they moved through the trees like great silent shadows, trunks swaying and stomachs rumbling. He thought about the flies, the stink, the death and the savagery. And it still seemed worth it. Anything would be better than this, the milling people, the greyness and the rain. The fucking rain that never stopped, but yet never rained really, not like over the bush velt. The huge towering black clouds that brought life to the parched ground, the sweet smell of that first summer rain that broke the back of the heat and brought grazing for the herds.

He watched a woman, bent with the years, cross with the lights below him. A car hooted angrily at her, but ignoring it she pottered on.

Seager walked back to the phone as it began to ring. It was the military attaché from the embassy and he was extraordinarily helpful. He was able to supply everything Pascoe wanted: six Brownings, the big thirteen shot nine millimetre handguns that were everyone's favourite, two H & K automatic machine pistols fitted with silencers. The man also provided Seager with the names of three men who had formidable abilities as enquiry agents, commonly known in television jargon as 'private investigators'. These men were all specialists in what they did, which was supply primarily confidential information about companies and dealings to anyone who would pay for it. They would research deeply and find things that only auditors and fraud squad people found without anyone knowing they had done it. They were worth their weight in gold when you needed one.

When he arrived, later that night, the man introduced himself as Student. He was slightly built and wore nondescript clothes, covered with a grey overcoat against the chill. He also sported a small goatee beard and rimless spectacles and, as he sat opposite Seager, his eyes blinked myopically.

"This man," Seager pushed a piece of paper over to him, "has extensive business interests in the Middle East. He is based in Beirut, although spent much of his time in the Gulf. The companies he has interests in are listed." The man blinked again. "I want to know everything about him. I want to know if he strays from the path of righteousness. I want to know the financial state of his organisation and his personal accounts. I want to know why he wouldn't pay a small ransom for his daughter's life."

The man nodded and then spoke. His voice was measured and careful. "My fees are high, but I understand you are not short of funds for this kind of requirement. Correct?"

Seager nodded.

"This would normally take about three weeks but you are very lucky. An American paid me for a search that involved dealings with this same man. That job was completed in March of this year. If I can restructure that data, then I can report within the next ten days, at half my normal fee. I am not a philanthropist, Mr. Seager. I have other work that needs doing so, anyway I can save time, I take. Without affecting my standards, you understand."

Seager nodded and wanted to smile. *Good*, he thought, *but why is he telling me he already has stuff on Adel Rakkafian?* "An unusual admission, that you have data already" Seager probed.

"Not really. I don't like Americans. What is it you specifically want to know? I specialise in the Middle East."

Seager told him and then he left.

That night, as Pirelli drove back to the Nolans to give Rob Stockly his gun, Seager sat down with Layla. They talked for over an hour, Seager seemingly asking silly questions and encouraging the girl to talk about her father, her childhood, even what she knew of Ireland, where she was born. They joined the others for dinner and, later, took in a floor-show in the restaurant. Seager and Layla went up to the suite just before midnight, Seager spending an hour on the phone to Svea and then going to the airport to meet the British Airways flight next morning.

When he appeared, Vickery looked as immaculate as usual and climbed into the BMW with perfectly creased pants after seven hours on an aircraft. "I suppose I'm paying for this," he said.

"Of course you are, silly boy!" Seager said, smiling as they drove away from a threatening traffic warden.

"Good work Max. I wasn't expecting anything for several weeks yet. Any problems?"

"Not that you don't know about. I have employed Student."

"Good, I was going to recommend him, he has worked for us before, twice."

"I want you to find us a place to live, a house or something, somewhere. About a week or ten days should see it through, but somewhere the boys can relax and keep an eye on Layla. She's a nice kid. I just want to know she's not going to have too high a profile until I'm back."

Vickery looked over at him. "Back? Where are you going?" he asked.

"Ireland," he said. "Some place called Tralee."

"Why?" Vickery asked.

"That's where it all began. That's where I will start. Student is covering the more recent stuff, and we'll meet in the middle. You said you wanted conclusive proof. I will find it. I will find out why it cost your boss a million quid to hire me and my men, when her own father could have had her back for two hundred thousand dollars – three times. I will also find out why he never discussed this with anyone, not even his old friend, a man who could have lent him money if necessary and never asked for it back."

CHAPTER SIXTEEN

Approximately thirty miles on the Limerick side of Tralee lies the village of Abbeyfeale. It sits on the border between Limerick and Kerry Counties and is noticeable, like the rest of Southern Ireland, for its fine horses. It serves the surrounding farming community as a market village and, a few miles on the Tralee side of the small group of houses and shops, there is a turnoff to the left.

Seager slowed the small red Allegro and took the bend at a prudent speed, dropping down into the rolling green fields. He had never seen a country so green or so hazy. Everything was round – the hills, the stones, the hedges and the trees – and it all had a damp softness about it, the air clean and slightly peaty. He drove down the lane several miles and studied the map again. He drove on slowly and, eventually, a large pair of pillars stood over an overgrown driveway. Turning into it, he saw the old hospital building ahead. By the look of it, it had been deserted for some time.

Seager stopped and climbed out of the car. The walls were covered with moss and the windows broken in places. One wing of the two seemed newer, the stone not as aged, but the grass that grew along the path edges was long and the once elegant gardens were overgrown. He heard the chugging sound of a tractor approaching and, as he walked back to the car, it appeared between the tall trees that bordered the road.

The driver, an ancient weathered man in a cloth cap, looked over and drew his smoking machine to a halt, its trailer of fertilizer creaking to a stop. The man looked at Seager suspiciously.

"I wonder if you can help me?" said Seager.

"You're not from round here to be sure," he replied.

"No. Australian," said Seager. The man looked again, fished in his frayed pockets for a packet of tobacco and a pipe and began stuffing it. "How long has the hospital been empty?" Seager asked pleasantly.

"My sister's niece went to New Zealand, must be three years ago now. The hospital? Closed it down in nineteen sixty-nine. Costing too much to run, they said. Now one has to go all the way into Tralee proper." He struck a match and began to puff at his pipe.

"I see. All the staff transferred did they?"

"Thems that wanted to go see. Others stayed. Village folk. Were a good while ago now. Some found other work." He looked away from his match and up at Seager, his bright blue eyes twinkling. "What would 'e be wanting with this old place then? Ain't for sale I don't think."

Seager decided to take a chance. "There was an accident in 1965. A motorcar crashed into a tractor hereabouts. Four foreigners. The two women died in the hospital, the driver, an Arab."

"Ah yes, I remember that night. It took place not far from 'ere, a third of the way back into the village. Some said the big man was a prince or sumsuch." He puffed away.

"That's the one!" said Seager.

"Was you eh then? Be a bit young," the man asked. To him, one foreigner was the same as the next.

"I wanted to talk to someone who was there that night. I'm researching an article on the Prince."

"Ah well. Now you be asking, let me think a minute. Most moved away when the hospital moved. Never many then, about thirty or so." He puffed at his pipe and then his eyes lit up. "You might try old Maureen Conners. She was the midwife hereabouts for many a year. She were attending then 'cos my daughter had 'er eldest girl that year. Old Maureen, she were a foin figure when she were young, she lives in t' village. The house is off the road with white gates. An 'orse is in de field beside the house. Can't miss it."

"Thank you" Seager answered. "I shall be there tonight in the village. Is there a place I can stay?" The sky was overcast and the damp dark was settling.

"There's rooms at the pub," he said, "and if 'e be wroitin about that noight be sure to get me name right, I was dere at the motor accident with de rest of the village. Sean Liogh, with a G and H." His eyes twinkled again.

"Thank you Seah Liogh with an H, I'll be buying tonight in the pub. Is yours Guiness by any chance?"

"Can't stand de mock! Gordons from across the water is my drop. I'll be there."

With that, he climbed aboard the tractor and set off down the road with a wave, his pipe still clenched between his teeth.

Seager turned and drove back into the village to find old Maureen Conners and hoped she was as talkative.

What other reason would a man have to hate his daughter? he thought. *Perhaps resentment.* He may have believed that his wife's death was attributed to the child and therefore blame the child. He would need to talk to the woman and see if Rakkafian had asked for a blood test on the baby, and if she remembered any resentment of ill feeling towards the child at birth. He found the house and, leaving the car on the road, walked down the pebble drive.

Knocking loudly on the door, he saw from the corner of his eye the lace-curtain move. He waited and presently the door swung open. "Maureen Conners?" he asked.

Her grey hair was pulled back into a tight bun and wrinkled skin now covered a once proud beautiful face. Her eyes were brown and now slightly rheumy and her hands were thick with arthritis. For all that, she stood straight and looked him in the eye. "I am," she said.

"My name is Max Seager. I wonder if you could tell me about the old hospital, and one accident in particular, treated there twenty years ago."

She looked at him warily then seemed to relent. "Come in. I don't get many visitors anymore, but twenty years ago?" She looked at him questioningly before asking, "Anyway, what's your interest?"

He followed her into a large warm kitchen, closing the door behind him.

"A man I am working for was in that accident. I'd like to get some details of the night. His wife had a baby immediately following the incident."

She settled herself into an armchair by a blazing fire in the sitting room and indicated a chair opposite. Seager launched into the story about the two young men with their wives in the motor accident.

"Oh yes, I remember, but I'm afraid I can't help you. I was away on leave. The one husband, he was still in when I got back, he was quite seriously injured I remember. Lower abdomen and groin ruptured and internal bleeding. He was a charming man." She looked into the fire. "Wouldn't he have been moved to a bigger hospital?"

"Ordinarily yes, but I think he liked the place. His wife had spent her last hours there, you see, and often that link is important."

"He would not have been moved if he didn't want to go," she said.

"I'm still interested in the first night when they arrived. Is there anyone who could tell me?"

"They have all moved on, now. The ward sister then was Mary Styles, but she died, let me see, the year before the fire. That would have been 1967." She got to her feet, tottered to the bookshelf under the window and withdrew an old photo album. Then she settled back into the chair, and carefully began leafing through the pages. Stopping, she pointed. Seager got to his feet, walked behind her and looked over her shoulder. "Yes," she said, "1967 it would have been. That is Mary there."

The photo was slightly blurred, and was of three women, the centre figure obviously a younger Maureen Conners. The fine bone structure was there and she was upright, strong and very attractive, although Seager estimated she must have been sixty then. The background was the hospital, immaculate lawns and clipped trees.

"Mary was a good Sister, very good indeed. Trained at Guy's in London. Terrible way to die, she should have known better."

"What happened?" Seager asked.

"Killed with a gun. They were at a shoot and there was an accident. The devil's work is a gun."

"Who was the doctor? You only had one at the hospital?"

"One full time, but a visiting gentleman came from Tralee and Limerick. Dr. Scott was the resident physician. He and a nurse by the name of Sowerby were courting and were in his rooms when the fire started. Never got out, although the two night girls managed to clear the west ward. They rebuilt the wing immediately, but only the next year the hospital was closed. Too much money to run, they said." She flipped a page and pointed to three pictures of the gutted wing.

"Only one ward there?" Seager asked.

"Yes. Only the one. The ground floor was the kitchen and offices and Dr. Scott's rooms were above the ward. He was a devil with the ladies that one." She rocked herself with the memories for a minute and flipped on a page.

"While you were away," Seager asked softly, "that year of the accident with the Arab gentleman, who did your deliveries?"

"You make it sound like newspapers young man! Midwifery is an old and special craft," she said sternly.

A picture fell from the back of the album. Seager picked it up and, just as quickly, apologised giving it back. It was a nude study of a young woman lying across a white sofa. Her firm breasts were large and her long legs neatly hid the pubic hair that glimpsed from the shadow.

"Don't be sorry," she said picking it up, "1934 that was."

"You?" Seager asked, looking up quickly.

"To be sure," she said, the brogue thick and proud.

Liogh was right, thought Seager, *quite a stunner in her day.* "You were quite something weren't you?" he said, looking her in the eye.

"Even twenty years ago the village women spoke of me as a threat!" she chuckled delightedly. "But time moves on. Lydia Morgan was the locum, got a card here somewhere, before I shock you with my stories."

They found it a few moments later. It was faded and dog-eared but the caption was clear, as was the name she had signed. *Lydia Conway (nee Morgan).* The postmark was a town in Lincolnshire, called Saxilby. Seager grunted delightedly. "This will be very helpful. Thank you"

At the door, he pulled on his coat and kissed her powdery cheek. "Thanks again Maureen."

She smiled at him. "Twenty years ago I would have asked if you wanted to stay the night," she said, her eyes flecked with mischief.

"Twenty years ago I would have begged to stay!" he said. "But I might be back, you never know."

"Promises, promises," she said, laughing. "Take care, Maxim Seager, and come by again when you pass through."

"I shall."

Seager walked to the gate and eventually found the right key for the car door. Then he drove into the village to find the pub to buy Sean Liogh his promised 'Gordons from across the water'. After the afternoon's despair at the hospital, and without the records and staff he had hoped to find, he was now pleased with his progress. Rakkafian may have had reason to believe that the child born to his wife was not his, and blood tests on a new baby may have provided a clue. He decided to contact Student and ask him to research the long dead woman's past and see if she had a lover.

He was back in England by eleven the next morning and phoned the Embassy for Vickery's new number. Hopefully they had all moved to a house somewhere. The telephonist gave him the number and he dialed a long code, zero seven nine with six and three digits. *Must really be in the sticks*, he thought.

"Ja."

"Who's that?"

"Who wants to know?" the voice said.

Seager recognised it and laughed into the phone. "Pirelli, you sawn off little prick, give me Vickery."

"Eh Max, howzit? Hold on eh, I'll get him." The pause was brief. Vickery came to the line "Got a pencil?" he said, and quickly went into detail of how to find a village called Duncton in Sussex.

Seager was there two hours later. The house was magnificent. Five bedrooms overlooked the downs with a huge garden. It was owned by Masters' brother, who was away in Spain for the winter and needed house sitters. Layla was in the kitchen, demonstrating that she could cook to win a five pound bet with Pirelli, and Buchanan was playing chopsticks on the baby grand piano in the drawing room. Pascoe and Vickery sat with Masters in the morning room watching television, as Seager walked in. "Where's Layla?" he said, without greeting anyone.

"In the kitchen," said Vickery. "All the doors are locked and Buchanan is next door." He paused. "Good evening Max!" he exclaimed, rather sarcastically.

They sat and talked, and were interrupted when Layla entered with trays of salads. She was back a minute later with fillet steaks and sauté potatoes and, as they ate, Seager seemed to relax for the first time in

173

two days. He left them early the next morning for what would be a three-hour drive up to Lincoln to try and find Lydia Conway nee-Morgan.

He was in the village of Saxilby at ten o'clock and phoned from a call box. There were two Conways listed and the second number bore fruit indirectly. According to the woman who answered, the Conways had moved. She gave Seager their new number and, when he asked what the code meant, she said, "Stamford. Just go back down the A1, and it's before the Royal Air Force Station at Wittering, left of the main road."

He left and headed south, the big Mercedes eating up the miles. Half an hour later, he drove into the village of Stamford. He stopped at a call box again and phoned the house. Lydia Conway agreed to see him, but only once her husband was home for lunch. Seager agreed and waited around the town until twelve. Then he drove onto an estate of semi-detached houses. Walking up the short path, he rang the bell and a woman in her forties answered the door and invited him in.

"What's all this about then? Are you police?"

From the kitchen, a man appeared. He was tall and wore corduroy trousers, suede shoes and a sweater. *A teacher,* thought Seager.

"No," he said. "I believe your wife may have delivered a friend of mine twenty years ago in a hospital outside Tralee in Ireland. I'd appreciate a few minutes if you can both spare it?"

After her years in England, her Irish accent was very soft, and when she spoke it was a warm and kind voice. "I delivered lots of babies, Mr..?"

"Seager."

"Mr Seager, what makes you think I will remember this particular little mite?" She was now smiling at him. "Come in anyway, sit down."

He helped her remember the night she was locum at the Abbeyfeale Hospital and they brought in the four casualties from the crash, the Arabs from the Rolls Royce that had hit the tractor. She did remember and was talking about that night when her husband popped his head round the door and said that he was going back to work. It was two o'clock by the time they were getting into the details. "I remember the babies. One loud, strong and tough, full of energy and the other, the little one with the birthmark above her ear, she was quieter. The second delivery was the problem. The mother was bleeding internally after the accident, and Dr. Scott was trying to stitch her up while I took the baby from the incision he had made. One mother died on the table and I believe the other died the next morning before dawn. One of the babies died too, I think, but I had gone over to Listowel for another delivery by then."

"The father, the one up and walking, was he concerned for the safety of his child or more concerned for the mother?" Seager asked.

"I don't remember. There was so much going on. Fathers react differently at birth time. Bernard fainted, poor dear, when I had Kyle. They all react differently. Women too. Some have a quiet strength and others yell and bellow away. The prince's wife, she was quiet and in great pain." She paused. "When I had tagged the babies and cleaned them up, I gave her hers. She looked like a Madonna there, cheeks flushed and the tiny little thing at her breast. I don't remember the father much at all. I was busy and the only one up in the west wing that night." She poured the tea from the pot after turning it three times, and handed Seager his. "The baby was tiny, but it's funny how tough they are when they want to live."

They finished their tea and, before Seager left, he asked the question he had been planning to ask all day. "In your opinion Mrs. Conway, from any indication you were given, did the father resent the baby for his wife's death? I believe some men do."

"Yes, it does happen, but rejection like that doesn't last long as a rule. Especially in this case, I would have thought."

"Thank you very much. Mrs. Conway, you have been very helpful." *Like shit*, thought Seager, *I'm back to square one.*

It was after nine that night, back in Duncton with the rest of his men, when Student phoned and said he was ready with his preliminary report, compiled from the previous study, and one artful piece of investigation by his Beirut contact in the law offices of the company that handled the Rakkafian Trust arrangements. A hefty bribe had been paid for information, and he wanted re-imbursement. Seager asked him to drive down the next day.

"Seems the marriage must have been arranged," Student explained when he came through the front door and settled in the study. "The will is heavily in Rakkafian's wife's favour and in any children she had. He would get nothing without a wife and child to inherit his father's estate and even half was to wait until the child reached twenty-one. Death of the child prior to that would leave the shares and funds to the trustees. Death after that age and the trusteeship would have been revoked and the contents of the old man's will would have eventually gone to his son by default."

"Why would anyone make a will like that?"

"It's not uncommon for exclusions with other factors to be in wills." Student paused and wiped his spectacles carefully. "In this instance the old man obviously didn't like or trust his son's acumen to effectively use the inheritance, and so offered it to his wife and child."

"And you say his personal finances are stretched?"

"To the limit. Several bad decisions over the years and a very expensive life style have all taken their toll. There is evidence that he was, in fact, involved in weapons, drugs and pornography in the last few years. All high risk operations, needless to say, producing huge profits." Student gave Seager several sheets of typed paper. "In there are the details, including his top people in the various sectors of his businesses. The top three are the ones involved in illegal weapons, narcotics and flesh. The rest seem, on the surface, to be legitimate employees of the enterprises they run, but I can't give up more at this time. We could do a search of the companies, but that would be time consuming and expensive. Do you want it?"

"No. It's the man I'm interested in. Any indications of psychological disorders, treatment for depression, guilt, anything like that?"

"No. Regular medicals at a clinic in Paris, but nothing else."

"If I asked you why this man wouldn't pay a ransom for his only child what would your guess be?"

"I don't guess and I don't surmise," Student replied flatly.

"Well, do it now," said Seager, just as flatly. "I just want to hear you answer the hypothetical question, not give evidence."

Student removed his glasses and wiped his eyes. "My summary would be basic. For the money. For the sixty million dollars she is worth in ships, investments, bonds and securities."

Seager was astonished. "Fucksakes! Sixty mil?"

"Yup," Student said, replacing his glasses.

"Do you think she is aware of this?"

"No certainly not. She would have been told on her eighteenth birthday that she had a trust fund, but not the extent of it, and if she has made a will then it would be binding after her death, even if it were signed when she was only eighteen."

"You're saying it wouldn't need updating after she reached twenty-one?"

"Correct."

"So, either way, if she dies after her twenty-first birthday, he gets the money."

"Unless she changes her will after her birthday and under Lebanese law, he would contest and win. They are still essentially Arab and a father is everything to them. They wouldn't conceive of a father allowing his daughter to die for gain, but put it down to The Will of Allah."

"Well," said Seager, "if ever there was a motive this is it."

"Not paying out two hundred to make sixty million, it's enough to tempt someone who wasn't fond of a relative."

Student stood to leave, buttoned his coat and closed his attaché case. He looked at Seager. "There is one more thing. Adel Rakkafian knows someone is researching him. I am safe as an employee, even if he knew who I was – but he is a man dealing in death and will not take it lying down. I would be very careful in any further dealings with this individual."

Seager looked at the small man, his eyes flecked and angry, his voice low and quiet. "How did he find out? I thought you were supposed to be the best?"

"I am the best, Mr. Seager. Someone else is involved. Possibly a Government Agency or something similar. They are never very subtle, but be warned." He put his hat on and walked to the door. "My fee?"

"See Mr. Vickery," stated Seager. "He has a cheque for you."

Student nodded and closed the door behind him and Seager crossed to the window and stood watching the rain and thinking.

CHAPTER SEVENTEEN

Student's warning to Seager had come too late. That morning, as people were just getting up to go to work, a laundry van stopped outside the redbrick mansions where Maggie lived with her mother. Stockly was shaving in the bathroom, the third room down the hallway that opened onto the main door. Mrs. Nolan didn't send out her laundry, but she wasn't aware that no-one else in the building did either. When the voice on the call phone said it was for 46, and the occupants had gone to work, she did the neighbourly thing, forgetting Stockly's express instructions not to answer the door to anyone. He would do that. That was why his gun was in his jacket pocket by the door and why he was not there to reach it when a master key opened the door in one full twist, and three men came through fast.

Stockly was still shaking his razor clean in the sink, and wiping the condensation off the mirror, when he heard the crash. As he hurled himself into the hall for his Browning, he was met with a stream of C.S. gas and a punch in the face that would have felled an elephant. The fist was sheathed in a brass knuckle; he felt his jaw shatter, his teeth break, as an incredible pain filled his eyes. As he fell to the floor, he lashed out one kick at the nearest figure and felt it connect. Then he was hit again and lost consciousness.

The man grabbed Maggie as she ran from her bedroom and, covering her face with a dressing soaked in ether, she ceased her struggle very quickly. Her mother was close behind her, as the last man – smaller than the first two – closed the door and produced the bags from the truck. He was the paymaster, the other two hired muscle from the East End of London. To them this was a snatch with one bloke as a minder – and, if he had a shooter, they could stop him before he could get to it. Simple enough, when one was an ex-heavyweight contender seven years ago and the other an ex-Royal Marine who had slipped over to the wrong side of the law after a bungled attempt at the payroll vehicle at Portsmouth docks. Yet, hard as they were, they would never have stood for what was to follow, so it was just as well that the smaller man with the foreign accent had waited until they had carried their cargo out to the laundry truck and driven away to deliver to the waiting trailer unit on the Dover Road. What the small man with the scar on his lip did shocked even the hardened men of the Murder Squad of the Metropolitan Police, men who thought they had seen most things.

Dragging Stockly's comatose body into the kitchen, he walked back to the hall and picked up a tool chest he had brought in from the truck with the body bags. He began, they later surmised, by forcing a dishcloth into Stockly's mouth, obviously to prevent any screams alerting others in the building. Then he spread the man's shoulders back down on the Formica-covered wooden bench top and drove six inch nails into his hands and forearms. After this, he took a cigarette lighter and a Stanley knife normally used for cutting linoleum, and began to undo his victim's trousers. It was then that Stockly's mind was brought back to consciousness by the unbelievable pain in his eyes and arms and hands. He struggled for breath, the blood rising in his mouth and nose, the dishcloth still crammed into his mouth. Through his pain, he lashed out with his foot and hit something, still fighting although he knew it was over. Then, the small man with the scar put down the knife and, reaching into the tool bag, produced a heavy hammer and smashed it down cruelly on the struggling kneecaps. They shattered in an instant and, through the gag, Stockly moaned. It wasn't a human sound, but one of an animal in enormous pain, deep and primal.

"Where is Layla the whore?" the small man said, his voice guttural and dry all at once, his eyes betrayed his excitement. He enjoyed the groans and the look in his victim's faces. He always had.

Back in Duncton, Pascoe walked through into the kitchen of the house. Seager was there frying eggs on the stove. They sat down and ate, and soon they were joined by Vickery and Pirelli.

"What did Student have to say?" Vickery asked, reaching for the water jug.

"Quite a lot," Seager replied. "Motive certainly, but not evidence as such."

"We can't use too much time on this. Sooner or later, Maggie and

179

her mother are going to have to be allowed back on the street, the press advised they are back, Layla's father, however much of a prick, advised of it." He lifted the glass to his lips and drank in measured sips.

"I know, I know, but it still doesn't gel." Seager stopped and looked at Pascoe. "Ken, I want you to go up to London and bring Maggie and her Mum down here. Student says Rakkafian knows he is being watched. Let's let him cool down a bit and, if nothing breaks in the next few days, then we can announce we are back and have the tearful reunions, and see what happens next. That might draw him out."

"I'll take Keith and Louis, they're going stir crazy here. You be okay here with James Bond?" Pascoe had taken to ribbing Vickery's constant perfect grooming.

"I'll shoot them with my wristwatch or something," Vickery replied dryly.

Seager nodded, smiling at Pascoe. "Who's got my gun?" he asked.

"Dunno. Ask Louis, he's got the arsenal. Probably got yours too."

"You won't have room for them both, not if you're bringing Maggie and her Mum and Rob back. Take one, take Louis, he needs the culture." Seager bit into his egg, and swallowed. "I'll give them a ring and tell them you're coming. Go on, pack a bag."

They left twenty minutes later, and Seager and Vickery walked with Layla down into the village to the shop. It was a small shop-cum-post office selling everything you could want and on the way back – laden with newspapers, milk and bread – Layla talked them into stopping at the pub for a drink.

It was quite ordinary as English village pubs went, lots of hidden lighting, comfy chairs and a huge hearth where a fire burned cheerfully on the grate. Seager rang Masters, who drove down with Buchanan, and they settled in for a lunchtime session, Layla relishing the atmosphere but drinking only tomato juice. "I'm Muslim," she said to Seager's quizzical look. They ate there again, Buchanan powering through both his and Vickery's, who had declared it inedible like all pub food. A little over an hour later, they drove home. It was getting colder and Masters tried to work out the central heating system, while Seager and Vickery sat down with the papers in the morning room, the television on with the sound down, flickering in the corner.

Pascoe was driving when they pulled up in front of Albany Mansions, Pirelli fiddling with the radio. It was digital and he couldn't make it go. "Fucking thing," he muttered.

"Probably cost a grand," said Pascoe. "Leave it. Stick another tape on, I'll go over."

He climbed from the car and, buttoning his coat, walked across the street to the building. He rang the bell and waited, then rang again. He rang a third time, and still the answer-phone remained quiet. He was becoming concerned, so he walked back out of the building and crossed onto the grass to look in the window, thanking his luck that it was a ground floor flat. Looking about to make sure he wasn't being observed by half the joggers in Battersea Park, he put his face to the window and looked in.

In the car, Pirelli chose that moment to look up and saw Pascoe peering through the window. *Jesus*, he thought. *That's not right.* Scrambling from the car, he ran across the road and Pascoe stepped back, shaking his head. "See if there's a window round the back?" Pascoe said.

Pirelli nodded and jogged up the street, counting the blocks so that he knew where to come back to once at the rear. Finding a service alley, he ran round the side, counted his way back and then stopped. He pulled his gun clear and cocked it, and moved to the first window and looked in through the curtains.

It was a bedroom, chintzy and soft, with photos on the dressing table. When he saw no-one, he moved to the next window and followed the same procedure. Here the blind was down hard and he could see nothing, so he moved forward to the last window at the end of the narrow courtyard. Another bedroom sat empty.

Fuck it, he thought, and as gently as possible, he jabbed out a hole in the glass by the sash lock. Unlocking it, he opened the window and climbed in. Quickly, he moved up the hall to the front door as quietly as he could and let Pascoe in.

"Anything?" Pascoe mimed.

Pirelli shook his head, held up one finger and then nodded to the passage and shrugged. Pascoe nodded and pulled his own gun clear, and together they moved down the passage, past the first bedroom through which Pirelli had entered. Pascoe nodded at his companion and crossed to the door; then, checking Pirelli was ready, he swung it open.

Bathroom. Sink of water, shaving cream on the floor, razor by the door. He crossed back up the hall, took Stockly's jacket from the peg by the door and hefted it. There was something heavy in the pocket and, when he reached in, he found Stockly's gun falling into his hand. He pulled the gun clear and showed it to Pirelli, before pocketing it and moving back down the hall to the third door.

The house was very quiet and overly warm, heated the way people do when they are old and their blood is thin. It was then they smelled it. Death has an odour peculiar to itself, and what they smelt was the smell of the slaughterhouse. The mixture of offal and faeces and bodily fluids, in the warmed confines of the blood-splattered kitchen, gave a smell that was unmistakable. Pirelli looked at Pascoe, his eyes saying *please no, let it be someone who came for them, let Rob have lead the girls out of here, and left a stiff behind.*

Pascoe's eyes said *now!* He swung round and pushed the door back.

Pirelli saw it first. His eyes tried to take it all in but his senses were retreating from the horror. Pascoe swung his head round with his gun ready and looked for a moment. Then he turned back to Pirelli, the man who had fought beside Stockly for five years, drank with him, laughed with him and shared moments when their lives were on the line. He sank to his knees still holding his gun, his eyes brimming, his lip quivering. In front of him, his friend lay disemboweled, the subject of mind-bending physical atrocities. He seemed to slowly draw breath, and then began a long moan that said he didn't believe what he was seeing.

Pascoe crossed and pulled him to his feet roughly. "Get back to the car, wait there. Move!"

Pirelli stood up, never taking his eyes from Stockly's body.

"Move it Pirelli!" Pascoe snarled.

The man lifted his eyes from Stockly's body and he looked right at Pascoe. "Sir? Who would do a thing like this? It's Rob. He never hurt a fly outside his job. Jesus sir, they fucking gutted him, they-"

"Get to the car NOW!" Pascoe said. "They've got Maggie, they've got her mother. They have moved and fucking caught us with our pants down."

Pascoe pulled Pirelli behind him to the window, pushed him out and followed. A few minutes later they were in the car and heading along the Great South Road looking for a callbox. They found one beside a sweet shop and Pascoe went in for change. The short fat Indian behind the overloaded counter refused his five-pound note.

"Not unless you're buying something, good sah!"

Pascoe reached across the counter and grabbed him by the scruff of the neck. "Gimme the change!" he roared, and threw him back without further threat.

Once the change was in his hand, he hurtled to the call box and dialled the Duncton number.

"Give me Max," he said when Buchanan answered. A moment later, Seager arrived at the phone.

"Ken."

"Max, we've been hit, sometime early this morning. Rob is dead. They have Maggie and her mother."

Back in Duncton, Seager's mind reeled. "Tell me briefly what you have?" he said, calm again.

"Empty house, Rob's body, nothing else. They did things to him, Max."

Seager knew from the strained tone that it was something extraordinary.

"O.K. Head back here now, leave the rest to me and Vickery. Is Louis with you?"

"Yeah."

"How is he?" Seager knew the two men had served together and been close. He would have to tell Buchanan.

"Shocked. It wasn't very pretty. We will have to watch him when we close. He will want to even the scores a bit."

"O.K. Head back now."

"One hour," Pascoe said, his voice flat. Seager knew him well enough that he too would need watching when they closed.

It was Vickery who broke him from his thoughts. He was still holding the phone in his hand and staring into space, his mind racing, when the man approached. "Well?"

"We've been hit. They have Maggie and her Mum. Robert Stockly is dead. His body is in the flat. I'm not sure about the circumstances. Ken and Louis are heading back now. Christ, they moved fast. They must have been watching the flat for days. We'll need to involve the police, have Rob's body taken care of. They may have tortured Rob. I don't know what he told them but we must assume he did."

Vickery took the phone. "I'll call a policeman I know. He's with Special Branch, he can advise the other lot without compromising us. I suggest we go back up to London, and think this out. It's our move, I believe."

As Vickery began dialing, Seager went to find Buchanan and Layla. They would need to pack, and he would need to tell Buchanan that his friend was dead. *It's our move indeed,* he thought, and began to plan it. *Maggie is the bait to draw us in. So be it. It's not just the ransom, it's more now. Why? They've killed one of my men and kidnapped two women to draw us out. They must really want Layla dead. Christ, I underestimated them, I underestimated how far they will go to get what they want. WHY? The money? Layla's birthday is when? When is she twenty-one? When is the money available to her grieving father? Sixty million dollars.* His mind raced across all he knew, a turmoil of conflicting details, a tangled web. *Layla's birthday, when is it?* He went to find out exactly by looking in her passport. Vickery was most pedantic about these kinds of things. He heard him talking fast into the hall phone and saw Buchanan and Layla step in from the garden into the drawing room.

"I have some bad news, I'm afraid," he began, and finished by telling the stunned girl, and told the big brooding giant to go and pack.

Buchanan helped Layla up the stairs as Seager lifted her passport clear from her handbag on the foyer table. *22nd September 1965.* She had been twenty one for just over three weeks. Her will would now be read and she was assumed dead by the world. It would be most inconvenient if she suddenly appeared, however altruistically intended by a well meaning friend like Rashid Al Khadem.

"When we get up to London tonight, I want the name of the Investigating Officer. A case like this will get an Inspector probably. I want his name and some background," Seager said to Vickery.

"Why? It's easy enough to get, but why?"

"Because," said Seager, "we are going to get Maggie back. The police will have a fairly good idea who does this kind of job, but they may not be able to make a case good enough for court. I want the suspect's name, and with a bit of luck he'll lead us to Maggie."

"And then?" asked Vickery.

"And then I'm gonna kill him. Or let Louis or Ken do it, but only after we have what we need. Until this morning, my advice would have been to get Layla's will changed, and presented to the Trustees, notarised by the relevant people, but now, fuck 'em! We are going to take Maggie and her Mum back. I'm not negotiating, and I'm not waiting about for them to make contact."

While they waited for Pascoe and Pirelli's return, Seager sat down with Layla in the drawing room. He told her what the enquiry agent had found, and what he suspected her father's motive was.

"Sixty million dollars," she said incredulously, "that's ridiculous!"

"No it's not. The full extent of your Trust was never made known, but your father must have a fair idea of its scope. He is short of money and desperate."

"It's only money," she said sadly, as those with money do. "For God's sake, I'm his daughter!" she finished bitterly.

"There are people who would kill a relative for a thousandth of that amount. Now they have Maggie. It can only be them. Now, we are going to get her back, with her Mum. However, we can only do that while you are safe, and with us, O.K.? You will have to stay with us a while longer."

The girl nodded sadly, the tears still rolling down her cheeks. She still couldn't believe her own father would want to kill her.

Soon after, Pascoe and Pirelli arrived back. Their faces had lost the ashen look; now they were simply angry, wanting someone's blood. Leaving Pirelli behind, Pascoe walked into the morning room to report to Seager. His voice was dry and edged with threat.

"They'd nailed his arms down, stuffed a tea towel in his mouth and gone to work. He was covered in burns. He'd been gutted. Everything was on the floor. Christ, they cut his penis off and nailed it to his lower chest. His left thigh had been skinned. Both eyes were out and his top lip had gone, Christ knows where."

For a moment, there was silence between them. Pascoe's voice was quivering with anger as he looked Seager right in the eye.

"Whoever did this, Max, was twisted. A psychopathically determined maniac. I have never seen anything like it and Max, I want the job. Robert Stockly was my Second in Command. Be clear on this! When we find them, I want this one. I'm calling favours, my friend."

"He's yours. I shall talk to Richard Vickery who represents our client and sort out a new contract for you and your men. I'd appreciate you sticking around. This could get nasty from here on in."

At that moment, Pirelli stepped in the door followed by Buchanan and spoke softly but clearly. "He was my mate, and Keith's. This is personal. Let's put these bastards to our Rhodesian sword. No more money needed, Sir!"

"Pack now," said Seager. "We move out in twenty minutes back up to London. From now on, Layla doesn't leave anyone's sight. At all times two guns on her, and don't fuck about – shoot, and we'll worry about the details later."

They left the country house immaculate, with the larder stocked as they had found it, Masters joining them that night in London. He had picked up a parcel on the way, some things he thought might be useful: three Motorola handheld radios, silencers for the two Heckler and Koch machine pistols, a laser sight that could mount on any of the Brownings they had, three sets of number plates and a half kilo of C5. All this came from a very enterprising little man who ran a business of sorts in Croydon, supplying people with unusual requirements at huge prices. He also offered Masters a new German stun grenade but was disappointed when Masters refused his seven hundred price tag. As it was, the order came to just under three thousand pounds. Seager had been most specific with his vetting of Pascoe's new shopping list. Nothing that made noise if it could be helped.

That night, when Seager and Vickery sat down to eat, Seager outlined his plan to Vickery and finished by asking him to contact Student and have all three of Rakkafian's senior men put under surveillance immediately.

"What do you want of the watch?" Vickery asked.

"I want to know where they are at any time in the next four or five days."

They drove back to the small family hotel in Bayswater with take-away food for the rest of the team. They had all but taken the place over, much to the delight of the owner, who had agreed to Seager's request to keep the small facility for their exclusive use. He was told they were the advance group for a film production company, and their patronage would be long lasting if their privacy were maintained.

Vickery was out bright and early the next morning and Seager paced the front room of the old building, awaiting his call. He was as out of place here, among the fraying floral curtains and damp cold, as Buchanan was out running through the park with Pirelli. The big man was like a caged animal in the confines of London, away from his wilderness spaces. Seager had heard him training that morning in the back yard, out amongst the rubbish bins, milk bottles and perpetual wet moss.

Vickery had found the name of the officer investigating Stockly's death after a conversation with his contact in Special Branch, and a few other details. He had advised Seager that the man was named Morrison and he was a career type, straight as an arrow and highly regarded. He had, however, been twice passed over for promotion after an incident with two subordinates, when a man had been beaten in the cells. The story had never come out, but none of the officers concerned had been promoted since. In fact, the two subordinates had been transferred into traffic division from C.I.D. – and this was a one way street.

Seager found him in a pub not far from the high rise offices of Scotland Yard. He was a slight, mild looking fellow with thinning hair and a pallid complexion, but offset with bright inquisitive green eyes and a sharpness that was evident when he listened or spoke. Seager moved alongside him at the bar, holding a half pint of beer.

"You Morrison?"

The man looked at him and nodded.

"I think we can help each other," Seager added.

"Like how?" The accent was clipped Scottish.

"I'm over there." Seager pointed to an empty table, and walked

187

away, knowing that the policeman's natural curiosity would bring him over. Moments later, Morrison excused himself from his companions and carried his drink where Seager sat.

"Right," he said, pulling up a chair "how are you going to help me, and what will it cost? Speak up."

This was the official routine. Seager wanted to smile, but he reacted differently.

"Listen, Inspector, I'm not one of your horrible little villains about to grass on his mate, so don't patronise me." He stopped and sipped his lager. The policeman looked at him and waited, now being the passive listener. "You began a murder inquiry yesterday. A man in a Battersea flat who was mutilated almost beyond identification."

Morrison lent forward, interested. "Now what would you know about that then, laddie?"

"I can tell you who he is, and why he was killed. I can tell you who I think is the man at the end of the line. In exchange, I want your help to nail him and, for that, I need to find the person or persons who took his orders and perpetrated the crime."

"Now hang on, son, we're talking about a murder here. We're talking about the most barbaric ritual killing I have ever seen. Now, if you withhold information from me, I will wring you out."

Morrison would have gone on, but Seager interrupted angrily, "Listen for a minute. His name was Robert Stockly and he was working for me, protecting two women who I believed were under threat of violence."

He paused and Morrison cut in. "Margaret Nolan and the owner of the flat, her mother Mary."

"Correct. We are also talking kidnapping. Now then, the odds are they're clear of this country. You can't get them back. *I* can. The chances that you can build a case good enough for a court, even if you have a suspect, are remote. So you aren't in a position to affect anything. Your hands are tied and we both know it. We both know what they did to Rob Stockly. Help me get this fucking animal off the streets, Morrison." Seager pushed an envelope across the table to him. "In there is some money. Quite a lot actually. I don't have any informants here but you do. Spread the money about. This job didn't go down without someone knowing about it, and someone out there will talk for a sweetener. In return for a couple of names that I can back-track against, I will remove this problem for you."

"You don't know what you're asking," Morrison said, looking at the envelope.

"Oh yes I do." Seager's voice slipped, now, back into his suave and powerful African accent, pronouncing each word deeply and slowly. "Don't tell me you've never wished you could just kill half the filth that roams the streets terrifying people, killing, maiming, and pushing drugs. You wouldn't be normal. All I'm doing is asking you to call me with a couple of names, and then leave it alone for forty-eight hours. There is another angle to consider. Rob has four friends who are a bit pissed off with this whole scene. Now, if you can't narrow the field for us, they're going to go looking all by themselves. I'm not talking about four yobbos with shotguns; I'm talking about four special forces veteran soldiers who will sweep through your manor and on into the East End like Attila the Hun, and you don't need that aggro do you? Mmmm?" Seager sipped his drink and watched the detective. He could see the man weakening.

"What force are you with?" Morrison asked, wilting.

"Retired. British South Africa Police Special Branch."

"Rhodesian?" Morrison asked.

"Yes," said Seager, the pride in his voice obvious.

"Who is behind the killing?" Morrison asked, resigning himself to breaching his code of ethics. He knew that Seager was right. Forensic exams at the Nolan flat had revealed very little to lead them. He could not ask what Interpol had to recover the Nolans, not if he didn't know where they were – and he didn't want any armed men doing their own 'search and destroy mission' through London.

Half an hour later, Seager strode out of the pub, confident that he would soon hear from the dour Scot.

That night, at about eleven o'clock, Morrison phoned. Seager took the phone from Masters, who was sitting in the darkened hall watching the street. From this position he could also see the kitchen door. Anyone coming through would have to pass him and the silenced Heckler and Koch that sat in a sling over his shoulder. They were now

189

taking their security seriously, although the chances they had been found were extremely remote in a city the size of London.

"Seager," he said guardedly into the mouthpiece.

"Morrison. Can you talk?"

"Yes, go ahead," Seager said delightedly.

"I spread some money about. Almost unnecessary. Seems whoever did this has scared everyone."

"I thought it might," said Seager. "Down in my part of the world 'run of the mill' villains have standards; this goes beyond what even the hardest of them would do."

"Same here, sonny. Now then. Three men on the job, two professionals from the East End, hard men, but straight. Apparently they were out with the girl and her mother, drugged, very quickly and left the third man there."

"Go on," Seager said.

"Then it gets hazy. All I have is a name. Doud. Got that?"

"Go on," said Seager.

"He was the third man. Not much on him, but we know he has a British passport."

"Doud sounds Arab."

"Yes and no. Born in Malta, hence the passport. But he is as Libyan as Gadaffi."

"Libyan?"

"Yes. Now then, one more thing. This guy is a sicko, that we know. It seems he is also a user, buys from a Jamaican called Winston. His girlfriend works in a pub called the Rose and Crown. Take this address down." He read the address, spelling the letters in phonetic style. "You can score from him and take it from there."

Seager was impressed at the speed with which the information had been gathered. It would normally take days to get this much. "You moved fast on this."

"He has some people worried. Stirs up the water too much. You have forty-eight hours, then I move. I can't hold it longer than that or my informant will smell a rat. The other two you can't have. In fact, if they get Doud first, they will kill him. He's done them damage as well. No-one likes a sicko, so do us all a favour and take this one."

Morrison paused. "Forty eight-hours Mr. Seager, then I will take him."

"Thank you Mr. Morrison. Let me know when I can return the favour."

"One more thing. Winston deals for a firm. He will have minders close by."

Seager smiled. "I have some minders of my own," he said.

Everyone was up early and ended up sitting around waiting for the pubs to open.

Seager was upstairs in his room, looking in the mirror and beginning to do what he could to make himself look like a junkie. Layla, who laughed cynically when told of his plan, assisted him. She suggested several little things that would all add up and look good. Below them, on the ground floor, the remainder of the group were watching a video that the hotel proprietor had selected for them. It was very arty and French with subtitles and had Buchanan gazing bored from the window, and Pirelli peeling the wallpaper in one corner. Buchanan stood, staring out of the window onto the wet slick street. A big red bus rolled past, its tyres humming on the slippery surface; a Volvo hooted angrily at the driver in the mammoth vehicle and two fingers were raised from the side window.

Buchanan turned and looked into the room as Seager entered. His hair was slicked with oil, and Layla had rubbed in crumbs and dust. It looked filthy. His eyes were red-rimmed from onion juice and he hadn't shaved. She had found a filthy sweater and donkey jacket, and with his jeans and tatty running shoes they made him look the part of a man who needed a fix.

"Right," he said, "let's go get this Winston bloke."

"How do you want to do it?" Pascoe asked.

"Buchanan and Vickery in the Sierra trailing us. Layla with them. You, Louis and Richard with me in the BM. I'll go in and bring him out. You blokes watch my back. This one has got mates and I don't want him loose before we have the gen. O.K.?"

"Yeah," said Pascoe. "Louis, Richard, bring H&K's. Leave the rest of the noisy stuff in the boot of the Sierra. You wanna pistol Max?"

"No." Seager still didn't like guns very much.

Layla was in the hall brushing her hair as Seager walked past. She slipped a rubber band around the thick black ponytail and smiled at him. The others were gathering their things and Seager took the opportunity to ask her about the will. "Did your father ever ask you to sign any papers in the last couple of years?"

She looked at him and, as she answered, she tucked one loose wisp of hair behind her ear. "Ummm yes, twice. He didn't come though. A lawyer from Larnaca was fawning all over me like a peasant to his master."

That's that Seager had expected. "Did you see what you were signing?"

"It was all in Arabic script which is difficult to read at the best of times, especially in its modern translation. I didn't take too much notice. A set of instructions with lots of Allah Willing and what have you."

Seager nodded to himself. *Get Student onto that,* he thought. *Let's have a translation from the lawyer in Larnaca.*

Vickery walked into the hall immaculate in a cashmere sports coat and fine wool trousers, brown brogues completing what was the most English set of clothing Seager had ever seen. Seager took him to one side and quickly explained what Layla had told him and finished by asking, "Can you get that verified?"

Vickery smiled icily. "Cyprus? No problem. Rashid owns half the place." Then he walked to the phone and began dialling as the remainder of the team gathered in the hall.

"Keith, you wait for Mr. Vickery and then take him and Layla over to the Embassy. Keep out of sight. Meet us at the Victoria and Albert Museum at noon. Park across the road, up on the pavement or something." Seager turned to Layla. Something he had seen was bothering him but he couldn't place what it was. He shrugged inwardly to himself and spoke. "Layla, wear a hat or something, dark glasses."

She nodded and handed him half an onion in cling film. "For your tears again," she explained, and delved into her bag for the large floppy hat she had worn the previous day.

"Let's go," Pascoe muttered impatiently.

CHAPTER EIGHTEEN

The pub stood on a quiet street just off a large roundabout in Upton Manor. Further down the street, a fast food restaurant did brisk business, but the pub seemed almost derelict. The door was ajar and looked as if it had been kicked open many times. A bright flower in a pot stood bravely against the autumn chill and grey stone walls.

Seager walked from the car into the brisk wind and, with his shoulders hunched, slipped into the warm interior. There were a few lunchtime drinkers in the public bar so Seager moved through the scratched door into the lounge, depressingly dark with fake carriage lamps and dark red vinyl seating. Standing at the bar, he waited for a middle-aged woman to look his way.

"Yes?" she snapped, her mean mouth set hard under tired eyes.

"Can I see Rose please?" Seager asked.

The mouth twisted at him. "She's got a job of work to do here yaknow!"

"I won't keep her a moment."

Seager smiled his best smile and the woman dropped the ashtray she had been cleaning and waddled back through the service door. A moment later, a much younger woman appeared. She was a slatternly blonde, with bruised upper arms and dark green eyeshadow. She walked to Seager's end of the bar and stood, her hands on the bar. Her knuckles were grubby and across her left hand was tattooed a word. Seager looked carefully and made it out. It said HATE.

"Yeah?" she said.

"You Rose?" Seager asked, hoping he sounded like a man with a need.

"Ooh wants ta know?" she asked.

"I need to see Winston.." he said, sotto voce.

"'E's not eah so naf off."

"Please. I need to score, I've got cash." He pulled money from his pocket. She looked at it greedily, and he sensed her weakening. "Please," he wheedled, "I am bad."

193

She looked him in the red-rimmed eyes for the first time, his hair lank and dirty, and he looked safe enough. "Wait 'ere," she said, and turned to walk away. If she had looked back she would have seen a new look in his eyes. She would have seen them glitter like an angry cat's, just for a second.

Seager waited patiently, and finally ordered a rum and Coke. He disliked rum but to order anything non-alcoholic would have been noticed in a bar like this. In fact, he disliked anything served with Coke but it seemed the lesser of the various evils on the shelf. He sipped it carefully, watching the other drinkers, and ten minutes later the door to the street swung open and a tall rangy black man entered. He had that confident well-fed look that minor success brings, and walked with a cocky swagger. His hair was held back in a knitted teacosy hat, the type favoured by West Indians. Lurid in colour, the hat contrasted starkly with the dreary workday wear of the other drinkers who seemed to stand back as he entered the room. He walked to where Seager stood and looked around.

"You de cat flashing money around? Wanna be careful around hea man."

"You Winston?" Seager asked cautiously, his voice perfectly blended with a mix of hope and desperation.

"Could be man. Wat you wan with him anyhow?"

Seager smiled, disarmingly. "Let's stop fucking around." He grabbed the dealer's filthy hair and slammed his head into the bar, twice in quick succession, followed by two huge jabs to the sternum. The Rasta's head flicked back and Seager swung him towards the door as the fat blonde behind the bar began to shriek obscenities. The man was almost limp in his arms except for a dry retching sound from deep in his pain-wracked body.

They reached the street and the BMW shrieked to a halt. Masters threw open the back door and, reaching out with one long arm, pulled the winded and bewildered loser into the car. Seager got into the front and, in the driver's seat, Pascoe accelerated into the sparse traffic. A few blocks down the street, he pulled into a quiet alleyway beside a rubbish skip.

Seager turned and looked at the man, who was now holding his face and writhing in the seat, as blood dripped down. Masters hand was wound firmly in his hair through his woolly hat.

"Listen carefully," said Seager. "Where I come from, people who sell drugs get hanged." It wasn't true but would serve its purpose. "So you tell me what I want to know or I will do just that." He paused for dramatic effect. "You deal with an Arab called Doud. I want to know where he is. That's all. Then you can go."

The man spoke for the first time, his breath sharp and words indistinct through his pain. "You can't do that man, I'm protected."

"Not from me you cunt," Seager snarled. "Where's Doud?"

The man moaned to himself through his short stabby breaths.

"I'll not ask again," Seager warned.

"Proteshun man. I'm safe. You better let me go."

Masters looked at Seager, his eyes questioning. *Shall I hit him?*

Leaning back looking out of the window, Pirelli suddenly spoke. "Better do as he says now! I don't think he likes you."

Masters joined in there. "In fact, you won't have any balls to hold soon, so why don't you tell Mr. Seager where to find Doud? I don't really care if you vote for the loony Left or not, or where you found that disgusting little slut you're rutting, all we care about is where to find Doud then you can run off and complain to the council or attack a milkman or something, mmm?"

The man moaned again.

"Doud, Winston," said Seager. "The Arab guy you sell smack to, big spender, Doud. Where is he?"

Masters leant across and turned the man's head towards him by twisting his wispy moustache. "Well?" he asked. "Answer the man. We are running out of patience."

Pirelli, still watching out the window, spoke softly again. "Company," he said, "green Jaguar, four men stopped on the road." He opened his door and stepped out, his Heckler and Koch suddenly appearing from between his legs as he swung it out from behind his back.

"I told you fucks," Winston muttered, more bravely now. "Now you gonna get it."

"From your mates?" Masters asked. "They have two chances, none and fuck all."

Masters emerged from the other side of the BMW, his own automatic weapon under his jacket. "I'll be back in a minute," he said, "don't get lonely."

Pascoe climbed from the front, just as the green car swung into the alley with an unnecessary burst of speed and screeched to a halt twenty feet behind the BMW. He walked forward until he was level with Pirelli. Seager sat where he was. This wasn't his thing at all.

Inside the car, Winston turned in his seat, still holding his crotch, and looked from the window at his rescuers. Four men climbed from the car, three black and one white. The driver, a big man in his twenties, looked with savage eyes at Pascoe, his jacket buttoned, his hands empty, his complete trust in his two soldiers evident by that alone.

"You got summing of ours," the man barked. "We want it back."

The others spread around him now, both sides of the car.

"This has nothing to do with you," Pascoe said, his voice feathery and menacing all at once. "Just leave us alone. GO AWAY."

"You didn't 'ear me white bwoy!" the man threatened.

"Don't disobey me pal," Pascoe replied, menacingly. "You won't live to do it twice!"

"FUCK YOUR MOTHER!" the man shouted and reached for the shotgun he had under his coat. His companions did the same, the movements fast and urgent and violent in themselves. It was a mistake. Pirelli and Masters opened fire together, the incredible silencers muffling the rapid firing to a dull thudding, inaudible thirty yards away. The rounds tore into the surprised group like terrible invisible punches, each hit throwing the victim back a few inches in a twitching, gyrating prelude to death.

A few rounds from Pirelli's guns shattered the windscreen as he swung left to back up Masters, but the men were already down and dead or dying. One man arched his back and clawed at his perforated chest in disbelieving horror, then settled back in final acceptance as his brain registered that his heart had stopped beating.

Suddenly the alley was silent, except for the sound of a sheet of newspaper blowing with the wind towards the corpses.

Pascoe, Masters and Pirelli climbed back into the car without a word and Pascoe started the engine. Seager never took his eyes off the man in the back seat. He had begun to make a gurgling, terrified sound in his throat, unable to believe what he had seen. Four men, the protection supplied by his boss, the hardest men in the north of London dead in as many seconds.

"Doud," Seager asked, "where is he?"

"Lupus est homo homini," Masters said. "*You're fucking next.* Now answer him!" The man began to speak.

"Lupus what?" Pirelli asked later.

"Est homo homini," Masters finished. "Man is a wolf to man."

"Should have done Latin," the smaller man said. "Then I could say things like that to lowlifes too.."

"You are mocking a great education, Louis," Masters said smugly. They were pleased; they had Doud's address and a terrified Winston was going to have to go into hiding. His employers would sorely miss the talents that Winston had indirectly seen to the demise of.

Pascoe said nothing, just edged the big car through the Clapham traffic towards the museum, Seager deep in thought beside him. It was Brighton that they wanted. Seager couldn't really picture a psychotic Arab torturer in the sleepy old seaside town where they had first met Stockly. But at least it would be fitting, he thought.

On the other side of London, Buchanan sat parked in the driveway of a large old Edwardian building opposite the Victoria and Albert Museum, morosely eating a Flakey bar, not enjoying the bodyguard detail he had been set. Layla sat beside him talking every now and then, mostly to herself.

"Keith," Layla said, "we will get Maggie back. Now stop smouldering and talk to me."

"I know we'll get her back. We did once before. But if they have hurt her then there will be long culling," he muttered.

"Long what?" she asked, pleased to have had a response.

"Culling. It's what you do when you have too many of a particular kind of animal in one place. You select and then kill enough to relieve the pressure on the grass, the water, or whatever they're overdoing."

It was the longest statement she had ever heard him say and was about to try to change the subject, sorry she had raised it at all, when the man spoke again. He had seen Seager and the rest of the crew on the approach. "There at the lights, the BM."

He started the motor and eased out into the road so that Seager could see him and, as they rolled past, Pirelli raised one finger at his friend, in the traditional 'up-yours' gesture. Buchanan smiled and pulled in behind them as the lead car threaded its way through the one-way system towards the south.

Seager stopped on the road in Croydon and phoned the Embassy, leaving a message for Vickery to phone them that night at a hotel he had selected from a guidebook.

Seager had opted for Worthing as a base. Only a few miles from Brighton, it was near enough without being on top of their operational area. When he got back to the car, he asked Pirelli to go with Buchanan and purchase a few things on the way down. "Get me Tippex. You know, the white paper stuff for correcting typing mistakes?" Pirelli nodded. "Some glue or solvent, and a can of fly spray."

Pirelli smiled.

Vickery sat at a spare desk in the Emirates' small London mission jotting notes as he talked on the telephone. He was ignored by the staff but treated with respect when necessary. As a direct report to the country's ruler, he wielded enormous power and yet was loath to use it, something none of the staff understood. All he had asked for was an office with a telephone, and had sent the waiting secretary home.

That was where he was when an Embassy staffer put a note on the table in front of him, saying that Student was waiting in the foyer. Vickery indicated that he should be brought up and finished his conversation with the agent in Larnaca.

Soon, Student was ushered in, wiping the rain from his briefcase.

"Mr. Student, I want you to brief me on the three men that Max Seager has you watching. Who, what, and which one interests us? I think we will be looking for one or two of them any minute."

Student nodded and pulled a sheaf of telexes from his case. "Subject One," he began, "is Mohsen. He is the weapons' dealer. This morning, he flew to Stuttgart from Athens. He is being met at the airport by

Heinrich Muller, who buys that type of thing. Number Two is Abdullah Jumbladi, the pornographer who is now in Paris. The receptionist at his hotel has just sent his luggage down to a château in the countryside outside Bergerac."

Student paused to blow into a creased handkerchief and Vickery broke in, "What's he doing down there?"

"Apparently it's a small, privately-funded mental home and orphanage, but I should have more on that later."

Vickery nodded, adjusting the cuffs of his handmade shirt beneath the cashmere jacket. *Good,* he thought, *we have two of them nice and tight? But where is Rakkafian, where is the man? Come to daddy you stinking shit.*

"Subject number three."

Vickery cut in, unable to contain his prying for the information. "And where is Rakkafian himself?" Vickery asked.

"Beirut today, but going to Manama tomorrow for a week or so." Student paused there. "He did change his plans. He was due in Larnaca and then Riyadh, but he's cancelled those arrangements and will be in Manama till next Saturday at least according to our sources." Student stopped and blew his nose again.

Vickery rose and walked to the door and opened it. "Thank you, Mr. Student. Anyone moves, I want to know. I will be here until tomorrow and then I will be contactable in Ras Al Qaleem at the Palace."

Student nodded and left without speaking again.

After he was gone, Vickery began to study his notes. It was time to bring the Emir into the picture. If the scenario was moving into the Gulf then they would need his sanction and he would not be amused at being left in the dark for so long on a venture he had initiated. This was his time. Seager was the ground man and, with his team of more physical types, they could adequately handle things at that level. The Emir was his problem.

Two police Rovers stood in the north London alleyway, their blue strobe lights flashing in the drizzle. Beside them was a new four door plain car. Inside a policeman was talking into the radio while his three colleagues surveyed the scene. Further up the alley, two uniformed men were covering four bodies beside a green Jaguar while others held back the gawking spectators that blue lights always attract. An ambulance arrived and nosed its way up the alleyway. Behind it, yet another police car arrived, this time with only two occupants. One man in the passenger seat alighted and walked towards the scene.

"What have we here?" he said.

The other man looked up at him from the car seat, the radio still in his hand. He recognised a senior officer when he saw one, but couldn't place the face, so his answer would have to be sufficient without being elaborate. "Four hard men drive into the alley. Four shotguns that never got fired. No-one heard a bloody thing. I've got someone on my manor with a silenced weapon doing a bloody Charles Bronson on me!" He turned back to the radio as it squawked into life. "Course I'm 'ere" he snapped irritably.

"I wonder who would want to do a thing like that?" said Inspector Morrison of Scotland Yard, who then walked smiling back to his car. Climbing into the seat, he told his driver to drive on.

"What's happening?" the driver asked, pulling away.

"Four stiffs. Not our case. Serious crimes will handle this. Looks like a gang job." He paused. "Stop at the shop and let's get an ice cream."

"It's cold, boss. You really want ice cream?" his driver asked, thinking about a cheeseburger and how nice that would be. They only stopped once and this might be it for the day.

"Yes. Ice cream. It's going to be a lovely evening. Shake off your English pessimism, constable. Be like the Scots, a silver lining behind everything."

The constable wondered just what had made his normally dour inspector so convivial.

At that same moment, Seager was adequately handling the parking of the car outside W.H Smiths in Worthing. "This is a no stopping area," said Layla brightly.

"Show the man your passport and shrug like you don't speak English," he said as he ran across the road. He appeared a minute later and, jumping back into the car, pulled into the traffic, throwing a map into the back seat where Pascoe and Masters sat dozing.

"Find the street in Brighton?" he asked.

"What are we after?" Pascoe asked sleepily.

"Lonsdale Terrace," Seager said. "We want to be there tonight, late, when this animal comes in from wherever he's been for the evening."

"Max," said Layla softly, "What are you going to do to him"

He didn't answer for a minute, just wound his way through the narrow streets looking for the hotel. They appeared at the seafront again and, as he turned left, he spoke up. "What this man did was beyond forgiveness. I will not forget what he did to a man that I placed there, under my command. This man is not sane. I'm just going to tip him over the edge. And when I have finished, I am going to kill him."

"You can't!" she retorted. "You are just sinking to his level!"

"Don't give me that sanctimonious shit, Layla. The man he tortured and killed risked his life for yours, and mine! Don't tell me about sinking to any levels. What do you think this is? Bloody Disneyland? If you can't handle it, Layla, then stay at the hotel. I will come back and you can ignore me and sulk, but I will have done the world a favour. End of discussion."

The two teams arrived at the Lonsdale Terrace walkup just after midnight. Pascoe pulled the bodyguard duty at the hotel in spite of his rank, because Seager wanted the skills of the other three men more. That afternoon, Masters had found a deserted warehouse in a row alongside the main coastal road in Shoreham-by-Sea, a small largely industrial piece of ribbon development between Worthing and Brighton. He had forced the back door and had a look around. It was ideal for the interrogation session they had planned, and Pirelli had left the items Seager wanted in a cardboard box in the dilapidated bathroom ready for their arrival.

Masters had been the one who had produced a set of burglar's tools and let Buchanan into the dark first floor flat on Lonsdale Terrace. Pirelli and Masters came in behind him, armed and ready, but their precautions were unnecessary. The big man moved like a cat through the dark and, finding the figure asleep in a large bed, moved his hand over a pressure point and pressed firmly. A few seconds later, he turned on the light beside the bed and beckoned the other two men into the room. Masters produced a washing line from his pocket and trussed the small dark-haired individual like a chicken, a gag deep in his open mouth, and then hefted the comatose form over his shoulder. At one point on the stairs, he stirred and moaned and Buchanan's hand flashed, not a pressure point this time, but a blow to the base of the back into the kidneys.

"Quiet or I will kill you now," he snarled.

Masters kept moving the entire time and then they were on the street, into the car and moving.

"What's your name?" asked Seager. "Nod your head. You are Doud?"

The man said nothing.

"I will assume you are. Your silence has betrayed your stupidity, you pig!"

The man writhed, his eyes rolling in anger and struggling at his bond, groaning into the gag, the insult the worst imaginable.

"It's the right one," Seager said as they reached the bottom of the road and turned right for the Shoreham House.

"I thought it might be," Masters said.

Neither Buchanan nor Pirelli said anything. They were with the man who had killed Rob Stockly and the mood was tense. Pirelli was hoping the man would try to escape or fight back, and thereby give him an excuse to drive his new battle knife through the man's side and twist it, then watch his eyes fade and his blood gush onto the seat.

The car came to a halt outside the warehouse doors. Stepping out into the night, Masters carried the struggling figure through the back door and headed up the stairs as Seager turned to Buchanan.

"How accurate are these pressure points?"

"Pretty good," he said. "Quite how long they're out for is up to the individual and the pain varies considerably with which point you go for."

"I want this guy out but breathing steadily for at least a full minute," Seager said.

"A minute is hard, two or three is easier. Very painful though."

"Tough," Seager said, "let's start." Then he followed Masters through the warehouse door.

Inside, Seager surveyed the scene. An empty chair faced a large television, switched on, but tuned to nothing. He nodded at Buchanan. The big man left the room and was back a moment later with the unconscious figure of the Libyan over his shoulder.

"Quick now," Seager began. "Into the chair in front of the head. Tie him there, Louis. Tippex into a tissue and hold it over his nose, thirty seconds of that and then some of that glue. I want him freaking out when he comes to. Lights off. Head phones on him."

Pirelli rigged a cheap portable hi-fi and microphone to the headphones so that Seager would be able to talk to the man through the headphones at whatever volume he wanted. When he wasn't talking, they'd treat him to strains of heavy metal music at full blast. Hallucinating under the influence of the drugs, the noise and the blizzard of feedback on screen would be a disturbing cocktail. While they worked, Seager quickly re-read the Arabic phrase book he had bought along with the map in the bookshop that afternoon.

At last, the man began to stir. The effects of the drugs in his blood and the pain from his neck where Buchanan had pinched the nerve were intense.

"Lights," Seager said quickly.

Pirelli hit the switch and the room dropped into darkness, the TV casting a ghoulish glow over the room. Finally, the figure awoke – and Seager leant into the microphone to speak.

"Al shatan unedique!" he intoned. *Satan is calling you.* "Al shatan unedique."

The man began to shake his head, the message loud in the headphones.

"There is no place in Paradise for you," Seager continued. "You defiled yourself, you have killed men of the book." Doud screamed out loud now, shaking his head, his mind playing tricks. Seager turned up the volume on the hi-fi and watched as the man's face became contorted with fear. "You are going to hell, Satan is calling you."

The man twisted and fought the bonds as the vision tore at his sanity, the psychedelic properties of the drugs, making the threat seem real to him. *He was was surely facing damnation.*

Seager talked into the microphone again, "Satan is calling you."

"No, I will be in paradise!" He didn't sound like he believed it.

From the side Pirelli pressed the nozzle on the fly spray and held a flame to the pressurized aerosol jet. It caught immediately. Hellfire billowing across his face, Doud screamed. His skin and moustache scorched. Then the voice began again in the headphones.

"Feel the fires of hell, feel them!" The fire belched again and the Libyan screamed, his eyes rolled into his head and he blacked out.

"Keith, bring him back, quickly, he's on the run."

Buchanan moved forward, found a nerve and pressed. The man leapt into life as the searing pain lanced though his neck.

"The fires of hell. They are burning while you burn, you fucker. Who sent you to kill the man and take the girl? Who?"

"NOOOAA!"

"Who?"

The flame roared again, Pirelli careful not to burn him too grievously.

"NOOOO!"

Panicking, he strained at the ties around his wrists. Sweat dripped from him. He bit his tongue through, blood bursting onto his lips.

"Who sent you?" Pirelli squeezed again

"No," he moaned as his chin dropped to his chest.

It continued for two hours. Until his addled brain could take no more.

Drugged, terrified and scorched he gave them a name: "Jumbladi."

"Where is the girl, where is her mother?"

"Gone, gone." He slumped.

The fly spray was gone. Seager stood, turned on the lights and looked at Buchanan, Masters and Pirelli before speaking. "Jumbladi is a direct report to Layla's father."

No one spoke as they packed to go.

At last, they were ready. Seager walked out, disgusted with everything and nodded to Pirelli.

Pirelli walked over to the barely cognisant man and lifted his face. "Your time has come." Lifting the handgun he had held all night, he fired two rounds point blank into the man's face and walked from the room to the waiting car on the road. In the now silent house, a rat came from hiding and sniffed at something that dripped onto the floor from the wall. It was brains. It began to eat. Soon it was joined by others, all gorging on their unexpected bounty.

"Vickery?" Seager asked. It was five am and the voice sounded strange.

"Yes. Sorry, go." Vickery replied, now awake.

"Can you get me a location of Jumbladi? He's one of Rakkafian's top people. Student should be ab-"

"Got it," Vickery interrupted, "stand by. O.K., he is visiting a château outside Bergerac in France. Some sort of insane asylum I believe."

Seager thought for a moment and then spoke again. "We're on a roll here. I wanna keep moving. We are going to France. Can you find out exactly where this place is and I'll phone you later?"

"Yes, no problem. I'm going back to Ras Al Qaleem, but if you ask for Isa Zayani he will have the information for you. He was the chap who bought over your last set of requirements."

"I remember him, I was going to come to that. We'll need something similar in France. Can do?" Seager asked.

"Yes. but Bergerac may be a problem. Can you collect in Paris?"

"If necessary. We are close Richard, very close. It's definitely Rakkafian – but I'm still not sure of the motive, not for conclusive proof that would be admissible to the Emir of wherever."

"Ras Al Qaleem," Vickery said dryly. "For your fee you could re-member that. For that fee I would memorise the phone book."

"I'll be in touch," Seager laughed. "Go back to sleep."

CHAPTER NINETEEN

The château was outside the village of Campsegret on the road between Bergerac and Perigueux. It was, as châteaus went in France, unremarkable. Off the road it was very secluded and the locals avoided the place; its reputation as an asylum was enough to keep them away from the dark gates that stood shrouded in creepers on the narrow service road.

The Institution had been set up by the wife of a wealthy Parisian fabrics manufacturer ostensibly as a charity, something his accountants appreciated too. The tall yellow stone walls housed roughly seventeen inmates of various medical conditions, some unpredictably violent and others just incapable of existing outside the Institution. There was, however, no real charity in the motives. No altruism in any form. What was an excellent tax write-off for the husband was also a novel playpen for the jaded tastes of his wife. Years before he had admitted to himself that the woman he had married was, sexually, altogether too much for him, and they were now married in name only. She had her lovers, her liaisons, her groups and little swinging circles – and, as long as she was discreet, he left her alone. What he didn't know was that, as the years had gone by, his wife's perverse tastes had not mellowed; in fact, at forty-two years old, she was more inclined to the unusual than at twenty. If he had realised what took place at the château, he would have taken immediate action to have her curtailed, for even in the modern era there were some things that were not acceptable to indulge in sexually. Activities with the deranged and mentally disturbed was one of those things.

Madame de Marchaine was, among Paris's select circles, something of a legend. She was a stunning redhead with creamy white skin and available to anything or anyone at the parties, preferably more than one of each. The weekends she spent at the château were little diversions from the hectic social life of the City, diversions that a few selected friends delighted in joining her on. There were very few that were privy to the goings-on at the château, and in the last year she had taken one quantum leap nearer to the trouble she was eventually going to have to face. She had parties for fun and then for profit and had recently begun allowing the sessions to be videotaped. At first, the Betamax tapes were for her amusement, but she had been convinced that there were enormous profits to be made by inviting the right people to the château, indulging their tastes, and then blackmailing them. The man who had convinced her of this was Abdullah Jumbladi, ever on the lookout for a fast buck in his field.

He had been to the château one weekend and marvelled at the potential that lay in the custom-renovated rooms. There was a strengthened glass wall with apertures through it, sound facilities, viewing rooms and a compliant trained staff who knew exactly how to please the guests of Madame de Marchaine. He made his suggestion, carefully veiled, as he was being fellated by a young girl, while the redheaded woman sat opposite watching and enjoying the ministrations of another child of similar age. Now, a year on, they had duped four very wealthy people, three men and one woman. They had another lined up for this weekend and the Madame arrived in delicious anticipation of what was to come, both the sex and the outcome of the blackmail in the months ahead. She didn't need the money, but she liked the fear that generated it. She marvelled at people's desire to pay to have their peccadilloes covered. She wasn't like that at all – she would relish her picture in a magazine claiming something disgusting – but her husband, whom she still loved both for his money and his patience, would not approve.

Now, as her car rolled sedately up the long driveway, the weekend was about to begin. Her companion was the lithe small-breasted wife of an English banker, a recent convert to the scene in Paris and ready and willing for a weekend in the country. The Madame had titillated her with stories on the way down, stories of the mammoth penis of the patient called Chalore, and the sweet tongue of the Indian girls who arrived as illegal immigrants and were sold to the château as staff to be trained for the future. "Cheri, come, the staff will bring your bags, come and have an aperitif," the Madame said, taking her new friend by the hand. Jumbladi would arrive later and, from the viewing room,

207

would tape the proceedings. It would be a weekend of both pleasure and profit, thought the Madame as she felt the bottom of the English woman through her skirt, running her finger along the crease in promise of the night's pleasure.

*

It was later that night that Seager and his team arrived in Bergerac. Wasting no time, he woke the proprietor of a small rental car agency and took an ageing Peugot – and a big, even older Citreon – from the complaining man. Seager's French was appalling and he was rescued by Layla who, with her cosmopolitan Lebanese upbringing, spoke the language well. By two the following morning, they were at the gates of the château and eased the cars into the dark shadows alongside the high stone walls.

"I don't like loonies," Pirelli said.

"They'll all be locked up," Seager consoled. "She had an apartment here somewhere and our target is with her. Don't worry about the loonies."

Student's local contact had been resourceful. He had supplied information of a calibre that had surprised even Student. "Monsieur, our inquiries have revealed much. It is not an ordinary Institution," he had said. "The patron does pay for the care and welfare of the patients, but she extracts a price." He was a tall, stooped ex-policeman from Lyon who had served in Algeria and had never felt at home since arriving back in metropolitan France thirty years before. He disliked Arabs in general, Libyans in particular, and berated them constantly in conversation. "She uses them for her pleasure. The staff say nothing but the village people say they have money in their pockets. More money than these people usually earn. The wealthy, monsieur, have their ways," he added sagely, before continuing, "She has three men who work up at the château. One guard at the gate, and two in the wards. They double with duties in the apartment when she is there for a liaison."

"What's the layout?" Seager asked.

"The apartment is linked to the main complex. That's all I can tell you. But there was a supplier of special glass in Bordeaux who installed glass walls and viewing rooms. He suspected things at the time but was told it was for observation of patients. He was paid well and so." The man gave a Gaelic shrug that said everything.

"Thank you."

"You are welcome. When you find that filthy Arab in there, tell him that he is not welcome in France, nor any of his kind." With this, he nodded at Seager and walked back to his car on a damp Paris street.

Seager now looked at the wall of the château. It was high and slippery. "The gate," he said to Masters – who nodded, and walked nonchalantly towards the gate like a tourist lost in the dark, calling in pidgin French to the guard. The others, including Layla, moved to the wall and waited.

The plan was that Pirelli, taking his turn as bodyguard, would wait outside with Layla while the rest went in. He was not impressed with the task. "Max, I'm not a babysitter!" he protested.

"Neither am I pal," Pascoe muttered, "but I did my turn, so you do yours."

Pirelli knew his battle was lost. "Sir," he said, shrugging his shoulders to himself. "Come on foxy," he said, turning to Layla, who stood tapping one finger, unamused in the dark, "let's go and sit in the car and compare navels."

"You wish!" she retorted, following.

"Quiet!" Seager hissed. He looked at where Masters had disappeared round the curve of the wall. "Keith?" he called softly. The big man moved up beside him like a shadow. "See what's holding Richard up will you?"

Buchanan nodded and moved forward round the wall.

Around the bend, Masters stood talking to the guard. Buchanan heard them laugh as Masters indicated running out of petrol in mime. Suddenly, his hand flashed through the opening gate and, grabbing the guard's lapels, he jerked his head into the bars. Dazed and surprised, the man stood back – and Masters was through and on him in a flash, his gun drawn into the man's throat. "*Ouvre la porte,*" he whispered, slipping the pin back on his weapon. The guard did so, and – with Buchanan calling back for Seager – the four men shrunk silently into the courtyard, leaving the guard lying unconscious in a bush.

Once they had reached the château and stolen through its doors, Pascoe raised his pistol to his lips and moved down the entrance hall. He waited until Buchanan, Seager, and Masters were opposite the next door and swung it silently open. Buchanan and Seager entered quickly and crossed to the opposite side, checking the other doors that led off the main suite. Meanwhile, Masters waited in the corridor. There were still the two male nurses who would be in the apartment somewhere. The other staff in the main block of the château would not disturb them, but the two men would need to be found.

Seager listened at one door and nodded to Buchanan, who crossed the carpeted floor and took up a position ready to go in, then nodded. Seager swung the door back and they moved through together, Buchanan leading by inches, both with guns in their hands.

On the other side, two men sat in easy chairs watching a small colour television. They were both wearing trousers, bare-chested and relaxed, drinking beer from bottles. Hearing a noise from behind, they both spun around, startled at the intrusion. One was rising from his chair when Seager showed him the gun.

"Bang bang you're dead. *Comprendo*?" he smiled nicely.

"That's Spanish Sir," said Buchanan. "Masters!" he called.

Pascoe appeared in the door and Masters a moment later.

"Praat the taal," Buchanan said.

"Ask them where Jumbladi is," said Seager. "No hassles, I just want Jumbladi."

"O.K," said Masters. "*Parlez vous Anglais?*"

Both men shook their heads.

"*Aah Arabi? Homme Arabi Monsieur?*"

The men looked at each other and began chatting, then one turned back to Masters and nodded. "Jumbladi?" he asked.

"*Oui oui*," Masters said "*Oui?*"

They quickly conferred with much pantomime of guns and hands up. The one turned back to Masters again and indicated that they were to follow him.

"Let's go," said Masters, "I think they're on the level."

"You up front," Pascoe said. "Keith, watch the back."

They followed the two men out of the room, into the main suite and out into the next corridor. Here it was heavily carpeted in burgundy-coloured shag, and their passage was muted by the softness underfoot. That was why Jumbladi never heard them coming, although the breathing and moaning through the speakers had died away to a soft conversation on the other side of the glass.

Masters swung the door back on the oiled hinges and Buchanan and Seager burst through. Seager grabbed the man from the high stool and slammed him back into the wall, jamming his gun into his open, startled mouth.

It was a small room, overlooking a slightly larger one below, where the bodies Jumbladi had been filming were entangled with one another, just reaching their climax.

"Abdullah Jumbladi, this is your life!" Seager snarled. "Now you tell me what I want to know or I will kill you."

The Arab made a gargling sound in his throat.

"Max, you're strangling him," said Pascoe reasonably.

"Ken, check the ladies down there in the fun factory. Keith, go with him. Richard, watch my back. Mr. Jumbladi is going to sing to me and I don't want to be disturbed."

"You're still strangling him, Max," said Pascoe as he nonchalantly walked onwards, following Buchanan down into the 'fun factory' below.

Seager released his grip on the man's throat and pulled his gun clear of the twitching mouth, dropping him onto the stool. "You contracted a man called Doud to do a snatch. Who was it for?"

Jumbladi said nothing and just glared through red-rimmed eyes, massaging his throat.

"Where is the girl and her mother? Talk, you cocksucker, or I'll become your worst fucking nightmare." Seager jammed the gun into the man's stomach and he doubled over.

"NO, HE WILL KILL ME!" Jumbladi uttered, then leant forward and vomited.

"He won't because I will. Who was it?"

"How dare you! Who are you?" In the room beyond the glass, Rene de Marchaine was frightened and angry. She made no attempt to cover

211

her nakedness as Pascoe marched through, leaving Seager and Jumbladi behind, although the English woman she was with did, stretching one hand across her breasts and one leg across the other. She was wet with sweat and her cheeks were flushed with what Americans call afterglow. It was a small room, covered in mirrored glass, and a small very pretty Indian girl sat against the wall, head on knee.

Pascoe turned from the Madame and looked up at the mirrored glass where he knew the cameras were hidden, then back at the smaller woman sitting on the floor.

"Did you know you were on candid camera?" He smiled at her shocked expression. "Dear me, didn't you know? Pity and shame on your hostess." He turned back to the Madame. "You are Rene whatshername?"

The English woman had now put her hands to her mouth in shock and disbelief, looking at Pascoe and Buchanan, hoping it was all some terrible joke.

"I demand to know who you are and what you are doing here in my house!" The Madame de Marchaine had risen to her feet and stood in naked splendour, her large round breasts swinging in sympathetic indignation.

"Sit down," said Pascoe. "We came for Abdullah Jumbladi. He has been a naughty boy, and is seeing the headmaster up there now. We'll be on our way soon or should I say we *should* have been on our way soon but I'm afraid when the headmaster sees all this, he will have things to say, I'm sure."

"We are consenting adults," the redhead insisted.

"Have they lowered the voting age in this country, or is that a midget?" Pascoe looked over at the quiet girl sitting and watching in unnatural silence. "And don't claim innocence!"

The Madame considered him, calculating his character. "I can give you money!" she offered

"Yes, do that. You look like a well loaded tart. Make it out to 'Save The Children Fund.' Half a million dollars ought to do it."

"HALF A MILLION!? I don't have that much."

"Sell this place, bitch! That's the deal. You find legitimate spaces for the patients, and you pay the donation or I will be back. There are tapes up there, with enough stuff I'm willing to bet to get a lot of people in trouble. They'll know where the tapes came from and they will be looking for you. Comprendo?"

"That was Spanish, Sir!" said Buchanan, dryly.

"I know it's bloody Spanish!" he snapped.

Meanwhile, up in the viewing room, Seager continued.

"He'll kill me," Jumbladi pleaded.

"I told you. I will kill you if you don't tell me. WHO?" Seager jammed the gun butt into the man's stomach again and, as he doubled over, he grabbed him by the hair and pulled his head back. "Who?"

"Rakkafian."

"WHO?" Seager pounded.

"Adel… Adel Rakkafian!" the man sobbed.

Got you you bastard! I've fucking got you, he thought elatedly. "Where are they now? WHERE?" Seager applied more pressure.

"Manama. the villa in Manama."

"Why? WHY? Tell me you bastard."

"Trade. Trade Layla for the other two."

Seager stood back and put his gun into his pocket. "Tell Rakkafian I'm coming. If anything happens to Maggie or her mother before then, I will kill him. Do you understand? I killed Doud. I may do you yet."

"Please," the man begged. "Please, I told you what you wanted to know."

"Oh fuck off out of my sight!" Seager, sick of the killing and treachery, turned and looked from the window for the first time. Down below, he saw the two women arguing with Pascoe. Then he saw the child in the corner. "Who are you recording for?" he demanded.

"Please just let me go. I told you what–"

"Who?" He turned and looked at the Arab, his eyes flickering, the grey like flint in slate. "You don't record these just to distribute. You are the headman of the porno set-up. Blackmail, is it? SPEAK!"

The man nodded twice, hanging his head, defeated and broken.

"Your boss wouldn't like that. A nice semi legit porno business fucked up because you got greedy. You're in trouble son! Just wait until I tell him what you have done."

"NO! No, please, he will kill me."

213

"I hope he does, but you may be lucky. I might get to him before he gets to you. If you help me, that is."

"Yes! Yes, I will help you," he blathered, terrified of his master.

Seager smiled. "Then listen carefully. This is what I want. I won't ask twice."

Half an hour later, he was finished and walked back to the viewing room. Pascoe waved a cheque at him. Seager had heard the exchange and knew what it was. He smiled tiredly.

"Let's go. Lock 'em in here."

They were out on the drive a few minutes later, Pascoe with a cheque and an armful of videotapes, Seager with what he wanted and only Masters and Buchanan empty-handed. Buchanan was keen on raiding the kitchen. He liked French food and thought that, seeing as it was a proper château, it would have croissants, crème brulee and crepes.

"Keith, its a loonybin with a flat on the back," Masters said. "The food would be like school food, except these people just throw it at the walls instead of each other. There's no good graze here. Anyway, what do you know about French cuisine?"

"I had some in Jo'burg once," Buchanan said, nodding at the guard, still trussed up in the bushes. "Evening," he said politely as he passed by.

The car was only fifty yards away and they were away on the road within a few minutes, heading for Bordeaux and the train north to Paris. When they got there, Pascoe phoned a very irritated owner of the two cars and told him where to find them. They then sat in the pre-dawn cold in the drafty waiting hall at the station. Seager paced up and down the floor, his hands in the pockets of the trench coat he had picked up on the way. His hair was curling over his collar and he needed a bath, a sleep and a shave in that order. They all did.

As they waited, Layla dozed against Masters' shoulder, while Pascoe and Pirelli slept sprawled on the hard bench like drunks in absolute bliss. They were both those kind of people who could sleep anywhere. Buchanan tried to make sense of the remnants of a French newspaper, but eventually he contented himself with looking at the pictures and reading the personal columns.

Seager had reached the end wall and turned to pace the other way again when, suddenly, he looked at Layla, snuggled into Masters' comfortable bulk, and smiled a beatific smile.

He had done it. The pieces fit. Suddenly, in the cold hall, it all fell in place. He looked at Buchanan, the only one awake, and smiled broadly. He walked over to Pascoe and shook him awake. "Oi, shorty! Wake up! Stand to!" he whispered softly.

Pascoe's eyes shot open. Rolling over, he put his feet on the floor and looked about himself. Masters, nearest, remained asleep. Pascoe's eyes focused on Seager like a Cheshire cat.

"Still wanna buy my boat?" he said.

"Wahh, fuck off! AND DON'T CALL STAND TO UNLESS YOU MEAN IT!"

"Build your own then."

"What the hell are you babbling about, man?" Pascoe was usually short-tempered when he woke, but this morning was worse than usual.

"I've sussed him," Seager said. "I've sussed Rakkafian."

A comparatively huge bribe had the station restaurant open twenty minutes early and they sat eating everything put before them, the croissants hot and fresh, the coffee hotter and 'Anglaise' breakfasts on the way. Buchanan ate like a wolf – not surprisingly, as they had not eaten since early the previous day. Seager had said nothing since his announcement but his change of mood had infected everyone. They were all talking animatedly and Pirelli was tapping out a drum solo to a Phil Collins song on the cook's radio, his teaspoon crashing into his saucer with gusto.

"Manama next," Seager said through a mouthful of the sweet pastry, "but first a night in a decent hotel, and a few calls. Layla, you can have Vickery's gold card and go shopping again."

"Oh," she said. "Yes please!" Her brown eyes flickered with mischief. She wasn't sure what had set off the mood change in everyone but it was certainly welcome.

CHAPTER TWENTY

By the time evening came around, Seager and the others found themselves in a small white-washed hotel outside Paris. Seager asked the operator for a 'person to person' call to Richard Vickery and waited for the connection. The others, including Layla, were down in the dining room eating. Wanting privacy for his call, Seager had promised to join them soon.

The international operator found Vickery at the Palace in Ras Al Qaleem fifteen minutes later, and Seager began by allowing Vickery to update him on the Emir's current mood after hearing the news about his old friend.

"What's happening?" he asked.

"You may well ask. Outright disbelief, then anger," Vickery said tiredly.

"He's got every right to be pissed off. He got shafted. His mate is a bad bastard."

"He's pissed off that he got duped more than anything. He used to pride himself on his judge of character. You'll still have to prove it, of course. To an Arab a friend is just that, and no claims of infanticide from you or I, will really convince him that his mate is trying to kill his own kid."

"There's more, and if he's pissed off now, just wait for this." Seager smiled to himself, gazing up at the wallpaper. The stains from the leak above left a mark like Madagascar.

"What?" Vickery asked quickly. His voice said it couldn't get any worse. "Jesus Max, you were paid to get them back. What else?"

Seager began to speak and Vickery listened, first in disbelief like his employer would, and then in admiration at both Seager and his quarry. Seager spoke for several minutes, and then for several more, answering the probes from Vickery, who tried to find holes in the theory.

"What do you want to do?" Vickery asked.

"I want him to admit it," Seager replied. "Set up a swap somewhere out in the open, where I can see who he's got with him."

"He's in Bahrain at the moment. What about there?"

"Somewhere nice and open, but with something nearby for Keith and a long rifle to cover my back."

"The Fort," Vickery said quickly.

"The what?"

"The Fort built by the Portuguese hundreds of years ago. It's not far from town and should be quiet enough. I'll pull some strings. Get it quiet. I'll also get you some serious backup."

"Mine is good enough. Just get us into Bahrain without Rakkafian knowing. I want the initiative. Every minute he doesn't know where I am, or where Layla is, he weakens."

"O.K. Fly in here and I'll ask the boss to get you a boat. You can go into the Marina Club there. If you fly tomorrow night, you can run in on Friday with the other boats from Jarada Reef."

"I'll make sure you don't get hassled by anyone. Do you want a skipper?" This was Vickery's forte, putting men in the field.

"No, but have some hardware on the boat," Seager finished.

Madagascar had become larger and looked more like Greenland now. Seager put the phone in the cradle and stood up, tucking in his shirt. Friday would see it finished, Saturday at the latest. Then it would be home to Svea and Sarah, Jannie, the boat, the cat, and his own bed. He sat down again, telephoned home and spoke for a few minutes; then he finally walked down the narrow stairs towards the ground floor.

The smell wafting up from the kitchen was enough to whet his appetite and he jumped the last three stairs in high-spirited anticipation of the menu. The others were already on their third bottle of red and on their main course. Masters was holding the chair with a story about a fat lady and a milkman and Layla was huddled between Pirelli and Buchanan, looking stunning in a black sequin dress that was as incongruous in the small family restaurant as Buchanan's handgun beneath his thigh.

Layla looked up at Seager as he entered and waved happily at him, escargot fork in one hand and glass in the other. He slipped into the empty chair, stole Pirelli's bread and bit into it hungrily.

"Snails are good boss," Pirelli said, his mouth full of garlic bread.

"No thanks. Slimy little things. I'll have-"

The waiter appeared, a middle-aged man with a large Gallic nose and sad eyes. He looked at Seager and raised an eyebrow without speaking.

"Cold chicken, green salad, German lager and bread rolls?"

The waiter nodded and walked away without writing anything down. The food arrived a few minutes later, exactly as ordered but included a bowl of soup.

"It's *fais froid, le marie*," the waiter explained.

"He said it's cold and his wife wants you to eat soup too," Masters explained.

"Thanks," said Seager, touched by the gesture. He looked back at his companions. "We leave tomorrow night. Gulf Air through Bahrain to Ras Al Qaleem. Leaves at about nine I think. Then we go and get Maggs on Friday or Saturday." He dipped his spoon into the steaming consommé. There was a muffled cheering from around the table. Layla remained silent and seemed to have accepted, at last, that her father was cast as the villain.

Seager stood on the flying bridge, the wind in his face and hands on the big aluminium wheel as 'Shamar' powered her way westward. The boat was a fifty foot Hatteras and belonged to the Emir himself. It was sleek and powerful, with high freeboards; she would make the run without problems. Her tanks were good for eight hundred miles, but planing across the Gulf at twenty-four knots, her operating range would be half that. The men had drawn weapons from the Emirates Royal arsenal and the choice had been vast. Now, a hundred miles out, Seager handed the wheel to the Somali crewman and throttled back. The big boat chugging gently along at five knots, he threw a selection of corked bottles over the side and nodded to Buchanan and Pirelli.

"O.K.," he said. "Let's see how they look."

The next twenty minutes were spent shooting the rifles in, only Buchanan adjusting the scope on the rifle as necessary. Both Masters and Pirelli were happy with their weapons, and Pascoe had fired his on the range at the Palace the night before. Buchanan made another adjustment, chambered another round and settled over the transom. He waited until the last few bottles had trailed four hundred yards astern and fired three times at each bottle, creating a wave. Each time, Seager checked the hit with a telescope from the bridge.

"Hit all three!" he shouted down.

Buchanan nodded and, clearing the magazine, slipped the rifle back into its felt cover, then back into the metal case it came in, and settled back into a deck chair.

Seager eased the throttles out again. They need to be off Jarada Reef by dawn. They would anchor and play the fool and eventually, later in the day, run into Bahrain with the other big pleasure boats. Their berth was organised and the right people would take no notice of the boat's arrival. Rashid Al Khadem was calling favours and had not yet had to resort to an outright request for help from the Emir of Bahrain, not that it would be refused. They were old friends and had much in common.

Seager's meeting the night before with the Emir had left the ruler deep in thought – and now ready to put all his wealth at Seager's disposal to see the truth.

Layla arrived up the steep steps onto the flying bridge, balancing a plate in the hand, the contents sensibly covered in cling film. She staggered to him at the high chair and offered it, one hand holding the grab rail. "Thanks," she smiled and walked forward of the control panel to look over the bows as they raced over the waves. Seager watched her lean into the wind as the hull danced and shivered beneath them.

"Layla!" he shouted into the wind. "Come and sit with me."

It was time, he thought. *Time to come clean.*

*

The Somali guided them into the shallow waters off Bahrain's coast in the blackness before the dawn. Pascoe was at the wheel caressing the big throttles, easing the boat's deep hull nearer the markers. Ten minutes later, she was anchored and rocking gently, her bows into wind. The only noise was the auxiliary generators that powered the air-conditioning and riding lights. By mid-morning, the shallows of

the sandy reef were scattered with big pleasure craft with their atten-
dant ski-boats and jet skis, bikini clad girls and gin and tonics. There
was a thriving social scene, with many small boats coming very close
to 'Shamal', curious eyes looking her over and trying to identify who
might own her and where she had come from. Several invitations were
issued to come aboard other boats but Pascoe and Seager declined all
with thanks. Only Pirelli seemed upset; he had seen the girls on the
other boats and, ever the optimist, he fancied his chances with one
somewhere in the fleet.

They ran back into Bahrain's Marina Club that evening, close
enough to the others to seem one of the normal homecoming craft.
Then they waited. Well after dark, a black Mercedes pulled to a halt
in the car park above the basin and two men crossed the area and began
to walk over the pontoons towards 'Shamal's' distinctive profile. Both
men wore thobes and guttras, the national dress, and raised their thobes
to cross the transom and step into the cockpit.

Seager greeted them guardedly. "Can I help you?" he asked.

"I am Mohammed Jalawi. I am from the Ministry of Interior. This
is Hamid. He doesn't have another name. He is the cloak and dagger
man from the office of the Emir!" The speaker burst out laughing and
shook Seager's hand. "Welcome to Bahrain. You have a problem, I
believe. We have been sent to assist. I suggest we retire to the bar
where you may drink whatever you like, and I will have a scotch!" He
laughed again; it was an infectious sound that had Seager grinning in
seconds.

"This way gentlemen," he said.

At the bar, Seager poured drinks and made introductions and finally,
with everyone settled and the Somali crew on the pontoon checking
the lines, he told his story. Both men listened intently and eventually
Hamid spoke. "This man Rakkafian has considerable influence on the
island, or did have until today. But his influence will extend for the
next few days. Enough to effect you anyway. He has a villa here and
spends considerable money locally. We have considered him, how you
say, suspect yani, for some time. He sells guns to people who shouldn't
have guns and sells drugs to anyone who will buy them but not here,
so we have left alone." The man sipped his orange juice and looked at

Layla, who was sitting cross-legged on the floor at Pascoe's feet. "I am sorry to speak of your father this way."

"Rarely can one choose one's parents," she replied profoundly. "I have lost something I never really had."

"Allah is great," Hamid replied. "Everything has a purpose."

"If you people knew that he has been a naughty boy, why didn't the Emir of Ras Al Qaleem know it?" Seager asked. "He thinks this guy has been his friend and confidant for all these years."

Hamid shrugged, "Maybe his desire for a friend clouded his judgement. Maybe he took counsel, maybe he gave the benefit of the doubt too often – or maybe it is a case of the messenger fearing for his head."

"So what now?" asked Seager. "I am free to finish this thing?"

"You are, as long as you do not involve or harm any nationals," Hamid said, handing Seager a piece of paper. "On there is my number, and the numbers of his villa here in Manama. Keep me informed of what you think I should know. Give my regards to Vickery. Tell him my debt is now paid. There will be a squad of six Bahrain Defence Force Special Forces people at your disposal should you wish. If there is to be any violence, I would rather they were there and in control."

"They may stand by, but I have my own men, who react faster than I can. If anything starts, they will finish it," Seager said firmly.

"As Allah wills," Hamid said, standing. "Again, welcome to the Pearl of the Gulf."

An hour later, Seager walked into the clubhouse through the easy throng of people and up to the phone booth in the lobby. He looked at the number Hamid had given him and began to dial. The phone was answered immediately.

"Nam."

"Rakkafian," Seager said.

The voice switched to English. "Not available," it said.

"Get him! My name is Seager. Tell him my name! MOVE."

He heard the phone being put down on the table and waited a moment. The hubbub of playing children came into the booth and Seager held the phone tighter to his ear.

"So," the voice said, "Mohammed has come to the mountain."

It was a very civilized, educated voice. The accent was almost unplaceable, but beneath its urbane charm it was a voice of steel.

"I'm here in Bahrain," Seager said.

"Oh, that's nice." His surprise was evident but carefully concealed. Someone had slipped up. He was supposed to have been told when Seager appeared in the Gulf.

"Don't play games with me, Rakkafian. I have something you want, so don't fuck me about."

"What have you got that I would possibly want?"

"Your way to sixty million. She's not dead yet."

"You have established your credentials well. Please allow my daughter to come home."

Nice try, Seager thought, *the concerned father*. He laughed into the phone. It was a short, dry, mirthless bark. He paused and breathed hard. "You have something I want. Anything happens to either of them and I will emblazon your story across the sky. I will explain to your daughter your desire to have her home in person and why."

There was a pause and Seager could almost hear Rakkafian calculating the odds. "I'm sure we can come up with some accommodation," he said casually.

"A swap," Seager said, "at the Portuguese Fort. Tomorrow night, nine o'clock."

"Agreed," Rakkafian said too quickly and hung up.

Got you, you prick. You really think I'm going to bring your daughter along to a lonely place alone.

Seager knew Rakkafian would suspect something. He thought quickly and dialled again.

"Tell Rakkafian I also want something else."

Rakkafian came on the line again. "What now?"

"I forgot something," Seager said pleasantly.

"Yes."

"Bring a million dollars," Seager said. He could feel Rakkafian recalculating the new perspective. Seager had placed himself into a league Rakkafian would understand, a motive that was real. Money. From now on, Rakkafian would think that Seager had sold out the Emir.

"I don't have a million," he said.

"Come along, come along. One for sixty odd? Find it. Be there!" Hanging up, he walked back to the boat through the starry humid night. The old feeling was rising. He had closed on the quarry, and tomorrow it would be the kill. He flicked his cigarette into the black inky water and walked on to 'Shamal'.

The Somali sat on the flying bridge, eating something, and nodded to Seager as he boarded. Below there was ribald laughter and shouted jibes. Seager opened the companionway door just as Pirelli threw a bread roll at the screen of the television, amid laughter from the others. Seager looked at the flickering image. A group of men ran across the screen, firing from the hip, mowing down dozens of enemies. A grenade was thrown and several bodies were blown skyward. Another burst of laughter erupted from the watchers.

"What's this?" Seager asked.

"It's called *Wild Geese*," Pascoe answered, grinning.

"Wild wankers more like it," Pirelli said, "what a load of shit!" The men laughed again as yet another single man killed dozens of enemy from a gun with a nine round magazine.

Seager joined in with the laughter, walked below into his cabin and drew the big tote bag from below his bunk. He was due to phone Vickery at midnight and tell him what more he needed and when the swap was arranged for. Vickery would be accompanying Rahid Al Khadem, who had refused to sit back at the end. Seager had fought against that. It would be complicated enough placing Buchanan, Pirelli, and Masters where they could react without compromising his efforts, but the Sheikh would be even more of a problem.

He walked back upstairs, and into the lounge-like saloon. "Tomorrow night at the Fort. You guys will deploy with Ken early afternoon. Let's do a plan and let's do a good one. We get one crack at this."

Two hours later, he finished with a closing remark looking at the photos.

"Vickery says there are several vantage points both close and at a distance. Keith, you shoot first if you are clear. Make no mistake. It *will* start. Rakkafian has a couple of heavies. Apparently he only has one travelling with him who is any good. Tall guy, very tall, wears a leather jacket and uses a long-barrelled light calibre gun. There might be another two or three. Louis, Richard, they will be your problem. Keith, you take the tall bloke, he worries me. Layla will be in one of those new nylon-armoured vests but he may go for a head shot – so blow him away if he blinks." Seager looked across at Pascoe. "Ken, you're with me, and take your chances. It will look all wrong if I'm there alone with Layla."

Pascoe nodded. He also had one of the new vests, and as long as he had a weapon he was afraid of no man, not even three up very close.

"I have to get him to speak. I have to get him to admit it so the tape will get it all. Otherwise, I have no evidence. Try not to initiate anything until that's done or we have lost."

"Why?" Pirelli asked. "We know what he is, let's finish it and go home!"

"I want him to admit it!" Seager's eyes glittered for a moment. "We do it my way. I want to confront him with it and have him say it in his own words." His eyes softened and he spoke again. "For Layla, for Maggie, for that dead boy in the Bundu, for Tim Sibanda, and for Rob."

The men all stared at him, letting it sink in. Then Seager got up, walked out of the saloon and back into the club to phone Vickery.

CHAPTER TWENTY-ONE

Buchanan chose to deploy before the next morning, high on the crumbling battlements of the Fort. It was for several reasons. He wanted to check the scope image on site in the dark, and settle in well before anyone might happen along. During the daylight hours, he would sleep and read on his stand. He would also report to Pascoe any visits from people who did not look like the usual visitors to the historic site, on a small radio purloined from the Emir's palace. By the time the sun was up, he had checked his rifle and pulled the greyish-brown bivouac cover over the small U-shaped rings that supported it. It meant that he could turn, roll and stretch below the camouflaged cover at will, safe from prying eyes.

Below him, only two hundred yards away, Seager would wait with Pascoe and Layla in the open, vulnerable and totally reliant on his judgement and accuracy. He adjusted the cover, settled back on his side, and opened a paperback book, much dog-eared and well fingered. It was an Oxford University Press edition entitled 'Venomous Snakes-Sub Sahara' and his favourite book.

On three occasions during the day, vehicles not containing bored Bahrainis drove up and around the Fort. Two had descriptions that Seager had warned Buchanan to watch for: men, no women, late model car, and the occupants looking at the access to the site, vantage points and cover, rather than the towering walls and the view. The cars both circled slowly and drove away and, the second time, Buchanan fancied he saw someone looking up at the walls.

Rashid Al Kadem arrived at the airport in a private jet soon after three, Vickery following him down the steps and into the black Mercedes that belonged to the Emirates Embassy. The Embassy staff had made it very plain to the Protocol Officer in the Ministry of Foreign Affairs that this was a private business visit, and no official functions would be entertained. The black car swept out of the V.I.P. gates at the airport, following Hamid from the Emir's office in his more humble Audi, down to the

Marina Club and the final meeting with Seager and Pascoe. Layla had been moved into a private villa for the day, a large elegant building occupied by an Australian expatriate who also owed Vickery favours. The meeting was brief and the Sheikh angry as he paced the saloon below decks, declining the offer of a drink from his own cocktail cabinet with the shake of a royal hand. Below, Pascoe expertly cleaned and re-cleaned his own and Seager's weapons, his own ritual pre-firefight action. Then, at 1620 hours, Buchanan watched another car covertly. It had been there already that day, he was sure of that.

He pulled his hat askew to alter his profile against the afternoon sky and watched it closely. It disappeared around the back of the Fort and, when it reappeared, it had lost two occupants. Buchanan smiled to himself. *Naughty, naughty,* he thought, *they have put some people in early.* He knew that the stand of trees behind the Fort was mostly out of sight of the exchange point – so, if whoever had left the car was going to see the swap and be in a position to become involved, they would need to be high and on his side. That meant along the same wall as he was on. He rolled back the bivouac cover and drew the sidearm he had chosen and looked at it, shrugged and replaced it. Then he bent down, took off his shoes and socks and rolled his trouser cuffs clear of his ankles. He went through a thirty second high speed warm-up routine of short sharp punches and high kicks, stretching his cramped muscles, and then dropped the twelve feet from the high battlement onto the lower level like a cat, graceful and light in spite of his size.

Back at 'Shamal', Pirelli and Masters set up the inflatable tender that lay in the stern lockers of her wide transom. Careful not to attract too much attention, they inflated the side walls on the seaward side of the big boat, clear of sight from shore. Pirelli had laid out his favourite track shoes, as much symbols of his psychological preparation as Pascoe's cleaning and re cleaning of his weapons. The sweaty old Adidas shoes were covered in the dirt of the bush and were laced with leather reims. He never wore socks and the shoes moulded to his feet perfectly. Masters, meanwhile, completed his preparations with a Walkman Stereo set playing into his ears; the tape was a popular rock opera soundtrack and was being played loud enough for Pirelli to identify the tune from where he was. He knew that Masters would cease the listening two hours before they went in, and sit in total silence if possible, allowing his hearing to readjust to the critical sounds that save a life. They were ready by the time the Somali crewman handed down cups of tea and sandwiches just before five.

Buchanan eased his way around a parapet, moving slowly. He had given whoever it was time to arrive at their stand and begin settling in before he moved further. Now, half an hour later, he moved faster, judging from below the best vantages from this side of the high walls. He stopped, almost nodded to himself, and began to climb the rubble of a collapsed section. Then he grinned widely as he found tracks in the dry dust covering the ancient clay bricks. Veering left, he rose still higher, hoping to come out above wherever it was that the others had chosen. Once at the highest point, he slithered forward on his stomach and peered over the short drop to the level below. There was a figure, a lithe dark-haired man, unfolding a packet of the flat local bread. He had set out a folding stool and a long object lay wrapped in his coat at his feet. A stand-up thermos stood beside a bag. He was settling in and the object in the coat was a rifle.

Buchanan looked slowly around for the second man. He was nowhere to be seen and the contents of the bag looked as if they were intended only for one. Somewhere, however, there was a second hostile. Buchanan waited for a few minutes, hoping the other man would return, but knowing he was going to be disappointed. Eventually, dark drawing in, he decided to move. He dropped from the wall above the relaxing man and, in the same moment, he rose from his crouch, grabbed the man's head with one hand around his mouth and twisted hard. The perpetrator kicked his legs out and only stopped screaming into Buchanan's palm when his neck snapped . His body went limp immediately.

With trepidation, Keith let go; it had been years since he was in a situation that demanded the most primeval subduing of another human. Checking the pulse of this man, whose tea was still hot, he did not feel any pride. This was war, in its rawest form. Swearing to himself, he began to rifle through the man's bag. He was looking for a radio, or some means of communicating with the other man. He found nothing and assumed that they weren't that organised.

At the same time as Buchanan was breaking the man's neck, Seager and Pascoe were looking at an aerial photograph of the Fort with Hamid and Vickery. On the small coffee table beneath then, the small radio crackled into life. They looked at each other.

"Zulu One Zulu One, this is Two."

It was Buchanan's call sign, and that meant something had to have happened. Had nothing taken place, he would have maintained his silence. Seager swept it up. "Go Two," he said, trying to sound calm.

"One, have some hide and seek here. Two, but one has dropped out of the game. He's not feeling well ova."

"Copied that Two, how about the other? Ova."

"In the trees three o'clock to my locstat. It's the only place he can be. Warn Three and Four ova." Buchanan hadn't raised his head but the only place was the trees away to the right, which would put the man behind Seager and Pascoe as soon as they arrived. That was bad.

"Roger Two. Three and Five will tell him about his friend ova."

I'll bet, thought Buchanan. Pirelli liked shuffling round in the dark, a knife in his hand and a game to win.

Pirelli and Masters were briefed as the sun dropped below the horizon. Pascoe showed them the trees that Buchanan thought might contain the second man.

"No probs," said Pirelli, putting on his shoes. They would be leaving in the boat to do a seaward approach in the next ten minutes. "There's a coastguard guy outside who will take you in," said Pascoe. "Take care of the playmate and be in position by eight. We'll be there at nine. The Sheikh will be there somewhere, so don't for fucksakes drill him O.K.?" Both men nodded. "Right, on your way!" he ordered.

"Turn here," said Pascoe.

The building ahead was the International Hospital and their turnoff was immediately right before the building. Seager turned the corner, the ordinary saloon from a rental fleet completely inconspicuous on the suburban Bahraini road. "Where are the troops?" he asked.

"Only six as promised," Pascoe said. "They'll be at the road and make sure no-one comes in after Rakkafian."

They drove on down the winding road towards the sea and eventually the Fort stood stark against the night sky. Seager drove to a parking area and stopped in the centre, the car pointing front on, like he had seen in the movies.

As they alighted, Layla adjusted the jacket she wore against the night air. It wasn't necessary, except to cover the outline of the armoured vest Seager insisted she wore.

Vickery walked from the shadows of the ruined house on the edge of the complex. "Ready?" he asked unnecessarily.

"Yeah. Where's the Sheikh?" Seager asked.

"Back there with a pearl-handled Beretta and hate in his heart."

"Tell him to stay out of this," Pascoe said firmly.

"He will." Vickery walked back.

Pascoe stood one side of the car and Seager lounged on the bonnet, leather jacket zipped up, and the outline of his Browning indistinct in the overlarge pocket. Layla sat in the back seat, the door open. For a time they waited, Seager hoping that the man in the trees was taken care of, not wanting to be shot in the back. "What's the time?" he asked.

"Look at your watch," said Pascoe, who was relishing in Seager's discomfort. "Don't worry. Louis and Richard have taken care of that."

"How do you know?" Seager asked, feeling the microphone in his lapel with one hand.

"I do. That's all."

He did, and they had. They had moved silently through the trees in the almost complete darkness like the arrival of night itself.

They stopped to listen every few feet and it was Pirelli who had smelled the man first. He had been smoking in the lower branches of a tree, cupping the butt to cover the light, but too slack or badly trained to think about the smell. To Pirelli it had been like a beacon, and he and Masters had covered the last sixty yards quickly, stopping below the tree. Behind its spreading branches, Pirelli had picked up and thrown a rock the size of a grapefruit at the silhouette watching the car park. He had grunted, and slid to the ground like a bundle of washing, holding his side where the rock had hit him, fast and silent and heavy. His mistake had been in reaching for the bulge beneath his jacket and he had died with Pirelli's knife, a new knife, in his throat.

"Where's the rifle?" Masters had asked, looking about. He and Pirelli had both looked upward and there, still resting in the crook of a branch, was a hunting rifle complete with scope. "He's our boy," he had said and then they had split up, moving into their respective positions to await the evening's outcome.

Masters was only forty feet from Seager by the time the car arrived, lying in what had once been a deep ditch below the wall. He could see everything at eye level but did not signal or move in case there were other watchers. Above him, seventy feet up and way back, was Buchanan, rifle now out, drinking water from a bottle. Pirelli was on the roof of the building housing the Sheikh and Vickery was off to Seager's right.

The men were ready and they were not kept waiting long. Soon, Rakkafian climbed from the back seat of the big American sedan that had brought him to the Fort, and stood upright, giving Seager his first look at the man he had chased half way across the world.

In the back of the car, Seager could see Maggie, her hair wrapped in a scarf, and beside her a smaller figure he knew must be her mother. The driver climbed from his side and stood threateningly beside his master. A second car arrived and three men climbed clear, walking up to the bigger car that had ferried Rakkafian.

Shit, thought Seager, *four plus the two we have had already. They are serious these boys. But so are we.*

Seager stepped forward arrogantly, dragging Layla at his side. "You must be everyone's favourite Lebo," he said. The remark was intended to anger his opponent, rattle him a little from the start. "Did you bring the money?" Seager asked.

Rakkafian walked forward. He was wearing evening dress with a black bow tie, his iron grey hair carefully combed back, looking every inch the successful business man.

"Good evening Layla," he said, "how nice to see you."

"Cut the shit!" Seager snarled. He disliked emotional tactics.

"No, I didn't bring the money," Rakkafian answered. "Why should I? Your suggestion was ridiculous."

230

"One million ridiculous?" Seager's voice dropped. Like a cobra's coils moving, it hissed. "Then let's make it two."

"Two, is it?"

"It's a long story" said Seager, "we both know it, so let's agree two million. It's worth it."

Rakkafian only glared at him. "I have a few minutes," he said. "Indulge me. Tell me a story."

"Only if you correct for me as I go. I'd hate to miss any details."

"Go on."

"Well, once upon a time, there was a young man. His father, a shrewd old man, didn't like his offspring very much. He had a son, a slippery little shit by all accounts, so he made sure in his will that he received nothing until he was married, and then only half of a sizeable fortune. Even that was dependent on an heir. Half when the child was born, and half to the child at twenty-one." Seager paused in the moon-light. "Still with me, Rakkafian?"

"GO ON!" Rakkafian's eyes were slits in his face and, in the light from the car doors, he looked evil. "Well, he was touring with a friend, both young men recently married and both with their young pregnant wives. There was an accident. Within hours, one woman was dead and only one premature baby struggled for life. Only, the young man was up and walking. His friend was seriously injured – in fact, an injury that prohibited any further children from his loins. The young man went to check on the babies and the surviving woman in the East Wing of the hospital. Then he had an idea. His baby was dead as was his wife. Was he struck down with grief? No. He was made of sterner stuff, this chap. You *still* with me, Rakkafian?"

"SPEAK ON!"

"Am I on the right track?" Seager asked softly.

"YES, SPEAK ON!"

"He looked at the two tiny babies. One dead, awaiting a trip down to the morgue; one alive. He remembered the will: no baby, no money. Well, here was a live baby but there was only one problem. The mother lived and she would know her baby. There could be no mistake. The child even had a birthmark. So our chap," Seager paused. "So *you* went back up the ward to a terribly injured woman, the wife of your friend,

231

and you killed her. Isn't that right, Rakkafian? You killed her, you changed the tags, you said the baby that survived was yours. After that, you were in the money." Seager's eyes glittered like wet flint and his voice was like a rasp. "How did you do it? Strangle her? Would have been easy. Your style."

Rakkafian began to laugh. It was mirthless but admiring. "You are very good. I did it. An injection of air into the blood. Very easy. It looked like a heart attack. So. That's that."

"No it's not. Because it didn't end there, did it, Rakkafian? A year later, you went back to the hospital and put it to the torch, killing two of the staff on duty that night. You were covering your tracks. You even arranged for an accident to befall the other duty nurse. A gun accident. Very convenient. Then, when Layla, Maggie and a young man called Edward were abducted on the road this year, it must have been like manna from heaven for you. She had signed the papers you gave her. It was time for her to go anyway. You were sixty million better off, and the dissidents down there would do your dirty work for you. They demanded a ransom, but instead you sent word back to them to kill her. They couldn't believe it. Being simple people who love their own, they couldn't believe it. I shot him. The man you asked to kill your Layla, sorry, not *yours*, but Layla all the same. As he was dying he said, 'I should have killed her,' like he was paid to do, but he grew fond of her and couldn't understand any man wanting his daughter dead."

"Enough!" Rakkafian barked an order and, suddenly, everything happened at once.

Buchanan, who had been watching the tall man on the left, went onto second pressure. The Parker Hale 270 bucked into his shoulder and below, milliseconds before they heard the report, the gunman's head disappeared from his shoulders as the hollow point round hit him square in the temple.

Masters and Pirelli opened up together, making a murderous crossfire into the three remaining men. Rakkafian span in terror as his plan went horribly wrong. One of his guards managed to get his weapon clear and seemed to be looking for support from the battlements as Pascoe fired three rounds into his chest from a kneeling position thirty feet away.

232

In the car, dangerously close to the hail of bullets, Maggie – who had suspected something – pulled her mother to the floor as Buchanan fired his second and last round into the kneecap of the man who had kidnapped his friend. Rakkafian fell screaming to the ground, clutching at his shattered knee, looking with wild eyes around him at his dead and dying bodyguards.

Seager pulled his gun clear of his jacket. He still hadn't fired it and, as he walked forward, he cocked the action.

"Adel Rakkafian, I arrest you for kidnapping and murder."

He paused and then spoke again slowly and softly, "You will be tried in the Shi'ia court at Ras Al Qualeem, and they will probably cut your head off."

Seager looked around as Vickery appeared, and watched Layla run for the car where her friend sat still holding her terrified sobbing mother. A hand touched his shoulder and he turned. It was Sheikh Rashid, his head held high and proud.

"I sent you to find the daughter of a man I thought my friend. You brought me betrayal, so close that even I never knew. You brought me back my life in the form of my daughter. Now, I have something before where I had nothing. It will take time, to bring her home. She has much to learn, but nothing is as important as the love of her father. I am indebted to you. You name it and it is yours."

Seager didn't know what to say, so he said nothing and watched Masters move among the bodies, checking that the threat was truly past.

It had been fifty-one days. It was time to go home.

Milton Keynes UK
Ingram Content Group UK Ltd.
UKHW011820131023
430526UK00001B/37